TROPHY WIFE

Ifeoma E. Nero

First Published in Great Britain in 2024 by
LOVE AFRICA PRESS
103 Reaver House, 12 East Street, Epsom KT17 1HX
www.loveafricapress.com[1]

YADILI SERIES

---

1. https://www.kirutaye.com/duke

2. https://www.kirutaye.com/xandra

3. https://www.kirutaye.com/bad-santa

4. https://www.kirutaye.com/rough-diamond

5. https://www.kirutaye.com/tough-alliance

6. https://www.kirutaye.com/trophy-wife

TROPHY WIFE

Ifeoma & Nero

DEDICATION

TO THE BUTTERFLIES who love my stories as much as I do and keep coming back for more. I love you all.

BLURB

***HE NEEDS HER TO ELEVATE** his status. But she will be his downfall.*

Finally, Ifeoma is ready to fully embrace the freedom of singlehood. Her ex-husband has moved on and remarried, and her son has flown the nest. With the intention of self-discovery, she embarks on a worldwide adventure, determined to fulfil three items on her wish-list: to experience pure joy, to find laughter in every corner, and to revel in her own sensuality.

Then she meets Nero, a mysterious Black Italian whose charm captivates her instantly. And for twenty-four hours he fulfils every item on her wish-list. But he wants more, more than she's willing to give. So, she ends it and goes home.

Months later, Nero turns up in Nigeria, more detached and ruthless than the man she remembers, intent on destroying her family business and legacy. And only one thing will quench his bloody feud—Ifeoma as his trophy wife.

Still, Ifeoma is a titled woman who isn't easy to control, if she can keep Nero out of her bed—the one place his passion burns hotter than a forge at dawn, consuming her restraint.

***Trophy Wife** is book 6 in the Yadili series. In this enemies-to-lovers romance, the air crackles with tension and the chemistry between the characters is scorching hot, cre-*

ating a story that will leave you breathless. Themes include unrequited love, he falls first, touch her and die, blended families, and the intoxicating darkness of a mafia romance. A full-length novel. No cliffhanger.

ONE

Nero stood at the floor-to-ceiling window overlooking the illuminated skyline of the city he'd called home for the past twenty-five years. The sunset gave dramatic lighting from the dark blue and orange sky. Lush greenery lined both sides of the glittering river with the grey mountains in the distant background. Meanwhile, twinkling streetlamps captured the beauty of the urban architecture around him.

Turin's grandeur was etched in marble and wrought iron. Palaces stood tall, their facades adorned with intricate carvings—each telling a story of dukes, kings, and clandestine affairs. The Mole Antonelliana pierced the sky—a spire of ambition and architectural audacity. Its glass dome caught the sun, casting kaleidoscopic reflections onto the cobbled streets below. Piazzas emerged unexpectedly, framed by colonnades and arcades.

In the distance, the rhythmic clattering of the tram echoed through the tree-lined boulevard, carrying stories of workers, lovers, and dreamers, crisscrossing the city like musical notes on a staff.

Despite the breathtaking beauty of the city in front of him, his stomach remained tightly knotted. The image of *the woman* lingered in his mind, refusing to fade away.

He'd made a splendid life in this country by anyone else's standards.

Yet he missed his fatherland, the place he'd spent his formative years. The country he hadn't visited for over two decades ago.

Yet there was nothing back there for him ... except a burning desire for revenge.

The impending arrival was undeniable. Dark clouds loomed in his mind, ready to unleash his fury. Anticipation made him close his eyes and sigh. The world should hold its breath and prepare for what was to come.

There were things he needed to put in place first.

Things he'd been working on for years. Since he boarded the airplane which brought him here.

Away from everything he knew. Away from her.

But he'd built a good life. Made a reputation for himself.

He was Nero to his close friends, or *il Re Nero* to close associates. It didn't escape his notice they'd named him after one of Rome's Caesars, who was notorious for being cruel and eccentric.

Some called him the Cash King because finance was his thing and he'd made them tons of money. Billions in any currency worth owning.

He'd once told an associate that his ethnic surname meant King of Loathing. Afterwards many started calling him King Loathing, mostly rivals, because he never forgot a slight. He was detached. Brutal. And he always retaliated, making them pay in all kinds of excruciatingly painful ways.

"We could be good together again," the velvety smooth voice cut into his thoughts.

He ignored it. When were they ever an item? A one-night stand didn't count as *together*.

His reputation meant people feared him. No one dared to cross him. Although it didn't stop some from seeking him out. Women especially. Like this one currently in his penthouse. There was always one who thought they could tame him, rehabilitate him, something.

It was laughable.

Some women liked the challenge of a bad boy. Like Alina, his ex and baby mama.

Except he wasn't just a bad boy. He was a dangerous man.

Anyone with any sense would want to avoid him.

But he had money and power.

Those things were intoxicating, addictive.

His association with the most powerful cartel in the region certainly meant people lusted after him and doors opened easily for him.

His ability to turn business opportunities into gold meant people sought him out from across the globe. However, there was one place where his reputation had yet to make an impression.

His fatherland.

But there was no escaping it. His name would strike terror in the hearts of his enemies over there, eventually.

They could continue living in blissful ignorance, which allowed him to maintain his advantage.

Meanwhile, he'd made a two-phase plan.

To build successful business ventures and amass a fortune exceeding his wildest dreams.

He had successfully accomplished the first phase goals.

Now for the next stage of his strategy.

Determined to reclaim his fatherland, he would unleash his icy revenge on those who destroyed his family.

"Are you even listening to me?" Alina let out a high-pitched whine, her frustration evident.

Irritation coursed through him, causing his grip on the rum tumbler to tighten and his spine to stiffen with the interruption.

The click-clack of her heels on the hard flooring filled the air as she came into view. She wore an off-shoulder, long-sleeved, knee-length red dress which clung to her skinny body, showcasing her boobs and narrow waist. Her eyes gleamed with a seductive expression that should have him chasing the pleasures they promised.

Instead, his dick barely twitched. She leaned into him and tried to kiss him. He turned his head away. He wasn't a kisser. Not like that. He didn't even like touch most days.

Alina knew this. They'd fucked, made an unplanned baby together. But they hadn't shared the intimacy of a tongue kiss. Had never even shared a bed for the entire night.

"You seem too tense, Nero baby. Let me help you with that." She lowered to her knees, staring up at him with a coquettish smile and flicking her ruby-red lips with her tongue.

Not going to lie. The sight of her on her knees with those lips opened seductively made pleasure uncoil in his gut.

In the past, he'd let her suck his dick. Yet he'd never allowed her tongue to invade his mouth.

Still, it had been a while since he had a woman moaning and vibrating in ecstasy around him.

A part of him wanted the follow through. For her to unzip his trousers and take his already throbbing dick out. He knew what she would do because they'd done it before. She would take his engorged dick into her willing mouth and massage him with her tongue and lips. She would open wide and take him all the way deep. He would reach out and grab a fistful of her hair. Make her take his girth until the swollen head hit the entrance to her throat. Make her gag on it and whimper enthusiastically as he fucked her hard, thrusting, straining, groaning, chasing release. Ejaculating and leaving the darkness behind for the brief encounter.

He took another sip from the glass in his hand and closed his eyes, allowing his mind to paint the picture.

However, the image in his imagination was of a different woman. One from a long time ago. One he hadn't seen in over twenty years. The one who reminded him of his quest for vengeance.

The one he wanted on her knees with her lips swollen from taking his punishing thrust. The one he would paint with his release as he fisted himself.

Hands made contact with his thighs and he opened his eyes, bringing with it a cold, heavy dose of reality. It wasn't the object of his desire in front of him. His dick deflated.

"You know better than to touch me." He growled, barely containing his annoyance.

"Come on, Nero. Let me do this for you. I'm sure it's been a while for you. For us." She batted her long fake lashes at him.

She wasn't wrong. It had been a long time since he'd been with a woman.

His first encounter with Alina was supposed to be a one-night stand. Afterwards she'd tried to initiate a do over and he'd shut her down. Then she'd shown up three months later at his office and had announced her pregnancy. After the initial shock of finding out she was carrying his baby, he'd accepted his responsibilities and had planned to co-parent with her. He would provide everything mother and baby needed, set them up in a new home in a safe neighbourhood.

However, she'd insisted on moving in with him and had threatened to have a termination if they didn't move in together. For the first time in his adult life, fear had iced his veins for his unborn child. Much as he accepted she had the rights to a termination, using his baby to blackmail him into cohabitation had seemed manipulative.

Then again, who was he to judge? He blackmailed others when it suited him.

Still, concern for his unborn child had superseded his ego. He'd accepted her terms of cohabitation and had moved her into his apartment. However, they still hadn't shared a bed or the same room.

Then his daughter Lucia, named after his late mother, had arrived. He'd fallen in love with the little bundle with light caramel skin, a shock of curly brown hair and hazel eyes from the moment he'd set eyes on her.

Instantly, he'd been glad for the decision to let mother and baby stay in his apartment. He'd employed a nanny for Lucia and spent the next decade becoming an integral part of his daughter's life as she grew from infant to adolescent.

It meant that he also shared a house with Alina, which made her feel entitled to him and his time. Never mind her entitlement to his money and influence.

He hadn't been involved in any romantic relationship since and he wasn't actively looking.

He'd had a few casual one-night stands, but Alina always made a fuss whenever she found out his sexual partner, confronting and threatening the woman to keep away from him.

He'd thought all the drama was an African thing. But his central European baby mama had plenty of it.

"Get off the floor," he ordered and walked away, heading to the desk. He sat in the leather armchair and swivelled it in her direction.

She rose to her feet, her face displaying a determined expression. Not ready to give up yet, she sashayed towards him, hips swinging, and leaned her butt on the edge of the desk.

"What is going on with you, *Il Re Nero*?" She purred his nickname seductively. "People might think you're gay or something."

"I don't care what people think," he replied nonchalantly, and he didn't. Even if he were gay, no one would dare say anything to his face, anyway.

"Come on. You know I've missed you inside me. You always do me so good. Give your baby mama some love." She pouted this time and fluttered her long lashes, pushing down her dress to reveal her braless boobs.

A smile twitched the corner of his lips.

She knew how to stroke his ego. Knew how to get his attention. She was beautiful. It was how he got involved with her in the first place when they'd met at a club. She said she'd been a Slovenian migrant working at a restaurant. She'd been bold, in his face and he'd found it attractive. They'd ended up in his apartment for what he'd thought would be one night only.

Fast forward eleven years and she was still in his apartment.

Not for long. He wanted her gone.

He drained the rum in the glass as the darkness returned to his mind, sinking its claws into him.

"Alina," he said in a quiet voice, waiting until she met his gaze to see his serious expression. "I'm never going to fuck you again. I told you this years ago. The only reason we share an apartment is because of Lucia. I wanted to get you your own place when she was a baby, but you refused."

"I—" she started, and he raised a hand to shush her.

"I agreed for you to move in here on the condition that we will live separate lives. You signed a document to that effect. Over the years, you've been with other men."

She gasped, eyes widening.

"Yes, I know you've been with other men and frankly I don't care, as long as you don't put our daughter into situations where she is in danger. That's the whole point of living separate lives."

He paused, holding her gaze, and she shifted from the edge of the desk and walked over to the armchair as if wanting to distance herself from him. Good. Her presence was beginning to get on his nerves. This den was his sanctuary in this apartment, but she'd invaded it without permission.

"I also know you've been harassing the women linked to me. I haven't bothered to warn you to desist because none of those women mean anything to me."

"That's because you care about me," she said it as if it was a gotcha moment.

"I care you are the mother of my child. Lucia needs you as much as she needs me. Beyond that, you mean nothing else. You are not my friend, lover, partner, or spouse."

A scowl deepened the lines on her forehead.

"*Baraba*!" she shouted in Slovenian, insulting him as she reached onto his desk to grab the spherical hand-blown glass paperweight.

He reacted before she could fling it at him, clamping her arm down and wresting the heavy decorative object from her. If she flung it at his head, he would have a concussion.

He liked spirited women, but hers was too much.

She had a temper and had a habit of flinging objects when she threw tantrums. He'd learned not to keep anything that could become a weapon within her reach.

Except this was his den, and she wasn't usually allowed in here.

"Alina, behave yourself," he warned sharply.

She glared at him, tugging her arm free.

"You are a cold-hearted bastard!" She snapped and headed toward the exit.

He said nothing about her accusation because it wasn't a lie.

She stormed out and pulled the door shut with a slam.

TWO

"Girl, you are free. Finally!" Nkoli's words sent a wash of liberation over Ifeoma's body as they clicked their wine glasses together in celebration.

Soft jazzy music played through hidden speakers in the hotel bar lounge, low enough for people to have conversations and laughter.

Her lungs expanded as she sucked in a deep breath. "Eziokwu, I am free at last. O bụghị obere ife." *It's not a small thing.*

On vacation for a month, she'd travelled across the Middle East, Asia and Europe, determined to see as much of the globe—the northern hemisphere—as possible. She'd arrived in Rome a few hours ago and would fly back to Nigeria in a few days.

She'd become friends with Nkoli at university when they'd pledged to the Yadi sorority. They'd remained close friends through the years, although they lived on different continents now—Ifeoma in Africa and Nkoli in Europe.

"It's not a small thing at all," Nkoli spoke with an amused gleam in her eyes. She raised the glass of sparkling prosecco. "Considering you've been divorced for over twenty years."

Ifeoma leaned into her chair at the corner table. "Nwanne, o di kwa egwu o." *Sis, it's truly amazing.*

They burst into laughter, loud and joyous, probably drawing attention, but Ifeoma didn't care. They were middle-class, middle-aged, professional women who looked well and dressed well, with successful high-flying careers.

Ifeoma, as an educator, now ran her own private school franchise as the principal and proprietor, while Nkoli headed an international NGO as Chief Executive.

Although they were divorcees, both had raised children who were now young adults. Hence, their lives were pretty much their own these days.

"But Ifeoma, on a serious note," Nkoli leaned closer, putting her elbows on the table separating them as they faced each other. She lowered her voice. "What do you really think about Maddox getting married again? Because I know how much you resented that he never came to beg for you to come back after you left him."

As the question sank in, a sombre feeling washed over her, causing her to stop and contemplate.

Her friend wasn't wrong.

Fed up with the responsibility of raising a baby alone while her husband fought in a war, she left her marital home and move back to her parent's house. She had married at a young age, in her mid-twenties, and it wasn't until the loneliness struck that she truly grasped the challenges of being a military wife. Although she was never far from her family or his, she despised her husband's frequent absences. Adding to the challenge, when he came home during those days, she would intentionally start arguments with Maddox, causing their time together to be anything but enjoyable.

One day, after he'd returned to the frontline, she'd packed up and moved to her father's house with her baby. Maddox came home. However, when he finally found her at her parents' house, she met him with an unexpected revelation: she wanted a divorce.

What she longed to hear from him was that he would sacrifice his military career. That he would go to great lengths just to have her back in his life. That he would follow her to the ends of the earth.

Instead, his reply had been an unexpected and soul-crushing "Okay," leaving her stunned.

Once he left, she retreated to the solace of her bedroom, tears streaming down her face as his heartbreaking reply echoed in her mind. The threat of divorce was merely a test she had employed against him. It was probably the most foolish thing she had ever done, and she regretted it.

Realising her mistake, she could have sought him out to offer an explanation. However, her stubbornness was both a strength and a weakness, defining her character. She was determined not to beg him, especially since he had already agreed to divorce her.

The lingering resentment she felt towards him persisted for years.

After a while, she couldn't sustain the resentment because she had played an equal part in the divorce as Maddox. In all fairness, he was a responsible man who always fulfilled his obligations. Raising their son, Abuchi, together, they flourished as co-parents, fostering a strong bond and instilling important values in him. Maddox and his family, despite the divorce, remained a strong support system for her. He not only paid for the house she currently lived in but also gifted her a partial school franchise, thanks to his mother's kind contribution.

At one point when Maddox left active military service and set up his own security firm, she entertained the idea of them reconciling. Neither of them had engaged in serious relationships or remarried. Her close ties to his family led others to believe they would reconcile.

However, the lingering issues from their troubled marriage would persist. Maddox, a steadfast protector, played a crucial role in their community. He was constantly on call, ready to assist anyone who required his help, and he frequently journeyed to different destinations. He would never be fully present for her.

"My sister, you're right," she finally answered. "There was a time when I resented him and hoped he would come back to beg me. But the truth is, I was being self-centred. Maddox is great at his job. The Umudike community, both home and abroad, needs his expertise. It was selfish and foolish of me to ever want him to quit it. He would have probably been miserable doing anything else. Now I wish him all the best. He's happy with his new wife. Zoe is a handful, but he seems more patient, more tolerant with her."

"He's in love," Nkoli said tentatively, as if not wanting to hurt Ifeoma's feeling.

"Yes, he is." Ifeoma's throat locked tight briefly, and she had to force air into her lungs again. "I've met her. She loves him too."

Nkoli reached across and gently placed her hand over Ifeoma's, offering tremendous comfort. "And we must find you someone who loves you with the fierceness you deserve."

"Me, kwa." Ifeoma shook off the melancholy with humour. "I'm not interested in finding anyone. I mean, do you know how long it's been for both of us? We must be rusted or something."

Both women burst into laughter again.

"Speak for yourself o. Me, I have someone who oils my engine and keeps my motor running on a regular basis." Her friend preened.

"Eziokwu? So quick? You kept this hidden. Tell me more. Who is this person? Where did you meet? I want the full gist." Ifeoma giggled.

Nkoli had recently gone through a divorce just five years ago. Her husband had been secretly involved with a woman from his workplace. Upon discovering the truth, they attempted to mend their relationship. Nevertheless, she couldn't have complete faith in her husband of twelve years again. He'd shattered her self-esteem, leaving her feeling inadequate. With this understanding, she took the steps to initiate a divorce.

Half a decade later and it seemed Nkoli had found her confidence to date again.

"His name is Lorenzo, and we were introduced at a charity event about a year ago."

"Lorenzo? Onye ocha?"

"Yes, he's Italian. A businessman and widower with grown children."

"How old is he?"

"Fifty-eight."

This meant Lorenzo was older that Nkoli by ten years.

"Wow. So, tell me. How is he, you know?" Ifeoma winked.

"Lorenzo is a total gentleman with me in the streets. But he's an absolute freak between the sheets."

They burst into more laughter.

"Seriously, you need a man like him in your life."

Ifeoma opened her mouth to argue, but Nkoli waved her off.

"I'm not saying you should remarry. I'm just saying you should get someone who oils your engine every now and again."

"But where is the time for all that? Between running the school and Abuchi—"

"Abuchi is living his own life. He lives with his father when he's not at university and you only see him for a few weeks a year. So don't use my godson as your excuse for not getting laid."

Ifeoma laughed because her friend was calling bullshit on her. One reason they got on so well. Nkoli always spoke the truth to her.

True talk, she was afraid to get involved in another relationship because she would never get someone who would love her the way she needed to be loved. Someone who wouldn't give up on her because she was being too difficult.

And she was a troublesome person, stubborn and set in her ways.

Who would want to put up with her? Best to stay single.

She had money, family, friends, and her career. She didn't need a man.

"Ciao, NK."

Ifeoma glanced sideways at the sound of her friend's nickname.

A smartly dressed Caucasian man with dark hair interspersed with grey caught their attention as he approached their table. A Black man, dressed sharply in a navy suit and black shirt, walked alongside him. They exuded confidence, and their impeccably tailored clothes told a story of refinement.

"Lorenzo!" With a gasp of surprise, Nkoli rose to her feet. "What are you doing here?"

They embraced tightly, and he planted a gentle kiss on both of her cheeks.

So, *this* was the famous Lorenzo.

Ifeoma watched as her friend's eyes lit up at the sight of the dapper silver fox, understanding the allure he possessed.

"I'm here to meet a friend." Lorenzo turned, motioning towards the man standing beside him. "This is Nero. Nero, this is NK."

"Nice to meet you," Nero said as he shook hands with Nkoli and kissed her three times on the cheeks.

"Nice to meet you, too. And this is my friend, Ify," Nkoli introduced, saying her shortened name to sound like Izzy, which was how Europeans pronounced it.

Straightening up from the chair, Ifeoma became the centre of attention as everyone's gaze turned towards her.

"NK has spoken highly of you," Lorenzo said, warmly shaking her hand and planting three kisses on her cheeks.

"Thank you. She said wonderful things about you, too," Ifeoma said with a smile.

"And this is my friend." He patted Nero on the shoulder.

Ifeoma turned towards him, her heart racing, as he reached out his hand to her. She placed her hand in his to shake him. A jolt of electricity seemed to travel up her arm, causing a frisson to run down her body.

In his custom-made suit and raven-black dress shirt, he exuded an air of sin and sophistication.

Their eyes locked, and a shiver ran down her spine, causing the hairs on the back of her neck to stand on end. He had an intense aura, radiating darkness and mystery.

A surge of exhilaration coursed through her, causing her stomach to flutter.

Completely entranced, she could not avert her gaze. The bar, along with its lively atmosphere and familiar faces like Nkoli and Lorenzo, momentarily disappeared. They stood there, hand in hand, gazed locked, transcending time.

Her heart fluttered, as if awakened by some unseen force.

A distant recollection, buried deep in the recesses of her mind.

A name danced on the tip of her tongue.

A familiarity teasing her with its elusiveness.

A moniker belonging to a ghost.

She scrunched up her face, deep in thought, but the memory remained frustratingly out of reach.

"Ify, are you okay?"

The sound of her name snapped her out of the dream-like state, bringing her back to the bustling atmosphere of the bar.

"Yes, I'm fine," she replied with a slight tremor in her voice. She quickly withdrew her hand, feeling a sudden jolt of unease. It had been a while since she'd encountered such an unusual response to a man.

"Do you mind if we join you?" Lorenzo asked, his eyes darting back and forth between the two women.

Nkoli's eyebrow arched as she gazed at Ifeoma, silently questioning her. If she disagreed, she knew her friend would promptly dismiss the men. Nevertheless, she didn't want to rob Nkoli of the chance to enjoy Lorenzo's company. Her friend was evidently smitten by the man.

"I don't mind," she replied nonchalantly, shrugging her shoulders.

Nkoli cheered and took a seat beside Ifeoma at the four-seat table.

The men occupied the seats directly across from them. Lorenzo facing Nkoli, with Nero opposite Ifeoma.

Swallowing nervously, Ifeoma's heart pounded and her hand grew clammy. Her body's reaction suggested she had never encountered an attractive man before.

What was happening to her?

THREE

Three months earlier

A quick tap on Nero's office door distracted him from the laptop he was working on, making him look up.

Lorenzo Piedimonte appeared at the opened entrance and crossed the threshold. "Working late again?"

"If I don't work late, I won't be making you so much money." Nero closed his laptop and stood. He wouldn't be doing much work on it anyway with the new arrival.

Lorenzo was a business partner, and Nero's closest relative, although there was a fifteen-year age difference between them. Twenty-five years ago, when Nero's world upended, Lorenzo had become his mentor, taking him under his wing. Recognising Nero's aptitude for numbers, he'd moulded him into his protégé. Lorenzo never made a business investment without consulting Nero first.

"But what's the point of making all that money if you're not out there enjoying it?" Lorenzo grinned and sat on the sofa, stretching out and spreading himself like he owned the place.

"I get by okay," Nero grumbled. What he really wanted to say was that he made all the money so he could exact revenge on his enemies, not so he could spend it frivolously.

He strode across the office to the bar, the hard flooring muting his steps. With a steady hand, he poured a generous amount of rum into two tumblers, the ice clinking as it hit the glass. Then he handed one over to Lorenzo, who still wore a cocky grin on his face.

"What?" Nero growled, although a smile played on his lips.

"You look so tense," Lorenzo stated. "Maybe you should allow Alina to give you the blow job she's dying to give you. You really need to get laid more often."

"Did she tell you that?" Nero grimaced, settling into another sofa.

"Yes, she came to complain that you were being a cold-blooded bastard and won't have sex with her."

"Having sex with her is the reason I can't get rid of her, much as I love Lucia. I don't even understand why Alina is suddenly pestering me for sex when we haven't done it for over ten years."

"Hmmm." Lorenzo lost the grin on his face. "I think I know why."

"You do?" Tension built on Nero's spine. They were close enough that he recognised the expression on Lorenzo's face and it made dread coil in his gut.

"Lucia will be a teenager soon. When that happens, according to the co-habitation contract, Alina will have to move out," the older man said. He was a lawyer and had advised Nero on legal matters. He'd drafted the co-habitation agreement.

Suddenly, everything clicked into place, and coldness returned to his core.

"Alina wants to get pregnant again, so she doesn't have to move out," Nero said.

"Precisamente!" Lorenzo confirmed. "She lives in an expensive apartment, has her expenses paid, and can pick her lovers. She has the best life. Why change it?"

"Why change it indeed?" Nero said. His mouth dried out, and he took a sip of rum.

Alina was manipulative. She'd proven it often. This was the next level plan. To get pregnant and sink her claws further into Nero.

He would not let it happen. His focus was the businesses and revenge, not relationships or pleasure. Alina had no chance in hell of getting into his bed.

"I will handle Alina. But that is not the reason for your visit," he said, conscious there must be a weighty reason for his business partner's presence here.

Lorenzo crossed his legs as he studied Nero. He was good-looking with the dark hazel eyes, sun-bleached dark brown hair streaked with grey and neatly trimmed beard. He seemed effortlessly relaxed.

In contrast, Nero's muscles wound tight with tension, like coiled springs. It was the sacrifice he made when revenge became his sole driving force. The burden wouldn't ease until he destroyed his enemies. He would relax after he had the satisfaction of seeing them suffer.

"I thought you might like to know there's concern among some investors." One thing about Lorenzo, he got to the point. No time wasting.

"Oh yeah, how so?" Nero asked, leaning forward as he sipped his drink.

"They're uneasy with about your sudden focus on the African region."

"They were uneasy when I focused on South American businesses."

"They don't like change."

"And as I've always said, change is good."

Although Nero made money for them, many still saw him as an outsider because his father was not Italian, although his late mother came from the region. Of course, his skin colour made him stand out, too.

Lorenzo blended in and his family tree boasted the who-was-who of the Piedmont region. They went back generations to the original settlers of the foothills of the Alps. Hence the Piedimonte surname, which meant foothills. He was Nero's connection to the very traditional Mafia families.

"They don't see what your focus on investing in African businesses will bring to the table and it's making them nervous."

"Bring to the table? How about hundreds of millions of dollars? They didn't complain about the extra zeros in the bottom-line last year."

Lorenzo was *il presidente* of the businesses under the Piedimonte holdings and Nero was effectively his *amminis-*

tratore delegato. He'd diversified their wealth away from rack-eteering, trafficking and money laundering to controlling multinationals. Nero's investment portfolio spanned across multiple industries, including hotel chains, media companies, and a wide range of technology enterprises.

"You need to show them you will not pack up and move to Africa," he said. "They want you to set roots in Italy, in Turin."

"Set roots in Italy? What the hell have I been doing for the past twenty years?"

"They want you to get married."

Nero nearly spat out his rum. He reached into his pocket and pulled out a handkerchief. One of the things Lorenzo had taught him as a young man was to always carry a hand-kerchief. He patted his mouth to wipe the spill.

"Did I hear you correctly?"

"Yes, you did." He finished his drink and placed the glass on the side table. "The families meet in three months. By then, they want to see you making plans for marriage. You need to appease their restlessness. They think you and Alina make a good match because, just like you, she has Italian blood, although her father is Slovenian. You already have a daughter, so it makes things easier."

"Makes things easier for whom?"

"I'm just passing on the message. You already know this. The families are traditional in their outlook. When Alina got pregnant, they thought you would marry her. You know the fuss her brother made. The co-habitation agreement was a way to appease everyone. Now, your African interests are making our allies uneasy again, and you will have to appease them. Marriage is the only solution."

"Over my dead body."

"Be careful what you wish for. You know how bloody our allies can get."

"Not over a low-level Slovenian upstart."

Lorenzo shook his head. "Alina's brother Mitja has his uncle's ear and had risen in the ranks of the Conti mafia."

Tommaso Conti. Traditional, rich and a giant pain in the ass. Nero's dalliance with his niece, Alina, elevated his status within the Piedimonte alliance. And if Nero married Alina, it would further elevate his status and make him more powerful.

Nero would never let it happen. Not to mention that marrying the annoying, vain Alina would turn his life into a living hell.

However, the idea of getting married sparked a sizzle down his spine. Except he was thinking of a different woman.

"You can't wait much longer, Nero. Get married. Appease the families."

Lorenzo was right. Nero had lived in Italy long enough to understand the gravity and urgency of those words. He couldn't jeopardise the Piedimonte syndicate because of his personal scruples. Their lucrative alliances with the mafia families brought them both wealth and power. If marriage was the cost, then he would pay it.

The families had valid reasons to be concerned.

His new focus shifted to Africa, and majority of the businesses he'd invested in were owned by one man—Victor

Nzekwe. Although the man responsible for wrecking Nero's family was no longer alive, Nero was determined to dismantle everything he had built. In retaliation for Victor's actions against his family, he'd already taken steps to ensure the Nzekwe family's businesses would suffer complete financial collapse.

The man left behind a wife, two daughters and a son.

But Nero fixed his attention on one particular offspring.

The beautiful, indomitable Ifeoma Nzekwe.

As he recalled her lovely face, the memories flooded back, accompanied by a bittersweet ache in his heart. In a cruel twist of fate, she'd chosen the same night his parents died to humiliate him.

The night that set him on the path of revenge.

He had already taken the first steps in handling Victor Nzekwe's son, Afamefuna. The man's decision to invest in a doomed venture would have dire consequences and strip him of his family business.

Nero's lips formed a wicked smile, hinting at the darkness lurking within him. He was ready to set a new plan in motion.

Lorenzo raised one eyebrow, showing his curiosity. "Should I be worried with that expression on your face?"

"You? No. But someone else needs to be worried."

"Why?"

Nero raised his tumbler to his lips and, for the first time, his dick pulsed to life at the idea he spoke aloud.

"I'm going to get married."

. . ༄ . .

P *resent day*
         Low music filled the room from the state-of-the-art sound system, a steady throbbing pulse meant to seduce. Muted light cast shadows in the private office.

Earlier today, Nero arrived in Rome and settled into one of the recently acquired hotels of the Piedimonte Hotel Group. Now, he sat in an armchair in a sequestered room discussing business with Lorenzo, while drinking rum.

The premises was an important asset in his and Lorenzo's personal portfolios. The report they were reviewing showed it had been extremely successful since it opened a few months ago.

However, at this moment, Nero was reaping other benefits from it, too.

Nero kept his eye on the screens on the desk. The monitors showed the public sections of the boutique hotel.

"You look tense," Lorenzo said after they concluded the business discussion.

"Uptight is my middle name, remember?"

"Maybe, but not like this."

Nero stole another quick glance at the monitor, his heart pounding. He strained his eyes, but the person he was expecting remained out of sight.

To be honest, he would rather be numb right now, devoid of any feeling. Despite his best efforts, the anxious knotted ball in his gut refused to dissipate. With each passing month since his decision to get married, the uneasiness had intensified, leaving him on edge. As he made plans, the ball grew larger, the knot tighter.

Plans to wed the daughter of the person he hated.

He should feel nothing, since this was about revenge.

The thought of seeing her again stirred up a dark anticipation, a mix of excitement and apprehension in his mind.

Over the years, he meticulously documented every detail of her family's activities. To gather intel, he had enlisted a team to secretly monitor their activities. He'd devoured the updates, consuming images and videos of them like a ghost, unaffected, disconnected, and consumed by a hunger for revenge.

Despite the circumstances, he couldn't shake his intense desire for Ifeoma, his enemy's daughter.

Reaching across the table, Lorenzo poured himself another serving of rum from the bottle on the table. Then, using the tongs, he grabbed cubes of ice from the bucket to chill his drink. "The families are meeting next week. When are you going to announce your marital plans?"

"Soon," Nero replied.

"Alina?"

"No."

"Aspetta, sei seriamente intenzionato a sposare quella donna?" *Wait, are you serious about marrying that woman?*

"You know I think that's impossible," Lorenzo continued, glass in hand.

They both knew *that woman* was the daughter of his sworn enemy.

"Nothing is impossible. You know I'm tenacious as fuck and will do whatever it takes to make it happen."

Nero had been moving the chess pieces into place for the past year. Now he was about to wreak havoc on the Nzekwe family.

"Still..."

"Still, she'll make a wife which will calm the families down because I will be married."

"But Tommaso Conti won't be happy."

"He will be in the minority. Easily managed." He sipped his rum.

On the monitor he spotted two elegant Black women sitting at the hotel bar. The people he'd been expecting. His heart rate accelerated, and he took another gulp of rum.

Lorenzo nodded. "So, how do you plan on convincing the woman to marry you?"

"Just introduce me to her and leave the rest to me. Your girlfriend is at the bar with her."

Lorenzo narrowed his eyes and glanced at his gold wristwatch. "Of course, NK is never late." He looked up to meet Nero's gaze. "Are you sure you want to do this?"

Without missing a beat, he replied, "Absolutely," and rose from his seat. He couldn't wait to be face-to-face with the woman. To truly test her strength and determination. Her dossier showed she was intractable, and from their last interaction, she disliked him. Still, he wasn't that young man any longer.

She would fight him. However, would she standby and watch her family disintegrate? Or would she cave in out of duty to her family?

They'd soon find out.

Nero and Lorenzo exited the private lounge, their footsteps echoing in the corridor. The three bodyguards stood outside, their sharp gaze scanning the surroundings. One walked into the room to monitor the screens. The others followed Lorenzo and Nero in the lift down to the lobby. They kept a discrete distance once the men entered the bar lounge. Lorenzo and Nero didn't like to draw attention to themselves in public arenas. Since they were powerful men, they needed round-the-clock security.

Nero's gaze roamed the bar area, taking in every face, until it locked onto Ifeoma.

His body reacted immediately, tightening with an intense longing. He experienced a fluttering in his gut, accompanied by a tingling throughout his body.

Damn. He'd felt nothing quite like it before.

"They are over there." He gestured at the ladies because he couldn't wait to be within touching distance.

"I see them." Lorenzo navigated through the maze of tables to the cosy corner where the ladies were seated and enjoying their conversation.

Lorenzo's lady-friend, NK, stood, beaming a smile as soon as she spotted the men. She was beautiful, curvy, dark-skinned and in her forties. Same as her friend.

Yet Nero had eyes only for one of them.

With the introductions, Ifeoma stood up from her seat, mesmerising him with the sheer elegance she exuded. Despite the age difference, she looked absolutely stunning in the orange dress which complemented her dark skin and accentuated her figure. Her hair, usually left loose, surprised him with its wavy braids, giving her a fresh and unique appearance. Makeup flawlessly done, her glossy lips caught his attention and her compelling brown eyes hooked him.

Something stirred inside him as he shook her hand. Flooded with warmth, his dick hardening at the contact and the hairs rose on his nape.

Anger roiled in his gut at the unexpected eruption of emotions she roused in him.

It was wrong for him to feel anything other than hatred in her presence.

Yet he had a new obsession with her.

A twisted fixation.

Then again, his entire life was one mega addiction to revenge.

So, nothing new there.

FOUR

"*I'm not saying you should remarry. I'm just saying you should get someone who oils your engine every now and again.*"

Nkoli's words replayed in Ifeoma's mind as she sat across the table from the most handsome man she'd seen in ages, making her heart race.

Still, she was in Rome. And when in Rome, do the Roman.

A playful smile danced across her lips as she entertained the idea. When she'd booked this holiday, she'd promised herself she would rediscover her adventurous self—the young woman who'd spent a year in Brazil so many years ago.

Honestly, she wasn't usually this carefree or careless with her thoughts. Her life was quite regimented, as the principal responsible for hundreds of students at Hillcrest School in the FCT. Disciplined, she thrived in her job as an educator.

Highly respected as the principal and proprietor, she could never fully relax in front of other people back in Nigeria. Then there was her role as Ezenwanyi Ejiofor's enforcer in the Yadili sisterhood. Keeping all the women in their fold obedient and orderly was her duty. So, there could never be a question about her integrity and moral compass.

Her no-nonsense attitude and toughness made her stand out.

Despite her non-relationship with Maddox since the divorce, she hadn't let another man into her life. In the early days, some had attempted to court her and had even proposed marriage. They assumed that her divorced status would make her eager to remarry. Her mocking laughter had sent them running for the hills and they'd never returned. Of course, for a while she'd been labelled a difficult woman because she would not subjugate herself to just any man.

And why should she?

She was a titled woman in her own right, owned land and property, had her own more-than-modest income, career, etc.

She'd attained a certain status and rank in the Yadili. If she wished to remarry, she would only entertain a man of equal or higher standing within the organisation. Maddox as an enforcer was tiers higher than most others and was her standard. She wouldn't settle for anyone with less ranking or achievements.

Of course, this meant her choices were limited. The men who'd attained such levels were already married, and she was even less likely to accept a polygamous setting.

In the early days, her mother had warned her to remarry while she was still young. Because once she hit forty she would become *agbara*, untouchable, for some men looking for young women in their child-bearing years.

Still, she stayed single. To a certain extent, their predictions proved correct because after her fortieth birthday, she didn't receive any further proposals. She had male friends. Mike, her mixed double tennis partner, for one, whom she saw once a week on Saturdays.

Nevertheless, she'd closed herself off and became unapproachable. Her choice.

She'd known she had Maddox's protection. For as long as he was single, those who knew them regarded her as belonging to Maddox. Some assumed they would reconcile their differences and reunite.

However, it all changed when Maddox recently got married to mafia princess, Zoe Himba.

Now, Ifeoma was truly single, truly free. Hence her celebration with Nkoli earlier.

"Buona sera, signori, signora," a waiter arrived and quickly rattled out some more words in Italian.

Although Ifeoma had a basic understanding of the language, she found it challenging to keep up when natives spoke rapidly. In contrast, fluent Nkoli had placed their drink orders earlier. Then again, she lived in the country.

"Since the ladies are drinking Prosecco, we'll join them," Lorenzo spoke in English, probably for the Ifeoma's benefit since everyone else at the table was at ease in Italian. He truly was a gentleman. "Bring another bottle."

"Certo." the waiter nodded and walked towards the bar.

Interesting, Lorenzo had ordered for his friend. Did he intuit the man wanted the same beverage? Had there been an unspoken communication between them, as Nero had not uttered a word since they took their seats?

It implied that in specific situations, Nero placed his trust in Lorenzo and followed his lead. Suggesting a father-son or uncle-nephew dynamic between them rather than friendship.

There was no trace of deference in Nero's intense aura as he locked eyes with her. His presence made her senses come alive, leaving a lingering imprint on her skin.

Gosh, she hadn't felt this way in ages—her heart all aflutter, her skin tingling with excitement. Not for twenty years. Not since she was young and dating Maddox. She'd forgotten the emotions.

Even this Eurasia trip alone evoked unfamiliar sensations. On previous vacations abroad, she'd travelled with Abuchi. But Nkoli was right. Her son had reached an age where he preferred to pursue his own interests. Without him to fuss over, she felt like an empty-nester, adrift and unsure of what to do.

Hence the reason her friend had suggested she book this trip and travel alone. Of course, she'd included the stopover in Rome so they could catch up, since Nkoli couldn't travel with her because of work commitments.

So here she was, immersed in her adventure. Spending time with Nkoli filled her heart with happiness. Due to their busy lives and living on different continents, they rarely had the chance to see each other. Her friend's advice to embark on this solo journey was excellent.

The trip had been amazing so far, leaving a trail of beautiful memories in its wake. The northern hemisphere was basking in the heat of summer, with the weather being pleasantly warm. In some places, the scenery had taken her breath away, while the people had greeted her with warm smiles. The prospect of delving into the rich history of Rome for a few days before her departure to Nigeria filled her with anticipation.

Nkoli leaned towards Lorenzo and spoke to him in Italian, catching Ifeoma's attention. Lorenzo replied without hesitation, reaching for her hand. He couldn't seem to take his eyes off Nkoli, and her friend seemed to have forgotten there were others at the table. Their affection for each other was undeniable.

At their age, was it even possible? Was it possible to find love a second time with Nkoli as a divorcee and Lorenzo a widower?

For her friend, maybe. But impossible for Ifeoma.

She didn't have the time, energy, or inclination to get romantically involved again.

A prickling sensation on her nape made her look up. She met Nero's piercing scrutiny and swallowed reflexively.

Surely he was staring at someone behind her because he couldn't be looking at her like she was the most fascinating object on the planet.

She lifted her menu card and held it to cover her face as she glanced behind to see if there was another woman at the next table.

Nope. Behind her was the window and the garden beyond, which was partially obscured by a hanging plant.

Okay. So, Nero must be staring at her. Another glanced at him, showed him exploring the menu.

She used the opportunity to observe him. When he'd been standing, he'd been tall, slightly taller than Lorenzo. Even sitting, his broad shoulders and chest filled out the black shirt. He'd removed the jacket earlier.

His skin was ebony, yet his curly hair was light brown. Matched with his onyx eyes, sharp cheekbones and Nubian nose, he really was the finest man on mother earth.

And her body would not let her forget it. It showed in the powerful awareness of her thudding heart. The moistening of her mouth and the warmth flooding her body.

Goddess help her, but she was aroused.

She sipped her drink to quench her dry throat and stuck her nose in the menu card, trying to ignore her suddenly awakened libido.

She should decipher some of the meal options. However, her body was diverting blood to her nerve-endings rather than her scrambled brain, turning every word on the menu into gobbledegook.

Since her brain refused to cooperate, she diverted her attention elsewhere. Anywhere else but the handsome man in front of her.

She glanced around the restaurant and it didn't have the feel of one attached to a hotel. It was a stylish and welcoming space, just like the rest of the premises.

They sat in the corner overlooking the back garden, which had more tables and chairs. They could have sat out there, but the people outside were smoking and neither woman wanted to be amongst smokers.

Still inside was lovely, too. Dusk settled in, bathing the place in a soft glow, courtesy of spotlights that resembled delicate strands of fairy lights. The flickering candles on the wooden tables added a touch of romance to the atmosphere. The convivial laughter, loud music, and jovial conversations created a festive atmosphere.

A diverse crowd of stylish, middle-aged and young people mingled, the venue buzzing with activities. Although she couldn't understand all the spoken words, familiarity lingered. The people used exaggerated hand gestures, laughed loudly, told theatrical stories using their entire bodies. Just like Nigerians, they were full of vibrant energy and enthusiasm.

It seemed Italians and Nigerians had something in common. A penchant for the dramatic.

"Iffy, NK was telling me about your trip through Europe," Lorenzo said. "How has it been so far?"

It seemed he suddenly remembered the other people at the table with them.

Ifeoma curled her lips into a smile. "Oh yes. My trip. It has been wonderful so far."

"How long are you in Italy for?" Nero spoke English like an Italian. Like his friend. He dropped the H in 'How' and the i in 'in' sounded like 'ee'.

Still, his deep, husky voice played havoc with her core and her nipples hardened.

What would it feel like having him whisper in her ear while he was deep inside her? Her insides clenched tight at the image.

"Ify?"

Blinking, her cheeks heated. She'd been staring at him while daydreaming. She coughed, picking up her drink to hide her embarrassment. "Four days."

"Nero is in Rome for a few days, too. You must let him show you around," Lorenzo chimed in with a sly grin, as if he could tell she was attracted to his friend. "What do you think, Nero?"

"It depends on the lady. I don't want to take up her time if she has something else planned." Nero gave a slow, sexy smile, sending her stomach flipping.

So, he was a gentleman, just like his friend.

"I don't mind," Ifeoma replied before she could think better of it. "I was planning to do some sightseeing and perhaps some shopping."

"There you have it," Lorenzo said.

"It will be my pleasure," Nero added.

"That's great," Nkoli cheered. "Now I can relax, knowing you will be in safe, capable hands."

Ifeoma met Nero's ardent, hungry gaze. The last thing he projected was safety. He looked like he wanted to eat her up and right now, she wouldn't mind. He had her flustered and excited for the first time in ages.

The waiter returned with the dewy bottle of Prosecco and, after the ritual tasting by Lorenzo, he filled everyone's glasses. He asked if they were ready to place food orders, but Nero told him to give them a minute.

She glanced at the menu again, a little disconcerted because she hadn't chosen yet.

"Would you like some help?" it was Nero's gravelly voice again.

"Help?" Ifeoma resisted the urge to tremble. It felt like he'd traced a finger down her spine. Hell, yes, her body needed TLC. It had been so long. She could do with him in a bedroom, between her legs, giving her multiple orgasm. He looked capable.

"With the menu?" He pointed at the item in her hand. How could a voice, a smile, be so damned sexy? He was absolutely drop dead gorgeous—tall, dark, handsome. Why did he have to live all the way out here in Italy?

Then again, if he lived in Nigeria, she wouldn't be entertaining all the naughty ideas and images in her head.

"Oh, yes, please." She gulped the rest of her drink.

He chuckled as if he could read her mind, a deep, raspy laugh, making her insides quiver.

"The menu has six sections." He leaned forward, showing his menu. "Antipasti are the appetisers. Primi Piatti is the first course, Secondi Piatti—"

"Is the second course," she interjected.

"Corretta. Do you know what Contorni is?"

His smile disappeared and his eyes were assessing her, challenging her.

Her spine stiffened. She thrived at challenges and didn't enjoy failing at anything.

The others, her friend and her friend's beau, were watching too.

She glanced at the menu again. Surely it couldn't be all that difficult to decipher. He'd already told her what the three other sections were. From her basic translations, she could make out salads in the Contorni section, which meant, "Side dishes."

"Brava ragazza." The sexy smile returned, along with his praise. "Your Italian is improving."

Warmth suffused her chest, and she did a little internal dance. Perhaps her Italian wasn't so bad. She would keep getting better at it, if it meant having his attention for a while.

"So, Dolci are the desserts?"

"Yes, and you pronounced it correctly, too. So, what is Bevande?"

What else was left after eating a five-course meal?

"Drinks?" she said tentatively.

"Brava!" Lorenzo cheered, grinning.

"Well done." Nkoli clapped and giggled, leaning against her.

"Thank you, thank you." Ifeoma tipped her head and chuckled. She loved all the praise, although some people from the other tables were watching them. She loved learning new languages, and Nero was an excellent teacher.

That was one thing that made her great friends with Nkoli. Their love for languages. If Ifeoma hadn't met Maddox and become a teacher in his mother's school, perhaps she would have had a different career. Maybe she would've earned a PhD like her friend and become a professor of linguistics. But she loved being an educator to middle and high schoolers, so it wasn't a terrible life.

"We'll make an Italian out of you," Nero said, pulling her attention again.

For a moment, they stared at each other, and she imagined the possibility in his words. Spending the rest of her life in Italy with him, becoming Italian. Her heart thrummed hard at the potential.

Yet it was all impossible. Her life was in Nigeria.

Daughter. Mother. Principal. Proprietor. Enforcer.

All those roles and responsibilities were hers.

"Do you like seafood? Are you vegetarian? Prefer red meat or white?" he asked, and she blinked. His gaze dropped to her mouth suggestively, and she licked her lips. The man oozed sensuality, and every gesture seemed provocative.

What was happening to her? Why couldn't she get a hold of herself? It was getting annoying.

"Ehm. I like seafood. No red meat."

"Do you mind if I order for you?" he raised his brow.

Her hackles rose and her spine stiffened. She didn't allow anyone to do anything for her. She was intelligent and capable of picking her own meal. Was it because she'd permitted him to translate some items on the menu that he thought he could take over? Who did he think he was?

"No! I—"

"Gentlemen, excuse us. Ify and I need to powder our noses," Nkoli interjected, standing up.

"Of course." Lorenzo rose to his feet. So did Nero.

Seriously, where did these men come from? Chivalry seemed like something lost with her father's generation. Then again, she hadn't dated in over twenty years, so what did she know?

Nkoli looked at Ifeoma and tipped her head, indicating for her to join her.

Ifeoma didn't argue, although the sudden need to use the bathroom surprised her. She supposed her friend wanted to say something without the men eavesdropping.

Nkoli led the way down the corridor into the surprisingly quiet convenience, with shiny black tiles and a clear mirror running along one wall over the white porcelain sinks. Her friend checked the cubicles attached to the opposite wall were empty before turning to her.

"NK, o gini? What's the problem?" Ifeoma asked.

"I na-ajụ m? What were you doing out there?"

"What did I do?"

"You don't know? Hmmm. I've known you for over twenty years. I know your mannerism and moods. That man out there, Nero. He likes you. Everyone can see it. Even better, you like him."

"And so?"

"O si m, and so?" Nkoli shook her head in amusement. "And so, why are you trying to shut him down?"

"Why is he trying to order my food? I can do it myself."

"Nobody said you can't do it. That's not the point. The man asked your permission. He wasn't imposing it. You've been out of the dating game for so long, you don't even know how to relate to a man anymore."

"I can relate to men alright. I employ men. I have male ... friends."

"How many of them have asked you out on a date?"

"It's not my fault if we're not compatible. If they're intimidated by me."

"Nero is not intimidated by you. He's not. And the two of you seem very compatible. It was wonderful seeing the two of you interact. I saw your eyes light up when he was talking to you and teaching you the words on the menu. I saw some of my old friend. The woman with hopes and dream. The fun-loving woman I used to know. But somehow, over the years, you've lost some of that. You only let your hair down when you're with me, which is rare these days."

"It's because we're birds of a feather. You know me like no one else does. Better than members of my family."

"I know that." Nkoli cupped her shoulders. "But I want more for you. I want you to experience life fully. I'm not saying you need a man in your life full time to do it. I'm just saying you need to loosen up a bit and have fun. Remember, you're on holiday. Relax, enjoy the moment. It's fleeting anyway. If a man says hello to you, wave and say hello back. Don't walk around like a cobra waiting to strike the unsuspecting passerby. You can reserve that for your students and teaching staff when you return to Naija."

Nkoli chuckled.

"I'm not that bad." Ifeoma couldn't help smiling.

"You are, and you know it."

"Fair enough," she admitted. She'd spent so long being on the defensive and ready to battle anyone she didn't know how to be different.

"Look, I'm not asking you to date Nero or to see him beyond tonight. But we are all having a great night. Let's keep it that way. Relax. Be spontaneous. Accept his offer. Take it as an adventure. If you don't like his meal choices, you can reject them. And use it as an excuse to avoid him for the rest of your visit."

"True. You have a good point." Her friend knew how to hit the nail on the head. Everything she said about her was true. She couldn't even argue. What did she have to lose by allowing Nero to order her meal? Sure, it was the first time she'd allowed anyone to do it. But it wouldn't kill her to attempt it. "Okay. I'll try."

"Great. That's more like it." Nkoli nudged her playfully. "But that man is fine, sha."

"Eziokwu. Fine abụghị obere," she replied. "You own man is fine too."

"I hụ gọ nu ya. The equation is balanced."

They giggled as other women entered the ladies.

Ifeoma used a cubicle and washed her hands before they left. The men were talking in low voices when they returned to the table. Both stood until the ladies were seated.

"I hope everything is okay," Lorenzo asked, glancing from one woman to the other.

"Everything is fine," Nkoli replied. "We just needed a girly moment."

"That's understandable. Are you ready to order? Ify, do you need a moment to select?" Lorenzo asked.

"No. I'm okay." Ifeoma met Nero's gaze.

His expression was inscrutable, and his smile was gone.

Her heart dropped. She missed his smile. Her friend was correct. The man had tried to be nice, more than nice, and she'd snapped at him unnecessarily.

She swallowed before speaking. "Nero, would you please order for me? I don't mind the fish or vegetarian options."

"Come desidera, signora." *As you wish, madam.* Ifeoma could translate his words.

There was no humour or warmth in his tone. It was like the shutters had descended and he'd shut her out. Yet he would be a gentleman and order for her because she'd requested it.

He waved for the waiter, who arrived promptly. Then he spoke rapid fire Italian without even looking at the menu.

How did he remember all the items by heart? Perhaps he'd eaten at the restaurant many times before. But didn't Lorenzo say Nero was visiting Rome, too?

When he finished, Lorenzo spoke to the waiter too in Italian. Then the waiter thanked them and walked away.

"Are you not placing your order?" Ifeoma asked her friend.

"Lorenzo ordered for me. He knows exactly what I like." Nkoli winked.

"Of course I do." Lorenzo reached across, lifted Nkoli's hand, and pressed his lips to the back of her hand. Love was certainly in the air for those two.

Nero pulled his ringing phone out of his pocket. "Mi scusi. I have to take this."

He stood and walked away without glancing at her.

FIVE

A ringing phone woke Ifeoma the next morning. The room was dark because she'd closed the curtains before going to bed. But streaks of sunshine filtered through the edges. Who was calling her this early? Was it someone from Nigeria?

She scrambled for the phone sitting on the bedside cabinet. A glance at the screen and she didn't recognise the number, although it seemed to have the Italian country code. A local number, but not Nkoli's because she had it saved already.

"Hello?" she answered in a husky voice, still filled with sleep.

"Buongiorno, signora. This is Nero."

Before he said his name, she already recognised the deep gravelly voice and her sleepiness receded.

"Nero, this is a surprise. How did you get my number? Is everything okay?" she said, sitting up in bed and tugging the covers around her since AC was on.

Last night after he received a phone call and had stepped away, he'd returned briefly to bid them good night because he'd had a business emergency to handle. She'd wondered what kind of business emergency would require his attention so late in the evening, but had assumed they had offices in the Americas where it was still daytime.

"Everything is fine. I got your number from your friend, NK. I'm calling because I promised to be your tour guide today."

"Oh. But I thought you had a business emergency."

"I handled the emergency last night. So today I am at your service. Unless you've changed your mind, which is your prerogative."

"No. Of course not. I would love to have you as my tour guide."

"Bene. Can you meet me in the hotel lobby in thirty minutes?"

"No. That's not possible. I'm not dressed. Let's make it an hour."

"See you in an hour. Ciao." The line went dead.

Ifeoma stared at the phone in her hand for a few seconds. Her hands were shaking and her heart racing.

Nero had called her. Nkoli had given him her number. More to the point, Nero had called her to ask her out on a date. She wasn't inexperienced not to know that this was going to be a date.

A grown businessman like him wouldn't take time out of his busy schedule to show a random woman around a city if he wasn't interested in dating her. After the hiccup yesterday, he would give her a second chance.

And what was she doing? Sitting on the bed analysing it instead of getting ready.

A thrill ran through her. She scrambled off the bed and raced to the bathroom to shower, shave her legs and armpits and brush her teeth.

When she came out, she sent Nkoli a text:

Nero called. He's taking me out for the day. I can't believe he called after he disappeared last night.

Then she took care with her makeup and styling her hair with products. She picked an orange floral midi sundress with a deep V-neck that clung to her bodice and flared at the waist. She paired it with fashionable, matching white trainers with orange flowers. Since they would walk around the historic sites, she needed to be comfortable.

Messages buzzed from Nkoli:

That's great. I'm so excited for you.

Lorenzo said there was an issue with one of their offices in Sao Paulo. That's why Nero left last night.

Remember what I told you. Relax. Be spontaneous. If he wants to treat you and spoil you, let him. Let him rock your world.

Ifeoma chuckled while reading that last one and she sent a reply.

I will. Thank you.

Standing in front of a mirror, she surveyed her appearance, and doubt niggled.

The dress was a recent impromptu purchase. She loved it when she'd seen it on the mannequin in a Paris boutique. But had it been a good idea to buy it, considering how the deep V-neck showed a hint of her braless breasts?

Was she overdressed to play tourist for a day? Probably.

However, she was also going on a date for the first time in twenty years. She would rather be overdressed than under-dressed.

She was beautiful regardless, and Nero had better be ready for her.

Grabbing her purse, she ensured she had her credit cards, her lipstick and mascara and petroleum jelly. She made sure her valuables were locked in her suitcase. Sunshades on, she took the keycard and headed downstairs.

In the lobby, she glanced around and her gaze fell on Nero, who was sitting in a low chair next to a pillar of green-ery, staring at his phone. He was waiting for her. Even sitting, he looked amazing. Her heart rate kicked up a notch as she walked towards him.

He looked up as she approached, and his eyes widened. Surprise? Awe? She couldn't tell.

"Oh." He stood from the chair, the sexy grin curling his full lips. "Ciao, bella."

Did he just call her beautiful? She couldn't help the an-swering smile as she extended her hand for a shake. "Hi."

He took her hand and his touch tingled all over her skin. Same as when he stepped in and kissed her cheeks. The smell of his cologne was intoxicating, and she inhaled deeply, a lit-tle disappointed when he pulled back.

"You look stunning." His voice had gained the deep rumble.

The butterflies took flight in her tummy. "I thought I might be overdressed."

He was in a white shirt and navy denim with a single-breasted tailored blazer. He looked edible. Delicious. Total eye candy.

"Well, you are a little overdressed for the coliseum. But I propose a change of plans if you will permit me."

Her spine stiffened at the mention of change, but she shoved the feeling aside. Spontaneity and fun were the order of the day.

"Oh, what do you have in mind?"

"I was thinking of showing you Rome like a native rather than a tourist. We can drive to the beach and on the way, we will stop for brunch. Then later when we come back this evening, I will take you to dinner to make up for last night and then we can go dancing afterwards."

She chuckled. "You want to take me dancing?"

"Yes, it's been a long time since I did it. I could use some fun."

"I haven't been dancing in a long time, too. But I'll be happy to try."

"Eccellente! First, a little shopping. Come with me." He waved towards the exit.

"Shopping? Why?"

"You are mine for the day and I mean to start the way I mean to proceed."

The way he said 'you are mine' sent a sizzle down her spine.

"I'm yours?"

"Yes, you are my date," he said matter of fact, a brow arched.

She wouldn't argue with it. "Let's go shopping."

She wasn't sure what he was going to buy, but she'd promised she would be spontaneous and go with the flow, so here went nothing.

They left the hotel premises and walked along the pavement into the designer boutique a few doors down. Nero instructed the shop assistant in Italian, and they went about making a fuss over her as they brought out different swimsuits. She could have told him she had a swimsuit in her suitcase, but she didn't bother.

He seemed intent on treating her. Why should she deny him?

In the end, she selected a black halter tie tankini because she wasn't comfortable showing her tummy. Nero added a sarong and flip-flops as well as beach towels and a tote for all the items.

Once they were done, Nero took the shopping bags, and they headed outside. At the pavement, she wondered if he was going to call a taxi. But he reached into his pocket and then a car flashed and beeped. A bright red Ferrari.

Of course, he was Italian. But this looked new and very expensive. What kind of business did he run?

He put the shopping bags in the boot, then helped her into the car before going to settle in the driver's seat.

"Ready?" he turned to her and their eyes met.

Her breath caught. He really was the most gorgeous man she'd ever seen.

"Yes." Her voice was breathy, and she gulped in air. Taking in the scent of new leather. "Is this your car?"

"Yes." He turned away, pressed the ignition and the car kicked to life. "Don't you like it?"

She almost missed the question he asked in a low voice.

"No. It's not that. I've never been in one before. Never known anyone who owned a Ferrari." She swallowed at her confession, not sure why she was telling him.

"I've always been fascinated by Ferraris. I hope you enjoy the drive."

They drove through the city and he pointed out the monuments and places of interest in the way out.

"Do you like sports cars?" he asked when the silence stretched for a bit after they left the city.

"I don't have an aversion to them, but I won't spend my money buying one," she replied honestly.

"What kind of car do you drive?" he asked.

"A Toyota Landcruiser. But to be honest, I don't do much driving these days. I have a chauffeur."

"Why is that?"

"It's convenient and practical. I run a school in my home city and I can accomplish a lot during the commute from home to work and vice versa."

"Good point. I can definitely see you as a principal. The air of authority and determination about you mixed with the class and elegance."

"I'll take that as a compliment."

"It is."

"Thank you."

He nodded and said nothing else for a few seconds as he concentrated on the highway.

"What about you? What do you do for a living?" she asked, wanting to know so much about him.

He glanced at her with a smile. "I'm the CEO of an investment holdings which include international telecoms, media houses, and tech companies. Our servers went down yesterday in Brazil, which impacted transactions, which was why I had to leave last night."

His reasons matched up to what Nkoli had told her.

"Is it all sorted out now?" she asked.

"Yes, and they are working on clearing the backlog through today."

"Great."

As he promised, they stopped to have a late breakfast/ early lunch at a café with a view of the sandy beach and stretch of ocean. It was beautiful. But perhaps not as beautiful as the man sitting opposite her. Compared to last night with Nkoli and Lorenzo, it was amazing having him all to herself. He sat close, within touching distance, but he didn't touch.

The air crackled with electricity as they ate the food he'd ordered. She'd allowed him to order again, although he'd explained all the items on the menu. She'd loved last night's food, so didn't see the point in doing it for herself when he did a much better job.

"You've got food." He indicated her face, and she tried to dab it with the napkin. He shook his head. "May I?"

"Okay." She swallowed.

He reached across and swiped his forefinger on her cheek. When he lifted it, there was some carbonara sauce on the tip.

Instinctively, she flicked her tongue out and licked the sauce off his finger.

His eyes widened as he sucked in a breath.

Then she gasped, realising what she'd done. "I'm s—"

"Shhh. Don't apologise about that." He placed his thumb under her bottom lip and tugged, opening her mouth, while the other hand cupped her nape, pulling her closer as he leaned in.

He was going to kiss her. Her heart raced, her pussy clenching. She'd lacked this kind of attention so much that even a little of it was driving her insane.

"Can I tell you a secret?" he whispered, staring at her open mouth as if measuring something. "Perhaps it's a bad idea. I don't want to offend you."

He leaned back, releasing her, breaking contact and sending a rush of disappointment into her. Without thinking, she leaned forward, placing her palm on his arm.

"No. Tell me. I won't be offended." What she really wanted to say was, "*Touch me. I won't be offended.*"

Staring at her as if assessing her ability to not get offended, he stuck his tongue between his lips. It took all her willpower not to breach the gap and kiss him.

"You sure you won't be offended, even if it's vulgar?"

"Do I really look that prudish to you?"

She might not have had sex in a while, but she wasn't a teenage virgin.

He grinned, leaning forward again. "If I tell you mine, do you promise to tell me yours?"

"Yes, just spill already!"

His grin turned sexy, and he cupped her nape again.

She cheered silently at the body contact. She didn't care what he said as long as he kept holding her with the firm grip like he would never let her go.

"This morning, I did something I haven't done since I was a teenager," he said in a low husky voice for her ear only. "While I was in the shower, I jacked off, picturing you on your knees and my dick in your mouth."

He leaned back a little, his dark gaze holding hers captive.

Breath locked in her throat and she could barely whisper, "You did?"

That he could find her attractive enough to picture her in such a scene was blowing her mind.

"Yes, and it was the hottest thing. Picturing you taking my engorged, throbbing dick. I came so hard, my legs nearly gave way in the shower. And yet afterwards, after dressing, I wanted you all over again. And this time I want the real thing, not just my imagination."

"Oh," she whispered, her voice filled with desperation. A fiery sensation surged through her body, causing her eyes to flutter shut, longing for his lips to meet hers.

"Come, let's have a swim."

What? Her eyes fluttered open, and she glanced around widely.

He stood and walked to the counter to settle their bill.

How could he express all those desires to her and then shut down emotionally? Was he serious about swimming? All she wanted was to go back to the hotel, where they could recreate his vivid imagination and indulge in even more.

SIX

Half an hour later, Ifeoma and Nero were in bathing suits, sitting on loungers under an umbrella on the beach. She'd thought the man was joking about going swimming when they'd been in the café earlier. But it turned out he'd meant it.

He'd paid for the meal. Then they'd walked back to the car. He'd grabbed the tote with the swimsuits and they'd walked to the huts to change. The beach seemed empty, with only a handful of people. He'd said it was midweek and locals rarely sunbathed in the middle of the day.

They eagerly entered the refreshing water for a swim. She stayed near the shore, not wanting to soak her braids with salty water, while relishing in the cool relief from the scorching sun. He playfully chased her around, their laughter echoing through the air.

Leaning casually on the lounger, he exuded sex appeal with his sculpted physique and confident aura. His unbuttoned beach shirt revealed the radiant dark skin and seemed to pull her in, tempting her to reach out and touch him.

Disbelief made her light-headed as she admired the handsome man by her side for the day. Other women at the beach were giving her jealous glares.

Her energy was an electrifying mix of self-consciousness and desire. It was only early afternoon, yet he had already twisted her emotions into a knot.

She grabbed her tumbler, feeling the cool condensation on the glass, and took a small sip of the refreshing Mai Tai. In his glass, a Cuba Libre, a rum cocktail, sparkled with ice and a slice of lime. Their shared love for the liquor, which had its roots in the Caribbean, brought them closer. After a long day, she enjoyed a glass of rum on the rocks, and so did he.

However, the thing she couldn't understand was this whole lying on a beach lounger thing as leisure.

"Is this how you spend your free time lying on the beach?" she asked.

"Not exactly. As you know, I don't live in Rome. I live in Turin, which is landlocked. The nearest beach I go to is ninety minutes away in a village known as Spotorno-Noli. But of course, only in the summer."

His gaze trailed down her body, heating her skin, fuelling her imagination.

What would he feel like in bed? She would bet the sex would be bone-melting, earth-shattering, dripping with sweat, until exhaustion. He certainly had a vivid mind. *If you can think it, you can achieve it, right?* She certainly believed it.

"What about you? Do you live near a beach?"

Blinking, she realised he was still talking. What did he just say? Seriously, her brain must be on meltdown because it was taking so long to process simple things.

"No," she finally said when his words registered. "Just like you, I live in a landlocked city. If I want to swim, I go to the sports club or a resort."

"So, we're both on an adventure today because this is my first time coming to this beach." He smiled, nodding as he traced his thumb over his bottom lip.

The memory of him gently pulling her bottom lip in the café lingered in her mind, along with his candid remarks about indulging in self-pleasure under the shower. Her body warmed up once more, igniting her senses, making her heart race and her palms sweat.

"Stop it," she said.

"What." He sat up, looking innocent.

"Stop that thing you're doing. Touching your lips."

"Oh. Is it bothering you? As you wish." He picked up his drink, but the devilish grin on his face said he knew exactly how he was affecting her. Knew exactly what he was doing to her. He did it on purpose. Was he playing games with her?

Okay. She hadn't dated for a long time. But she wasn't Ifeoma Nzekwe for nothing. She was *agbara*, feared by many. She'd certainly tamed a few men in her lifetime. If Nero wanted to play games with a lioness, he better prepare to be mauled.

Needing liquid courage to up her seduction game, she downed the rest of the cocktail in one gulp. Then she reached into the tote and pulled out the bottle of sunscreen they'd bought at the local chemist along with bottles of water.

"Nero, will you rub this sunscreen onto my back for me?" she asked in a sweet voice and shifted. She lowered the lounger, so it looked like a flatbed, then she rolled onto her belly.

While the one-piece tankini covered her stomach, her entire back was on display, along with her shoulders and arms.

"Are you sure?" His forehead furrowed as he stared at her behind. For the first time since she met him, he hesitated, as if the idea of touching her skin was a temptation he needed to conquer.

And to be fair, she was laying a trap for him, and she intended to ensnare him. While other women were killing for BBL, she had the naturally endowed bottom designed to bring men to their knees.

She hid her smile. "Of course. I don't want to get skin cancer."

"Come si desidera." He puffed out a breath and moved over, sitting on her lounger. Then he typed briefly on his phone before putting it away in his pocket.

Her trip to Italy was short and she wouldn't see him when she returned home. Wouldn't interact with him beyond today, probably.

Nevertheless, he was hers for the day. This gorgeous man, the most beautiful in all of Italy, was hers and she would claim him for the time they had together. Afterwards, they would go their separate ways and she would chuck it down to an adventure.

But she craved his presence in this very moment. Craved every rugged fragment of his being. Whether his intentions were noble or playful, she didn't mind. Her focus was on the way his eyes sparkled when he spoke to her, as if she was the only woman on the planet. She hadn't desired anyone like this in so long, and she would be damned if she wasn't going to take what she wanted. Especially for one day only.

Her heart raced, and a surge of adrenaline coursed through her veins.

Their eyes met as he grabbed the lotion bottle, popped the cap, and tipped it. Cold oil drizzled down her back. However, her insides seemed on fire already. She laid her head on her crossed arms and closed her eyes.

His warm fingers untied the halter sashes, sending her pulse rate stratospheric.

Her eyes flicked open, and she glanced around, trying to see if anyone was watching. With the ties loosened, there was nothing covering the sides of her boobs since her arms were under her head.

Her mouth dried out with as the excitement ratcheted up to another level.

Oh god, he wasn't playing. No sirree. She'd challenged him and he'd taken it up a notch. Did she want him to stop? This was the time to call it off if she didn't want to be on public display?

Just as she was about to shift, he firmly pressed his palms onto her back, skilfully working the oil into her skin with slow, deliberate movements.

Damn. It felt so good. He felt so good. She closed her eyes again, relaxing into his touch.

His fingers drifted down her sides, ghosting the flesh of her breasts, making her clit tingle. Then his hands tugged down the swimsuit halfway down her butt and he was massaging her cleft and ass cheeks.

Damn it, she wanted him to squeeze them. Goosebumps chased over her skin and she struggled to breathe.

Oh, goddess. Was it a smart move to challenge him like this? Her nerve endings prickled, and her core pulsated over and over. The tingling sensations grew stronger, hinting at an impending orgasm. Did she really want to have a public climax?

"Bella, turn around," his voice was husky, and it took her a few seconds to realise he was talking to her.

She held onto the top half of the tankini as she rolled over.

His eyes were intense, dark, and filled with desire, taking her breath away.

"Let go of the straps," he said in a low voice.

"We're in public." Nervousness pulsed through her. She glanced around, clinging onto the swimsuit on her chest.

"No one else will see but me," he purred reassuringly and knelt on the sand beside the lounger, his body covering her side.

She didn't know why, but she believed him. Although logic dictated that because they were outside on a beach, someone else would come by any minute. Still, she let go of the tankini straps. Actually, pushed it down to her hips, exposing her breasts and tummy. What the heck, in for the penny, in for the pound.

He poured more sunscreen onto his palms, rubbed them together, and leaned over her. His hands caressed her skin, starting from her shoulders and collarbone. He rubbed down the middle of her chest and around her breasts, then trailed down towards her stomach.

Self-conscious about her body, she scrunched her eyes shut. She didn't mind showing off her voluptuous backside, which was perhaps her greatest physical asset. But her stomach was a different subject with the scar from her c-section and the fupa.

His hands massaged her stomach, down to her hipbones, over the scar and down to her legs, rubbing the cream over her thighs. Then he came up to her chest. It was obvious he wasn't just rubbing sunscreen.

He covered each breast with his palms, caressed and squeezed until she was panting. Then he tugged her nipples.

Moaning, she arched off the lounger, arousal spiking through her. She'd forgotten how it felt to be touched like this. Sensation surged, all her nerve endings primed. Blood whooshed in her ears.

He kept one arm squeezing and tweaking her breast. The other travelled back down her belly, around her navel, along the c-section scar, under the swimsuit, over her pubic bone.

"Ify, you are fucking beautiful," he whispered as his fingers parted her labia.

"As if," she scoffed nervously. "I didn't peg you as a sweet talker. You don't have to lie to me."

Not that she doubted her own beauty. She just felt self-conscious when he stared at her stomach and didn't believe he truly found her beautiful.

"Open your eyes," there was a sharpness to his voice, and his hands stopped moving on her skin.

Shit. She didn't want him to stop. Her eyes fluttered open. "What is it?"

"I don't like being called a liar," he said in a gruff voice. His expression was back to inscrutable, like last night after she'd argued about him ordering her meal.

"I—I didn't mean it like that," she stuttered, spreading her legs, inviting him to continue touching her intimately.

But he didn't budge. "How did you mean it?"

Did he seriously want to get into an argument in the middle of making out? She wasn't about to tell him that no man had touched her stomach since she gave birth.

Sure, Maddox had tried after Abuchi's arrival, but she hadn't let him touch her. Instead, she'd picked quarrels.

So, Nero was the first to see her belly and scar. And he couldn't blame her if she didn't believe him.

"I see," he said ominously and pulled away, withdrawing and standing. He began dusting the sand off his knees.

"See what exactly?" She sat up, tugging the tankini up to cover her breasts. It seemed they would not get any more love from him.

"I see that you really think I'm a liar." His eyes narrowed.

"Well, everyone lies sometimes." She said, suddenly annoyed he would take it this far. "So, you lied because you thought it would make me feel good. You had good intentions. I get it."

"For fuck's sake!" he sounded outraged and threw his hands up in the air, shaking his head. "You know what? Let's head back to the city."

"Yes, let's go back." Why did she ever agree to this date in the first place? This was why she never dated. Men were so fucking arrogant and demanding. Yet with fragile egos.

She'd called him a liar. Big deal! He should get over himself.

SEVEN

Nero's heartbeat pounded, and his muscles were tight. It made his manoeuvres jerky as he drove the Ferrari back towards the city.

Ifeoma sat beside him in the front passenger seat, doing her best to ignore him by keeping her gaze on the scenery whizzing past.

He avoided looking at her because every time he saw her, he seemed to forget that she was his foe. The daughter of his enemy.

It was bad enough yesterday when he'd met her in the hotel bar with Lorenzo and her friend Nkoli. As he'd sat opposite her, he'd maintained a detached demeanour, while scrutinising her and searching for the best way to execute his plans.

Their reunion had been long overdue—a quarter of a century in the making.

Yet, she hadn't recognised him. Granted, he was no longer the teenage boy hanging around her parents' house just so he could glimpse his friend's gorgeous, confident, off-limit older sister.

He'd watched her hesitation with the menu and instinctively he'd stepped in to help her. The sight of her responding to him so warmly brought back his old infatuation for her, if only for a moment.

The exhilaration hadn't lasted long. When he'd offered to assist her with ordering the meal, she'd spoken to him in the same condescending tone he remembered from old, causing his excitement to fade.

It had been his sign to retreat, a reminder that she wasn't his friend, would never be his friend. The subsequent phone call and issues with the server in Sao Paolo had been a godsend, giving him a reason to escape from her presence.

However, he couldn't escape for long. Lorenzo had reminded him later last night about his promise to show Ify around the city today. He'd passed on the phone number he'd collected from NK.

Nero was a man of principle. If he made a threat or a promise, he kept it.

So, this morning he'd called Ify, and she'd seemed happy enough to hear from him and had accepted to spend the day with him.

He'd steeled his mind, or so he'd thought. Until she'd stepped out of the lift in the hotel lobby and walked towards him.

Like a sudden collision with a truck, it came crashing into him, leaving him dazed and disorientated.

Despite his disdain for her family, he couldn't deny the lingering attraction he felt towards her, fuelled by her incredible beauty.

He'd accepted his attraction to her would never change. Instead, he would use it to his advantage.

Rather than wasting time at the crowded tourist attractions in the city, he had made alternative arrangements, and she had gladly accepted his invitation.

Things had gone well initially.

The shopping trip. Then brunch at the café.

While conversing with her, he observed her growing interest in him, prompting him to exploit the situation. He would bring her to the brink of desire and leave her yearning for more. Relentlessly torment her, pushing her to the brink of her endurance. Until she had no option but to invite him into her bed.

She still didn't know his identity or his history.

But he didn't just want sex. No, it would never be enough for him.

He wanted the ultimate vengeance.

Ifeoma Nzekwe as his wife.

His heart burned with determination as he imagined the day when she could no longer resist him, even after her disdainful rejection so many years ago. Fuelled by vengeance, he had the power to crush her family, just as they had destroyed his.

His torturous seduction had worked for a while. He'd told her what he'd done in the shower. Seen her practically melt with desire. Switched it off and invited her for a swim to cool off and then turned it up again as they sipped rum cocktails under the beach umbrella.

Then she'd given in and had invited him to rub sunscreen on her body.

He'd hesitated because he hadn't wanted to touch her. Not yet. Not until tonight. He'd wanted to string her along for a while.

But he'd capitulated. He could still use the body contact to his advantage. He had when he'd caressed her skin. It worked. She'd melted and moaned and invited him to touch her intimately by spreading her legs.

What he hadn't expected was for her to call him a liar, because he'd mentioned how beautiful she was.

That accusation had been a trigger. One he couldn't ignore.

The same way her father had lobed accusations at his father so many years ago when their business partnership had disintegrated.

It brought back the old nightmare and hurt, especially since she dug in her heels rather than acknowledge her error.

She'd accused him falsely of lying.

She. Was. Beautiful.

It seemed falsely accusing people was in her veins. Same as her father. No matter his attraction to her, he needed to remember it.

A ringing phone jarred him from his reverie, and he glanced at Ifeoma. She had her phone in her hand and swiped to answer it.

"Nkoli, hi," she said.

"Ifeoma, what happened?" her friend's tinny voice came through the phone speaker.

"Ka anyị suo Ìgbò. Achọghị m ka nwoke a ghọta ihe anyị na-ekwu." *Let's speak Igbo. I don't want this man to understand what we're saying.*

Nero didn't react but kept his gaze on the road through the windscreen where the building weekday evening traffic meant he had to slow down. He didn't want Ifeoma to know he could understand every word they spoke in Igbo.

"Okay, tell me what happened," NK said.

"I told you in the text already. We're in the car on the way back to the city."

"Was the date a bust? Why is it over?"

"The man got angry because I called him a liar."

"But why would you do such a thing?"

"We were having fun o. Then things got a bit handsy, and I took part of my swimsuit off and he saw my belly and scar. Do you know he had the audacity to say that I was beautiful? Of course, I told him he was lying immediately, and he got angry."

Nero had to bite his tongue to stop himself from reacting to Ify's rant. There was silence on the line, as if her friend was also struggling to find the right words.

"Ifeoma?"

"Eh."

"Ifeoma."

"O gini."

"Ifeoma, how many times did I call you?"

"Three times."

"So, you've started this your behaviour again. Didn't you promise me that you would be on your best behaviour during your date? That you would leave all your hangups and let the man spoil you for a day?"

"I did, and I was, but..."

"But you couldn't believe that a man would think you are beautiful even with your c-section scar? It's the same way you couldn't believe Maddox still found you attractive after you gave birth. That you had to push him away and test his commitment to you until it backfired."

Ifeoma sat silently and Nero had to glance at her to check she was okay. She looked harassed, sitting stiffly, phone in hand.

There was a heavy sigh on the line. "Ify, I'm sorry if my words are painful to hear. But you know they are the truth. Nero didn't do you any harm. He didn't tell a lie. So don't accuse him falsely. Don't punish him for something he had no part in creating."

Ifeoma sighed heavily. "I know."

"So, are you going to apologise to him?"

"Why?"

"Because he deserves an apology."

"Why?"

"Ifeoma—"

"I will apologise to him."

"Good. I'm still at work and I have to get back to it."

"Okay. Talk to you later."

"Bye."

Ifeoma exhaled heavily after the call ended and sat silently for a while.

Nero's mouth dried out, and his throat constricted. The telephone conversation between the two friends was revelatory, but also concerning. There was so much information he could use to his advantage.

Like the fact that it seemed no man had touched Ifeoma since she gave birth. Not even her ex-husband. That could mean she hadn't had sex for over twenty years, at least.

However, his overriding emotion was concern for her wellbeing. It seemed she had a form of body dysmorphia or body dysmorphic disorder because of the c-section scar. He knew about it because his goddaughter, Lorenzo's daughter, suffered from it. She was in therapy and used antidepressants.

It was a mental health condition which affected the way the sufferer saw parts of their body and was linked to genes, chemical changes in the brain or past traumatic experiences.

He wondered which one triggered Ifeoma's condition.

More importantly, he understood why she'd called him a liar. Her brain was tricking her.

"Are you okay?" he asked as his concern for her rose. Despite everything, she was the only one who seemed to get under his skin easily. His innate need to care for her overtook his anger at her.

She blinked. "Yes, I'm okay. I was talking to Nkoli."

"Is she okay?"

"Yes, she's fine."

"Good."

"I told her what happened. She wants me to apologise to you."

"But you don't want to," he said it with humour because he could hear her reluctance.

She glanced at him, saw his grin and a small smile curled her lips. "I'm not used to apologising. For two days in a row, I've had to apologise to you."

"That must be a record." He chuckled.

She giggled. "It is."

He said nothing, and they sat silently for a while.

"I'm sorry for calling you a liar. I shouldn't have," she said finally.

"Your apology is accepted," he said honestly.

"Good. Can we continue with our date? I mean, you promised to take me to dinner and dancing afterwards."

"Yes, the date can continue. I'll take you to dinner and dancing, on one condition."

"What is it?"

"You will accept everything I tell you to be the truth."

"What?" she frowned.

"That's the deal or no date and no orgasms for you."

"Or you—"

"Deal or no deal."

"Deal, damn it!" she growled.

He chuckled and continued driving.

EIGHT

At the tapping sound on the door, Ifeoma's senses heightened. She glanced at the mirror and hurried across the room to open the wooden slab.

Two hours earlier, Nero had dropped her off outside her hotel room and said he would return at this exact time. She used the time alone to make a few phone calls, check her online messages. Then she'd showered and changed into another outfit for the evening.

She peeked through the peephole, and sure enough, Nero stood on the other side of the wooden slab. She'd tried searching for him online, on social media specifically. Since she didn't know his surname, she'd searched for people named Nero in Turin. She'd had no luck. There'd been many people named Nero who lived in Turin, but none of them were her Nero.

Her Nero? She snorted. Since when did he become her anything?

She didn't even know him. Didn't know his surname. Had known him for less than twenty-four hours.

Granted, they'd been on a date earlier, and the laughter and connection they shared still lingered in the air. It filled her with excitement and happiness, leaving her with cherished memories. The attraction between them sizzled, a magnetic pull towards each other.

He stood outside her door, eagerly waiting for her to open it so they could embark on their evening plans. She appreciated his punctuality, a quality she highly valued in others. His consistent actions showed he was reliable and trustworthy.

Luckily for her, he'd become the perfect holiday fling. Although her time with him would be brief, she was determined to make every moment count.

As she twisted the lock and pulled the handle, her heart rate quickened.

"Buonasera, Ify." He beamed the sexy smile. "Sei bellissima."

"Ciao," she said, practicing her Italian. "You look lovely too."

In his black shirt, trousers, and navy blazer, he looked absolutely stunning. He smelled divine as he approached her, his scent enveloping her senses as he leaned in for a gentle kiss on the cheeks. It took all her self-control not to gulp in a lungful of air, desperate to capture his essence.

"Grazie. Are you ready to go?" his gravelly Italian accent was on point too. It had only been a few hours, but she craved the comforting sound of his voice.

"Just a minute." She turned away to compose herself, resisting the urge to drag him into the room and shut the door. To make him stay so they could order in. He'd promised her orgasms, after all.

Still, he'd also promised to take her dancing, and she wanted to have fun and see what else Rome had to offer.

She grabbed her purse, her skirt swirling around her bare legs. "I'm ready."

"May I?" He held out his arm.

"Of course." She slipped her arm through his as she shut the door and they walked to the lift, down to the lobby and out the exit. A black car was waiting, and he helped her into the back seat before climbing in next to her. The driver was in a chauffeur uniform.

About twenty minutes later, they stopped by a pavement. Nero came around and helped her out. He took her hand and led her towards the restaurant, her high heels clicking on the stone paving.

She assumed they would go to another Italian restaurant. However, as soon as she saw the name and flag above the establishment, her heart started racing. She could hear music coming from the inside.

"Are we eating here?" she asked, eyes widened, glancing around.

"Yes. Have you tried Brazilian food before?" he asked.

"Brazilian food," she giggled. "I lived in Brazil and travelled through South America for a year when I was younger. Of course, I've eaten Brazilian food. I love it."

She dragged him along in excitement as she headed to the door and he laughed.

"Welcome to Bento Steakhouse," the server greeted them at the reception.

"Boa noite," she said in Brazilian Portuguese, the language returning semi-fluidly, although she'd rarely spoken it in the past two decades. "Temos uma reserva..."

She trailed off and turned to Nero, who watched her with a smile. She'd been so excited she spoken before him without knowing if he'd made a reservation. But he appeared to be an organised man, so he would take care of it.

"Piedimonte. Nero Piedimonte," he said to the server, who checked the computer.

That was his surname? His father must be Italian. Which of his parents had the African gene? His mother? Was he adopted?

Curiosity niggled, leaving her with so many questions. She'd assumed he was the son of African immigrants but the surname didn't quite match.

"Of course. Please come this way." The server let the way.

Nero placed his hand on the small of Ifeoma's back and her skin tingled as they walked to their table. It wasn't in the corner. Instead, it was close to the middle of the restaurant and the dancefloor opposite a stage with a live band.

After they were seated, the server explained how to get service. It was a buffet-style, and the meals were centred around barbequed meats. They ordered drinks, and he left.

Feeling a surge of energy, she turned to Nero with a smile. "You really outdid yourself. Brazilian food and music all in one. I haven't experienced anything like this in so long. Just being here now brings back so many wonderful memories."

"I'm glad you love it," he said with a grin on his face.

As she breathed in the atmosphere, she felt a sense of rejuvenation, reminiscent of her carefree days before marriage and motherhood. A time when she'd been fun and light-hearted.

This place exceeded all of her expectations, with its captivating ambiance. The food was so delicious that every bite was a burst of flavour, the lively music filled the air, and the incredible atmosphere made it a night to remember. And, without a doubt, the company was exceptional.

"So why is a beautiful woman like you single?" he asked, his eyes fixed on her as she savoured the rich, chocolate taste of the Brigadeirao.

Her cheeks heated as she tilted her head. The way he called her beautiful still caught her off guard, leaving her torn between accepting the compliment and distrusting his sincerity.

His gaze held an undeniable conviction, revealing his genuine belief. A warm, comforting feeling settled in her heart.

"I don't know," she muttered, trailing off into a hesitant silence. As they sipped on the bottle of prosecco, her inhibitions melted away, allowing her to speak openly. A confident smirk played on her lips. "Some men are intimidated by me."

"I wonder why?" he teased, a mischievous twinkle in his eye. With a graceful motion, he tilted his head and took a sip from his flute, his throat bobbing as he swallowed.

"Hey, it's not my fault if they are not man enough to handle me."

"True."

"But you're not afraid of me."

With a gentle touch, he lifted her hand to his lips, causing a pleasurable shiver to run down her spine and settle at her most sensitive spot. "No," he replied confidently, "I'm not intimidated by you. I'm man enough for you."

His eyes glowed with tenderness as he watched her, causing her heart to constrict in her chest.

"You are?" she asked, her throat dry as her imagination sparked to life, anticipation fluttering in her belly.

"I am. You are so beautiful. I want to put my hands all over you. Dance with me." He stood, extending his hand to her, and she joined him.

They joined the lively crowd and were soon swept away by the rhythmic beats of the samba music. Within moments, she was in sync with the music as they gracefully spun around the dance floor. Nero's dance routine was mesmerising, showcasing his extraordinary talent as he seamlessly blended salsa and rumba into his performance.

Maddox had been a good dancer, but he hadn't been this superb or versatile.

Nero moved across the dancefloor almost like a pro. He was gorgeous, intelligent, seriously sexy. And right here with him, she felt incredibly sexy, too.

Maybe it was the music, the atmosphere. The man.

At this moment, she wasn't an educator or a principal or a mother. She was just a woman dancing with a man, having the fun of her life. She'd forgotten this feeling, and she had Nero to thank for it.

With his handsome face and sensuous lips, the compelling amused gleam in his eyes, he seemed happy and carefree. Surprising because of his intensity when they'd first met. Yet, he appeared to be having the time of his life, too, laughing and joking with her.

When the music slowed down, he pulled her closer and encircled her with his arms. His body relaxed against hers, making her relax into him too, her head just reaching his shoulders with the heels.

"I've wanted to do this for so long," he said in a husky voice in her ear, pressing a kiss to her lobe.

"Do what?" she replied, feeling all warm and precious in his arms. Her body was tingling, priming with the contact. Her hand was in his while the other was around his back, his on her waist.

"Hold you this close, feel your warmth, your rhythm."

The words made her heart pump faster, harder. The air crackled with electricity. All she could picture was having sex with him. Her body yearned, ached for him. She grew wetter, her nipples tightening.

He dipped his head and brushed his lips against hers gently. He didn't push in with his tongue, just waited for her to open up for him.

She didn't hesitate. She granted access and his tongue entered her mouth, bringing the spice and warmth that was exclusively Nero. The kiss was exploratory and erotic, an expression of intent, giving a precursor of their naked bodies joined and moving against each other.

This virile, sensual man awakened her senses, made her lose control. She didn't care that they were on the dancefloor in the middle of a restaurant. She didn't see anyone else, only felt Nero.

His tongue probed, their bodies entwined.

Everyone else faded.

She wrapped her arms around his shoulders, tugged his head down, and deepened the kiss. His hardening dick pulsed against her belly. His hand tightened around her, drawing her closer.

When he lifted his head and they caught their breath, his eyes had darkened even further. His need matched hers. Dripping wet, she was aching for him to touch her more intimately.

For the first time in years, her body longed for a man with a newfound intensity.

It could be the thrill of being in an unfamiliar place, away from home, bringing a sense of freedom and adventure to her. Maybe it was a spell. Whatever it was, she was determined to seize every moment before it slipped away.

She stood on tiptoes and spoke into his ear. "Can we head back to the hotel?"

Leaning back, he locked eyes with her for a brief pause before giving a slight nod. His kiss was delicate, like the soft brush of butterfly wings against her lips. "Let's go."

They returned to the table. He swiftly withdrew his phone from his pocket and spoke in a flurry of Italian words during the quick call. He took care of the bill and left a generous cash tip before they headed out.

By the pavement, a sleek black car stood waiting, its polished exterior glinting under the streetlights. It appeared to be a car service, as she spotted the same professional-looking driver waiting beside the vehicle.

In no time, they reached the hotel and stepped into the elevator, their fingers interlocked.

He stood outside her door, patiently waiting for her to open it. As soon as she did, he gently cradled her face in his hands and planted a tender kiss on her lips.

"Good night, bella," he said, withdrawing.

NINE

"Wait, what?"

Ifeoma stood in shock at Nero's statement. They'd had the most amazing evening which had culminated in kissing on the dancefloor in a busy restaurant. All the signals were there that they both wanted to make love.

She'd asked him to take her back to her hotel room to continue and take it to its natural conclusion.

Now they were at her door, and he was saying goodnight? No way. She didn't get all worked up for nothing. If he was playing gentleman, this was the wrong time. She needed the freak to get her into bed.

"Are you not coming in?" she leaned back, narrowing her eyes.

"Do you want me in your room?" he shoved his hands in his trouser pockets, looking relaxed, confident and yet withdrawn.

"Yes, why else did I tell you to bring me back here? After the way we kissed on the dancefloor, you're really going to ask me that?" Did she read the signs wrong? It had been ages since she dated, so perhaps she was out of touch with reading the cues. But she would have sworn he wanted her.

He was staring at her with such intensity now. "Kissing you was everything I wished it would be. And I'm sure making love to you will exceed my expectations."

The awe in his voice filled her chest with warmth, proving his attraction to her and her instincts.

"So why are we standing in the corridor talking about it instead of doing it in my suite?" she said with exasperation.

"Because you still haven't invited me into your room. I can't assume anything. You need to be explicit with the invitation."

"Why? You sound like a vampire." She burst into laughter at her own joke.

But he didn't laugh, and she stopped. "You won't enter my room without my invitation. Fine. Mr Nero Piedimonte," she said his name the same way he'd said it at the restaurant. "Come into my hotel room."

. . ✺ . .

"After you," Nero replied as he followed Ifeoma into her hotel suite.

As they entered, the door swung shut with a gentle thud. In the living space, she turned on the soft glow lights, illuminating the low sofa, wooden desk, and double bed. The place was immaculate, with plumped pillows and a neatly made bed. The perfectly arranged furniture and spotless surfaces suggested that housekeeping had probably come to clean up earlier in the day. He had instructed the manager to maintain the suite meticulously for their esteemed guest.

A heaviness settled in Nero's body as he watched Ifeoma walk deeper into the suite.

She was really doing this. Inviting him into her suite. She'd only met him last night, considering she didn't remember him or their shared past. He'd been a stranger yesterday and was little more than an acquaintance today. Yet she was ready to have an affair with him. A one-night stand?

His gut clenched, and he fought to control himself. His emotions always seemed to be rampant around her.

She appeared calm and nonchalant as she placed her purse on top of the desk.

Did she do this often? Take strange men to her bed?

Her conversation with her friend in the car earlier indicated she didn't bare her body to men, but it didn't mean she didn't have sex with them.

Had he misread her?

All the flirtation and seduction had been a setup, part of his plan to punish her for what she did to him years ago. What her family did to his.

Yet he'd expected some pushback. He hadn't expected her to invite him to her suite within twenty-four hours.

This was the same woman that had spurned his advances years ago.

Why was she now inviting him in to have sex?

Conflicted, he was caught between his attraction to her and his need for vengeance. Yet, his head ached with annoyance because she was giving in so readily.

What was the difference between him now and then? Sure, he'd matured. But he also had more money. Did she find him more attractive because he had more money?

She knew little else about him, beyond the fact he was a handsome CEO and drove a Ferrari. This made her no different to Alina, who latched onto him because of his wealth and influence.

The acid taste in his mouth burned all the way to his stomach.

Was this his luck at relationships? Was he swapping one woman with insatiable vanity with another?

"Do you mind if I have a drink?" He walked to the bar and grabbed a bottle of water. "Do you want some?"

"No. I'm okay." Her voice caught.

He heard the nervous edge and hope flared inside him. Was it possible she was uncertain about fucking him? Would she call the whole thing off?

A part of him wanted the confident, abrasive woman who spoke her mind and didn't care who got hurt. It would help him keep control of his emotions.

She turned her back to him, looking out of the window onto the city street.

He watched her silhouette framed against the window. Across the street was a bridal boutique with a mannequin in a white gown in the window.

Weddings. He was supposed to be planning one for himself.

The corner of his mouth curved as cold cynicism ate its way through his heart. If he had a choice, there wouldn't be a wedding at all.

"You know, I never thought I would do this," she said, still staring out of the window.

It took him a few seconds to rouse from his thoughts to understand her words. "What?"

"When I got married, I thought I would be married for the rest of my life to my husband, Maddox. Do you understand that?" She tilted her head, not looking at him.

"No." Nero shrugged. A sense of indifference washed over him, uninterested in discussing her ex-husband. He didn't want to know about that part of her past, about the man whom she'd readily given her affections while she'd spurned Nero.

The fiery sensation inside him compelled him to take a series of long, refreshing drinks. The cold mineral water failed to quell his rising temper.

Or his desire. He yearned for her, his heart aching. It was the worst insult. He couldn't comprehend how such intense anger and a burning desire for revenge consumed him, while he also felt an undeniable physical attraction to her. It was not right for him to crave her like this.

This wasn't supposed to happen to him. He'd sworn he'd never get trapped by a manipulative woman again.

Yet every word, every phrase she spoke, intrigued him. Held him captive.

"Even after I asked for a divorce and he agreed, I thought he would change his mind. That he would come back and confess his undying love. That he would never let me go. But he did." She sighed heavily.

Her pain slammed into him and his chest constricted and he took a long drink, and then another.

"Why are you telling me this?" he asked in a sharp tone. She swivelled, wide-eyed.

He moved toward her, stalking her, anger, desire, frustration coming together in a vortex of emotion. He saw a flicker of emotion in her brown eyes—shock? Fear?

What did she expect? Life was cruel and demanding. He'd grown up without the people he loved, without stability. Her father had denied him those things when he'd murdered his father. Her father had been eager to take everything away from him and his family.

"I'm telling you this because doing this isn't easy for me. I'm not asking for anything else. I just want to feel for one night. One night only. Tomorrow you can move on with your life and I can move on with mine." She tilted her chin up defiantly, holding his gaze.

Placing his hands on her shoulders, Nero fought his own conflicting emotions, torn between walking out the door and tossing her onto the bed. He wanted to hold her, touch her.

Yet her conditions didn't suit him.

She wanted no future with him. But he wanted one with her. She was the woman he had chosen to marry. He needed a wife, although he didn't trust her. But between her and Alina, there was no contest. He wouldn't even consider a different woman.

· · ❧ · ·

A strange mix of familiarity and unease filled the air. The weight of Nero's hands trapped Ifeoma's shoulders, making it impossible to ignore the palpable connection between them. Keenly aware of his intense desire for her, it filled her with both excitement and apprehension. It shone in his onyx eyes, the way they sparkled with affection, and in the gentle touch of his hands.

Still, there was an underlying shift in the atmosphere, something ominous. Something she couldn't name.

"What's on your mind?" she whispered as he drew her forward, pulling her toward him.

The silence in the room was suffocating, made even more unsettling by the lingering, heated stare. His presence had the power to make her feel as enticing as a gourmet dinner. Her throat tightened as she swallowed hard, feeling her heart race and panic escalating, causing her to wonder if it would have been a smarter decision to send him away.

"Ify, do you really want to do this?" he asked, his hands gently gliding from her shoulders, down her arms and encircled her wrists. The moment his fingers wrapped around hers, an intense jolt of heat travelled up her arm.

The sharp sensation coursed through her. Every nerve in her body was on fire, urging her to escape. But her body remained immobile, her muscles weakened by the overwhelming heat.

"Do you?" he repeated in a growly tone, holding her body against his.

Her breath trapped in her throat, bottled in her chest.

"Tell me something," she said, captivated by their contrasting features.

His muscles were taut and defined, showcasing his steely strength. His outfit, with its refined design, masked the powerful physique of his chest, stomach, and thighs.

"What?" His voice carried a hint of wariness and distance. His forehead creased with a smooth furrow, but his unwavering focus intrigued her. Like an agile wild beast stalking prey, calculating when to pounce.

He surely had no shortage of women vying for his attention. With his striking looks, sophistication, intelligence, and wealth, he exuded an undeniable sensuality.

Swallowing the butterflies back, her body buzzed with nervous energy. "You said earlier you wanted to put your hands all over my body."

His eyes locked onto hers, and he stayed quiet, waiting for her to continue.

The dryness in her mouth made it difficult for her to speak or swallow. She wished she'd accepted his offer of a drink. "And I was wondering why would you find me interesting? I'm forty-eight. Five years older than you. What do I have that appeals to you?"

He didn't answer, but his body language spoke volumes—his mouth compressed, and his silence grew heavier. In his eyes, she was nothing more than a meaningless fling.

Fair enough. It shouldn't matter to her. She only wanted a holiday fling. Yet disappointment settled heavily on her shoulders. She averted her gaze to compose herself.

He gripped her chin, tipping it until their gazes met.

"Ify, I'm attracted to you because you're beautiful, intelligent, successful, well-travelled, fluent in multiple languages. The list goes on."

"And I can dance," she added.

"Certo. You're a brilliant dancer." A small smile tugged at the corner of his mouth. "But none of those things are relevant."

"Why not?" she said, her tone tinged with a hint of defiance.

"Because all you desire from me is physical intimacy, not emotional connection." His cold, clinical, and blunt words left no room for misinterpretation.

Yet she could imagine having sex with him would be far from a frigid experience.

It would be a scorching, intense affair, leaving her with a lingering hangover for months. But she was well overdue for this hangover. "Then that's okay, because sex is enough for me."

He hung his head, shielding his expression. "I understand."

He sounded less than enthusiastic, like he didn't want to be here. Like he didn't want to have sex.

Because that would be crazy.

He wanted her. She'd seen the evidence repeatedly throughout the day.

Yet he didn't want her and was fighting the attraction.

Perhaps he felt a sense of duty to protect her in an old-fashioned way.

Shame, she wasn't someone else. Unlike her friend Nkoli, who had eagerly relocated after her divorce, Ifeoma couldn't pack up and move here. Her family, career, and life were in Nigeria. Italy and Nero were short, enjoyable interludes.

For a moment, indecision filled Ifeoma as the unknown yawned about her in every direction, and then she acted based on what she needed to do. She touched him. She placed her hands tentatively on his chest, needing to discover him, needing to rediscover herself, life and sex.

Yet touching him wasn't without pain. Was this how she was supposed to feel? Conflicted. Wrenched. Overwhelmed. She hadn't done this in so long.

Touching him made her come alive, and her heart felt so tender right now, all her emotions stirred. His hands moved to her back, and he drew her even closer, making her shiver.

"Cold?" he asked.

"No." Warmth emanated from his body, and the strength of his thighs and hips pressed against her. His body hardened with desire, and the unmistakable pressure of his arousal prodded her belly. "Just overly sensitive to touch."

"Sensitive?"

"Yes, from the anticipation." A mixture of fear and arousal pulsed through her as she experienced a surge of adrenaline. Anxiety. Excitement. "I'm—" She broke off, knowing she couldn't just tell him she was relatively inexperienced, that the only man she'd been with sexually was her ex-husband.

The last thing she wanted was to give the impression of being naïve. She was afraid of making him lose interest. If this was to be their only night together, she was determined to make it flawless.

"Never mind," she whispered, her voice barely audible in the silence.

His head dipped, so close to hers, capturing the warmth of her skin and the gentle rhythm of her breath, before his lips met hers in a slow, tender kiss. The caress was soft, but there was a hidden ferocity behind it, a searing heat that made her wary, prompting her to turn her head to escape its intensity. His hand glided up her back, brushing against her curly braids before settling at the base of her neck. His touch left a lingering tingle on every part of her body.

"Your pulse is thumping against my palm," he whispered, against her hair.

She nuzzled her face into his shirt, savouring the intoxicating aroma of his presence. Hyper-aware of his radiating heat, the firmness of his muscles, and the velvety texture of his skin through the partially unbuttoned shirt.

"That's what you do to me," she could barely recognise her breathless voice.

He tipped her head back, stared into her eyes. "Now, you're teasing me."

"No." She attempted to smile, but her lips only curved slightly. Instead, she reached up and caressed his face with her fingertips.

Her light touch caused him to startle, but he made no attempt to move away. Delicately, she ran her fingertips along his jaw, savouring the sensation of his stubble beneath her touch. The desire to uncover every detail consumed her, from the shape of his face to the intricate lines adorning his cheekbone and chin. And the alluring scent embodied a harmonious blend of his skin and the sunshine, smelling like the ocean breeze, musk, and spice.

"Has anyone ever told you how handsome you are?" she whispered, awed by the bristles of his beard, the firmness of his skin.

"Sometimes, but are you saying you think I'm handsome?"

"I don't just think it. I know you're handsome."

As his eyes locked with hers, his smile slowly vanished, and he leaned in, pressing his lips against hers once more. She relished the sensation of his lips against hers, enjoying the intoxicating scent of him and the gentle pressure.

Teasingly, he closed his eyes and tantalised her with a warm and fleeting touch. Like the first sip of a velvety red wine, the kiss was seductive, provoking the senses and sparking the imagination.

As his lips pressed against hers, she experienced the irresistible allure of pleasure in every contact. Their kiss intensified, his hand tenderly cradling her cheek while his thumb traced the outline of her lips, sending waves of warmth and desire coursing through her veins. The heat inside her body seemed to melt her from within, while her breasts throbbed with an ache and her nipples became exquisitely sensitive.

Her response stirred him, igniting a fire within, and the kiss transformed into something passionate. No longer tentative, or teasing, Nero's lips were firm, demanding, taking, tasting.

He tracked the upper bow of her lip with his tongue. As their lips met, he explored the contours of her mouth, relishing the softness of her lower lip and the warmth of her tongue. Without uttering a single word, his gestures conveyed his intentions to claim and take pleasure in her, but always under his conditions. He traced a path from her cheek, down her neck, and settled on her collarbone before finally cupping her breast.

His touch sent a shiver down Ifeoma's spine as his fingertips delicately brushed against her nipple. The sensation of his caress made her belly clench, a tight and hot ache that intensified with each stroke. His presence ignited a longing in her, fuelling her confidence.

This was how she should reclaim her sensuality with a man who ignited all her senses. Who made her quiver and throb with each caress. Someone as sexy as Nero Piedimonte.

His hand slid under her blouse, its warmth spreading across her bare abdomen, while his fingers delicately traced the outline of her slender rib cage. She took a deep breath, desperately attempting to clear her mind and ease the dizziness, but the warmth of his caress was intoxicating.

With the gentle lift of the silk of her bra cup, Ifeoma's body responded. Her breath hitched, her mind consumed by a relentless craving, as if she could dissolve into pure desire.

No one had ever caressed her with such intensity, leaving her simultaneously vulnerable and ravenous. Her imagination ran wild, conjuring up the sensation of his hands exploring every inch of her belly, hips, and thighs.

Nero pushed her backward, setting her firmly down on the edge of the bed. Head spinning, she braced her hands braced on either side of her hips. He towered above her, like a silent giant in contemplation.

Electricity crackled between them. A sheen of sweat coated his forehead and passion stormed his onyx eyes. He was breathing deep, his chest filling, rising, and his lips pressed hard. It was obvious he was at war with himself, conflicted.

He gripped her hair, tugged her head back and pressed his mouth to hers in a searing kiss, taking her breath away while possessing her body. With the kiss, he tore her open, rendered her vulnerable, and branded her all at once.

If she'd had any doubts about wanting him, they fizzled away. His tongue swept her mouth, probing, making her want to capture the fierce rhythmic thrusts, making her belly clench and clench again.

Her craving for him was fire in her veins and heat in her core, sensitising her entire body.

Then, as fiercely as it started, he turned his head and ended the kiss.

TEN

"Undress," Nero commanded hoarsely, the bristles on his chin rough against her jaw, his warm breath tickling her skin. The command, so hard, so direct, sent flickers of feeling everywhere.

Ifeoma shivered and clutched at the silk coverlet on the bed. Suddenly he oozed power, authority, control. Just like the night she met him. He matched her in this aspect. Liked that he wouldn't lose, much less give up control to her in this situation. In the bedroom. Still...

"No. You do it," she challenged because it was in her nature.

As he straightened, his imposing figure cast a shadow over her, and his piercing black gaze seemed to undress her with just a look. "That's not how this works. We do it my way or I walk."

She wanted this. She wanted to know life again. Wanted to know power and possession. Her existence had been suspended for twenty years. Sure, she'd done things, succeeded in others. Yet, her mind and subsequently, her body had been in a sort of storage, waiting for an old lover who would never return.

She had finally accepted that her ex would not be hers again. She had to rediscover her sensuality and her body. Nero was a tool to achieving this next phase of her life.

"Fine." Her heart thudded in her chest as she reached behind her, untying the strings of her blouse. His gaze bore into her, his intense concentration making her acutely aware of his presence. As she fiddled with the knot, her hands trembled, betraying her struggle to undo it. Time slowed down, and every second felt like an eternity.

As he stared, his gaze hardened, reflecting his resolve. The air grew hotter, making beads of sweat form on her forehead. With damp hands, she struggled to untie the knot and loosen her ties before reaching for the hem of her blouse.

If he was just going to stand and watch, then she would turn it into a striptease of sorts. Taking her time, she lifted it above her head and set it down on the bed next to her. Still, he didn't budge.

Self-conscious, yet determined, she continued, unfastening the snap and zipper of her skirt before pushing it over her hips and letting it float to the carpet. In only the black French knickers and matching bra, she stepped out, turned to the side and bent in half to pick it up, flashing her bum at him. Slowly she straightened, placing the skirt next to the blouse on the bed.

She glanced up at Nero, saw nothing encouraging in his face—no smile, no spark, just the inscrutable expression. Tears pricked the back of her eyes. Why was she doing this? What was she doing here? And yet she knew.

Maddox.

Scalding tears burned the back of her eyes and morphed into anger.

She needed to forget her ex. Forget the disappointment of losing him. Forget that he never came back for her.

Her anger blazed fiercely, threatening to overpower her passion.

She was strong. Capable. Beautiful, damn it!

She'd once been a passionate person, fierce and full of life. Now she wanted it all back. Her sexuality. Her prowess.

The tears continued to sting her eyes and collect on her cheeks. Her throat felt like someone had scraped it raw, constantly reminding her of the pain she tried so hard to ignore.

"I can leave if you've changed your mind." Nero's voice sounded faraway.

She blinked, pulled back to the present and her surroundings in the hotel room.

"No. I haven't changed my mind," she answered defiantly and yet her voice broke. She would be back in Nigeria in a few days. But today, tonight, she had him. She'd be with Nero, indulging in passionate intimacy to satisfy her desire for a special connection. It was just the thing she had been longing for.

Pulse racing, Ifeoma reached behind her back and unhooked her silk bra, peeling the delicate fabric from her shoulders and breasts. Defiantly, she lay on the mattress, lifted her chin, and searched Nero's face, looking for signs of disgust. Was he repulsed by her body, her wobbly tummy, the c-section scar?

Eyes dark, expression shuttered, he lowered his body next to her. Leaning over, he kissed her shoulder. Her nipples peaked, breasts aching as he straddled her legs.

His lips found the crazy pulse in the small hollow below her ear, and she drew another quick breath. The sensation tingled through her body. Need washed over her like molten lava, slowly consuming her. His lips moved down her neck, trailing a path of lingering kisses until they finally found rest on her collarbone.

"Remove my clothes," he said. His voice vibrated against her skin, sending shock waves through her.

"No." She glared at him, pushing back. No man had ordered her to do anything in years. Yet this one was pushing his luck twice in one night.

"Yes." He was leaning over her, staring down at her with those eyes that seemed to see everything.

She growled and all he did was grin, as if he found her response amusing.

Or perhaps the joke was on her. With her hair in disarray and her body laid bare, in nothing but her panties, leaving little to the imagination. If she wanted this show to move along, she had to obey him and follow his conditions.

Ignoring her lack of clothing, she attempted to concentrate solely on him. Leaning closer, she breathed in the scent of his cologne—ocean breeze and spice, concentrated on the seductive heat of his body. Her hands trembled as she reached for the first button on his shirt. She hadn't undressed a man in years. If she didn't do it now, she might never do it again.

With determination, she carefully unfastened the button, her fingers moving with precision. Time seemed to slip away as they shed their clothes, and she found herself beneath him, consumed by desire. His hand moved slowly, tracing each delicate contour as he glided it down from her chest to her waist. A shiver ran down her spine, causing her nipples to harden.

"Damn, you're irresistible," he said in a husky voice.

She had no verbal response for him as she tried to keep it together. Tried not to fall apart before it had started.

He took his time, gently pressing his lips against hers, causing her frantic pulse to slow. The world faded and everything was him. His taste, his skin, his heat, her desire for him.

His hands cupped her breasts, palms grazing her taut nipples and then skilfully shaping her ribs, waist, and hips. He had a way of making her feel malleable and feverish in the most enticing spots. The touch of his mouth on the hollow of her neck sent shivers down her spine, and she instinctively reached out for him, her arms encircling his shoulders.

She revelled in the sensation of his body, the taut, velvety strength beneath his flesh. Her fingers tightened around the bulging muscles of his upper arms as his mouth traced a path of kisses and nibbles along her shoulder and collarbone. Surprisingly, she discovered a realm of sensations she never thought possible as his teeth and tongue explored her body, igniting a symphony of pleasure in hundreds of nerve endings.

His hand moved between her thighs, parted her labia and found slick wanton flesh. She moaned, arched, opened wider as his mouth drew fire trails across her breasts. Overwhelmed, she pressed closer, aching, wanting more of him, wanting everything he had to offer.

"Oh," she gasped as his mouth sucked one swollen nipple.

He spread her thighs. The fresh breeze from the air conditioner washed over her skin briefly before he shifted his weight until his body nestled between her parted legs.

He lifted his head, his gaze moving from her face to her outstretched body, leaving her feeling exposed and uneasy. A strange sensation coursed through her, like she was a sacrificial offering.

"Are you okay?" he asked, his voice so husky it rasped across her senses, stirring her all over again.

"I'm fine."

He must have seen the frown on her face. "What's on your mind?"

She reached up to touch his face, trying to distract herself from getting unnerved. "Nothing."

His black eyebrow arched.

She smiled. "You don't believe me."

His shoulders rose and fell. "Trust is earned, not given."

"Touche."

This time, she didn't wait for him. She reached for his neck, brought his face down, and kissed him. He didn't respond at first, and she felt the tension on his shoulders. She followed his lead from earlier, slowing the kiss down until his taut muscles relaxed and a groan rumbled through him.

Leaning up over her, he shifted his position, his hips coming to rest against her pelvis. The insistent pressure of his solid shaft left her momentarily breathless, the firmness of his length pressed against her abdomen, radiating heat.

"Nero, I need you," her breathy voice conveyed her need as much as the words.

"I'm right here," his voice sounded on edge.

"I need you inside me, please."

As if he'd been waiting for her request, he positioned his hard length against her tender opening, his hips insistent. Despite her welcoming wetness, her body tensed at the unfamiliar solid invasion.

"Relax for me," his voice was a gravelly whisper in her ear as his fingers caressed her clit, making her moan and arch and open her thighs wider. He stroked his dick, rubbing it against her delicate folds, getting her juices all over himself.

Desperate for him, she lifted her hips, and with a jerk of his, he slipped inside her. Only the tip. Yet he was thick and snug, making her gasp in shock, reminding her of her first time with its discomfort.

Panting, she tried to breathe through it as he pushed in, a little at a time, stretching her, while his fingers circled her clit, trying to relax her.

With a powerful thrust, he entered, the sound of their bodies colliding, echoing in the air. The sharp pain made tears well up, and she whimpered.

He halted his movements and raised his head to peer down at her. "Did I cause you any pain?"

She willed her body to relax, to accept the feel of him. "You're huge."

"Do you want me to stop?"

"No." Too late now. She squeezed the muscles on his back like stress balls.

She should have communicated her lack of experience to Nero and admitted it had been a while since she had done this.

"I won't move until the pain subsides," he whispered in a husky voice, his head leaning down to give her a tender kiss.

He returned to kissing her, lip to lip, tongue to tongue. Distracting her, relaxing her. Arousing her. Her head spun, her body rippled with delight, and she shifted, the unease translating to a full, pulsating sensation.

With small thrusts of his hips, he started a rhythmic and sensual motion. She felt a ripple of excitement, a subtle shiver that danced along her skin. With a deep breath, she adjusted her posture and raised her hips, seeking the sweet ripple. As he thrust harder and deeper, the pleasure intensified, flooding her body with energetic vibrations.

Nero took the lead, his thrusts deep and powerful, leaving her breathless with pleasure. He traced his fingers along her skin, leaving a trail of goosebumps in his wake. This sexual experience was incredible compared to her previous encounters on a completely different level.

The quickening of her pulse made her skin feel hot to the touch. She tightened on the inside, clenching around him as he drove deeper, desperately longing to keep him with her. No matter how hard she tried, he refused to be restrained by her, persisting in his rhythm. The tension grew, her muscles tightening with each passing moment, a fierce heat building up inside her, ready to erupt.

"Ifeoma, I claim your body with my heart as the gift," he said in her ear.

His use of her full first name should have alerted her. But his words didn't register immediately, overtaken by the feel of him inside her.

The deep rocking of his hips made it impossible for her to escape the exquisite torment, intensifying her sensations. Just when she thought she could hold on, she soared through the air. The stinging flicker transformed into a raging flame, devouring her in an instant. Her body trembled beneath him, her grip on him tightening as her muscles sprang to life.

He buried his hands in her hair and groaned her name into her mouth as he arched and tensed and shuddered, pulsing inside her.

She must have blacked out for a while. When she stirred, feeling sated, Nero was still with her, in her, his gaze on her.

Something flickered in her mind, his words just before she climaxed.

"What did you say earlier?" she asked, stretching a little.

"I claimed you as mine." He said casually and dropped a kiss on her lips before pulling away.

Her spine stiffened, and she sat upright as he headed for the bathroom.

"What do you mean, you claimed me?"

"You should know exactly what I mean. You are Yadili," he said before he disappeared into her bathroom.

ELEVEN

Nero knew she was Yadili?
What? How?

Shit! She was in danger.

As soon as Nero disappeared into the bathroom, Ifeoma scrambled off the bed and grabbed her purse for the desk where she left it earlier. She unclasped it and withdrew her personal alarm, depressing it to send the silent signal to her security team.

As a senior Yadili and enforcer to Ezenwanyi Ejiofor, she always travelled with an entourage, although they were trained to be discreet unless danger was imminent.

Nero's last words to her proved she was in danger.

Her mind had already switched from wanton woman to crisis management mode.

How did he know she was Yadili? Only Yadili could identify other Yadili? The rules banned them from divulging their secrets to non-members.

So how did Nero Piedimonte find out about the Yadili and Ifeoma's membership?

Unless...

Before she could process the thought, Nero returned to the bedroom. For a moment she forgot the danger, distracted. He was big, muscular, and naked. Her pulse elevated, her skin flushing.

He'd been inside her, snug, hard, pulsating, lighting her up, making her come alive for the first time in decades.

"Come on. Let's get you into the bath," he said, leaning over her as if to scoop her up.

"What?" She backed away, eyes narrowing, remembering his earlier words.

"I ran the bath for you. A soak in it will help to soothe your soreness," he spoke with such casualness, as if it was the most natural thing in the world. As if they'd made love and he'd run a bath for her to care for her aches.

Well, they had made love—had sex—and she was aching.

But that was beyond the point.

"If you think I'm getting into a bathtub right now, you're out of your mind." She grabbed her discarded clothes.

"Okay." He sat on the bed, making no move to cover up. "What would you rather do?"

She tugged her clothes on without the undies. "I want answers, damn it."

He sighed, as if she was being petulant, bracing his elbows on his thighs and clasping the tips of his fingers together. "You will get answers in due course."

"In due course. Let me tell you something. Security is coming here any minute now." She crossed arms over her chest and wondered why they weren't here already. Their room was just next door.

"Oh, that. If you mean hotel security, then good luck with getting them to do anything for you without my permission, since I own this hotel."

What the hell. She reared back, eyes narrowed. "You own this hotel?"

She hadn't been referring to hotel security since she had her own personal guards.

"Yes. But if you were speaking about the two men who checked into the hotel in the room next to you, you should know they are currently indisposed and won't be making an appearance here tonight."

"What the hell? How did you know about my guard?" She shook her head. "More to the point. What did you do to them?"

"They are unharmed. Just detained in their room. I didn't want them interrupting our quality time together," he said nonchalantly.

Even sitting there indifferently naked, he oozed power, authority, control. Virility.

His total calmness was thrilling, scary, and annoying.

"Quality time? Who the hell do you think you are?"

"I'm the man who just declared Ifeoma Nzekwe as his life partner."

Okay. He had her there. She hadn't seen it coming. Had been so lost in the throes of passion, she hadn't known he would trap her with an oath of commitment.

"Life partner?" she scoffed. "I only want you for one night."

"And I want you for life. Get used to it. I'm not letting you go."

For the first time tonight, she had a wave of fear. "What do you mean, you're not letting me go? I live in Nigeria. My life is in Nigeria. I'm not moving to Italy. Not for you."

He flinched. The first visible sign of her words perturbing him. Well, tough. Whatever game he was playing had to end.

"I'm not going to be your life partner—" She didn't get out of one relationship, even if it ended twenty years ago, just to get into another. "—as I said, I only wanted one night with you. In fact, the night is over because this nonsense you pulled killed all the passion in me. So, get dressed and leave." She paused and remembered something else. "By the way, how do you know about Yadili?"

He shifted and stood, picked up his boxer briefs and tugged it on. Then his trousers. He was ignoring her.

"Answer me, damn it!" she stomped across the carpeted floor on bare feet and stood in front of him.

How did she not notice how tall he was? How imposing? He pulled his shirt on, muscles rippling as did the buttons, top to bottom. He sat on the bed and reached for his shoes.

She grabbed and tossed them across the room. "No. you're not getting dressed and ignoring me."

His eyebrows rose in warning. "Ifeoma, you told me to get dressed and leave, which I'm doing."

"I also asked you a question and you need to answer it," she bit out.

"Complete our ritual of commitment and I'll answer all your questions," he challenged.

"Ritual of commitment!" she yelled. "You're insane. I'm not doing it. You should rescind your oath of commitment. I don't want it."

"Then you should have rejected it when I said it while I was inside you."

Good point. But...

"You tricked me."

"I tricked you!" He shot off the bed, looming over her. "Be careful about accusing me falsely. I did nothing to you that you didn't invite. You invited me into your room, into your bed, into your life, into you. Our ancestors bore me witness."

As soon as he mentioned ancestors, she bit back the retort on her tongue. To falsely accuse him when he'd invoked the ancestors was to curse herself.

But his words were a revelation. He knew about the Yadili. He knew enough to tie her hands, to quake her foundations.

Nero Piedimonte was an enigma she needed to unravel. Was that even his real name?

When she said nothing, he grabbed his shoes and slipped his socks and shoes on. He was going to leave without giving her an answer. She had to change tactics. There had to be a way to reach him. She needed to understand what she was up against before he walked out of the door.

"Nero, I'm sorry," she started, hoping an apology would mellow him like it had done this afternoon. "I didn't mean to accuse you falsely. I'm just—" she searched for the right words "—confused. Your actions are surprising to me. Surely you can see that?"

He puffed out a breath, still watching her with narrowed eyes. "Yes, I understand."

"So, I want to understand where all this is coming from. Who are you really and what do you know about Yadili?"

"You deserve all the answers." Fully dressed, he stepped up to her and cupped her shoulders. His eyes softened, and it looked like he would explain.

How could he go from cold to hot in a blink of an eye? They just had an argument, yet he could still be gentle, even though she hadn't given in and he hadn't won. They were at an impasse. Her shoulders relaxed.

"And I promise I will tell you everything. But don't the rules say that only life partners or spouses can discuss Yadili? I don't make the Yadili rules."

"But—" she started, but he shushed her with a finger to her lips.

"I don't want you to get into trouble, love, you being an enforcer and all."

He'd trapped her well and good. The only way to get him to talk was to complete the bonding ritual. But it would never happen. She didn't know him. Hadn't wanted to know him beyond what was necessary to get him into bed. Now it had come to bite her in the bum.

Ifeoma, i zutala nsogbu. *Ifeoma, you have bought trouble.*

Stunned, she did nothing as he pressed a tender kiss to her forehead.

"Ifem, have a good night. I'll see myself out."

Did he just call her an endearment, which was a play on her given name?

Ifem. *My possession.* A reminder that he'd claimed her.

She swivelled, lost for words as he departed, the door swinging shut.

TWELVE

As soon as Nero left, Ifeoma grabbed her phone. She needed to make some urgent calls. She walked into the bathroom. Water covered in bubbles filled the sunken tub. Aromatherapy oils—lavender and something else she couldn't identify—scented the air. A jar of bath salts stood on the sink counter.

Damn. Nero had run the bath for her. He'd been serious about soothing her soreness. About taking care of her.

No man, no person, had done anything like that for her in twenty years.

She sat on the WC, emotions warring inside her.

What manner of a man was this? She'd only just met him last night. The attraction between them proved potent. Yet she didn't know him.

But he knew her. Identified her full name and status in the Yadili.

He'd prepared for her arrival in Italy. Her accommodation in his hotel was not a coincidence. In fact, their meeting last night was definitely not a coincidence.

Did Nkoli know? Had her friend set her up?

Her stomach curdled, an icy finger travelling down her spine.

Nkoli was her oldest friend and knew all her secrets because she was Yadili too, although in a different clan. She had suggested places for Ifeoma to stay in Italy, including this hotel.

Suspicion made her body tense. Would her best friend sell her out by revealing her secrets to Nero? But Nkoli was Yadili too and understood the serious consequences of sharing their secrets with non-members.

But who else was the culprit?

There was only one way to find out.

She dialled Nkoli's number. As it rang, she switched to speaker and placed the gadget on the counter.

"Hello, Ifeoma? O dịkwa mma?" Nkoli's voice sounded hoarse.

"Did I wake you?" It was the middle of the night—past two o'clock on the phone display.

"Not quite. But you don't sound good. Did something happen?"

"There's a problem. Did you tell Nero about me?"

"Nero, kwa? No. I haven't spoken to him since we met him last night. Hold on."

Her friend sounded sincere. Ifeoma couldn't detect any deception. If anything, she sounded confused.

Fabric rustled as if Nkoli got out of bed and walked around. Then a door closed, and she spoke. "Sorry, I had to go to another room. I didn't want to disturb Lorenzo."

"You're with him?"

"Yes, he stays with me when he's in Rome. Anyway, what's going on with you and Nero?"

"He knows about me, my full name, about my life, about the Yadili and my status within the network."

"What? How?"

"That's what I need to find out."

"Wait, oh. You thought I told him?"

"Well, somebody did."

"And you thought it was me?" Nkoli sounded horrified. "I never met the man until yesterday. The same time you met him! And you're accusing me?"

Ifeoma puffed out air. "I'm sorry. It's just that the man knows so much about me. Things that only Yadili should know. He knows about my security. He even owns this hotel."

"Seriously? Egwu di kwa!"

"I'm telling you. This is not ordinary. And he is refusing to tell me how he knows all these things."

"Is he there now?"

"No. I told him to leave, and he got dressed, kissed me on the forehead and left."

"Okay, I'm confused. Back up a little and explain. Last time we spoke this afternoon you were in the car with him and you'd had a quarrel. What happened afterwards?"

Ifeoma sucked in a deep breath and started explaining what had happened. Apologising to Nero in the car. Their date at the Brazilian restaurant, the dancing and kissing. Her inviting him to her room afterwards. The subsequent love-making.

"It was the most ecstatic feeling, having him inside me. I was high, floating. Then he spoke the oath of commit-ment—"

"Oath of gini?? Commitment? While he was inside you?"

"Yes."

"And you rejected it immediately!"

"Hian. Did you not hear me? I was high, soaring, chasing the best orgasm of my life. At least it felt that way at the time. I barely registered his words, let alone had the where-withal to reject them."

"Ewo! Nsogbu dikwa." *Wow! This is trouble.*

"I know. Afterwards I confronted him about it and the man calmly told me he'd claimed me and since I was Yadili, I should know what it means."

"Chere o. He mentioned Yadili?"

"M si gi, I have never been more shocked in my life. Even as I was demanding answers, he was spouting Yadili rules and regulations."

"Damn."

"He said the only way he would answer my questions was if I completed the commitment ritual."

"He has you there."

"I know. I'm not about to tie myself to another man."

"I understand. You have to get him to rescind his oath."

"The man refused. Point blank. He said he wants me for life."

"This is serious."

"Tell me about it."

"Then you have to find a loophole that will void his oath. Like if he coerced you at any point or you said no to him during your encounter."

"I already tried that. He didn't enter my hotel room until I invited him, didn't touch me until I asked him to. He knew the rules of the bonding ritual. Knew it wouldn't stand if I was forced during our lovemaking. His actions were faultless. The man invoked the ancestors when I challenged him. Mehn, I had to shut up before I put a curse on myself."

"No. this is not ordinary. The man has to be Yadili. Those are not things you read in a book."

"You're right. But if he is Yadili, how come you and I don't know about him? I couldn't even find him online when I searched on social media. Although that was before I knew his surname."

"What is it?"

"Piedimonte."

"What?" Nkoli's voice was shrill. "That's Lorenzo's surname."

"Exactly my reaction when I found out."

"But Lorenzo didn't say they were related."

"I don't want to say this since you're in a relationship with him. But is it possible that Lorenzo is involved, and they set this up?"

"Mba! Are you trying to accuse him as well?"

"But think about it. What are the chances of the two of them being in that bar at the same time as us?"

"Could be coincidence."

"Really? Knowing what we know about Nero now. Knowing Nero owns the hotel. That man specifically targeted me. He came at me with purpose. Nothing about our meeting was coincidental."

"You're right. It was an accurately executed plot. Definitely not random when you put everything together."

Ifeoma stayed silent, letting her friend get used to the concept and the implications.

"Lorenzo was involved, which means he used me to get to you," Nkoli said, sounding disappointed.

Ifeoma's heart hurt for her friend because she guess Nkoli had fallen for Lorenzo.

"I'm sorry. What are you going to do about it?" she asked.

"I'm going to talk to him. But it's making me question everything I know about him. Everything he ever told me. You know how hard it was for me after I found out my ex was cheating. I don't know if I can trust Lorenzo again if it turns out he is lying." Nkoli sounded crestfallen.

This was an enormous blow for her. Ifeoma didn't think she would get involved again after Nkoli's married broke down. Finding out she had a cheating spouse had been devastating. That she'd gotten so deeply involved with another man five years later was a feat of miracle.

"I'm really sorry that the explosions in my life are directly impacting yours," she said.

"No. This is not your fault. Lorenzo deliberately deceived me. And Nero, well, that man went to a lot of effort to get to you. He is up to something. Ify, I'm worried about you. You have to be very careful."

"I know. But I'll be fine. I can handle whatever Nero brings. But are you going to be okay? Do you need me to do anything?"

There was a tap on the hotel door.

"No. I'll be okay. I have to go. I'll talk to you later today," Nkoli said in her ear as she left the bathroom.

"Okay. Take care."

"Bye."

She hung up, peered through the peephole and saw it was her bodyguards. She opened the door and let them in.

"Good evening, ma," they greeted. They appeared intact, unharmed.

"What the hell happened today?" She sat in the armchair, glaring at them.

They briefed her on how they were ambushed on the way back from the restaurant and taken to an unknown location. Blindfolded and bound, they were kept there for a few hours and only returned to outside the hotel a few minutes ago.

As Ifeoma sat there listening to them, she understood Italy was no longer safe for her. She couldn't stay here any longer. It was time to get out of Dodge.

THIRTEEN

Ifeoma flicked her fingers across the screen of the digital tablet in her hand. She turned the page to read the resumes of the candidates applying for the position of her personal assistant.

It had been two weeks since her return from Italy, a fortnight since she last saw Nero Piedimonte.

. . ⚜ . .

She'd spent the night trying to find a flight out of Rome to Nigeria for the next day. When she couldn't, she fell into a restless sleep. Her bodyguards took turns on the night watch and didn't leave her alone.

The next morning, a phone call woke her. Still groggy from sleep, she'd answered before checking the caller ID.

"Ifem, good morning," the deep rumbling voice sounded cheerful.

"Nero, what do you want?" she grumbled, sitting upright.

"I'm just checking that you had a good night."

"No, I didn't have a good night, thanks to the stunt you pulled. So, what are you going to do to fix it?"

"I can come over and kiss it better," his voice acquired a seductive quality.

A warmth settled over her, but she shook it off. This was how she got into trouble in the first place. Allowing him to seduce her.

"No. I don't want you to kiss it better. If you want to make me feel better, rescind your oath of commitment. Are you going to do that?"

"No one in their right mind would spend a lifetime hunting treasure, acquire it, only to give it up," he said in a calm voice.

She frowned. Treasure? "You're not making any sense."

"All will be made clear soon enough. In the meantime, what is your plan for the day?"

She kept quiet, not about to divulge that she was trying to get on the first available flight out of his territory.

"I was thinking we could go visit some tourist sites together," he continued.

"I'm not going anywhere with you," she retorted.

"Okay. I suppose you want to head back to Nigeria as soon as possible. I will instruct our pilot to file a flight plan to take you back. It's the FCT you need to get to, right?"

Flabbergasted, she asked without thinking, "You have a private jet?"

"It's not mine, personally. It's a company asset, but we can borrow it for a day or two." He sounded amused.

"We?" her heart raced at the implication.

"Yes. You're my woman and I would like to make sure you arrived home safely."

"Firstly, I'm not your woman. Get that out of your mind. Secondly, in case you haven't noticed, I'm perfectly capable of taking care of myself. So just leave me alone."

He sighed heavily on the other end of the phone. "Ifeoma, I will leave you alone for the time being. But remember this, you belong to me. Our ancestors bore witness to my claim. You are mine to cherish, mine to protect. Woe betide anyone who messes with Ifem."

Shock ran through Ifeoma at his vow. He sounded serious, determined.

The oath of commitment was a complicated ritual. One had to give up their heart in order to claim a body. In Nero's case, he was giving up his heart to claim her body. In reverse, Ifeoma had to give up her heart in order to claim his body. Also, their minds and souls would be bound by completing the ritual.

Hence the reason she hadn't completed the bonding ritual. Giving up her heart meant loving Nero, and she would not make the mistake of falling in love again.

Definitely not to a man who lived across a desert and sea from her. Long-distance relationships were not her thing. It hadn't worked with Maddox, who had lived in the same country but worked away. It would not work with Nero, who lived on a different continent.

Not to mention she still didn't know him fully, and he was refusing to talk.

However, the implication of not giving up her heart was that she hadn't claimed Nero's body. This meant he could give *his body to others. Have sex with other women, as many as he wanted, and there wouldn't be any consequences for him.*

Meanwhile, she couldn't have sex with anyone else because of his claim.

Not that she was in a hurry to get in bed with anyone else.

But the idea of him with someone else made fierce anger boil her blood and her muscles quivered with agitation.

"So, you're saying no one can touch me? But what about you? Are you going to sleep with other women?" she finally asked because she couldn't keep silent about it.

"Without your claim, I can't guarantee that it won't happen," he said flippantly.

Her spine stiffened, and she shot off the bed. "You can't guarantee it? How is that fair?"

"I don't make the rules. Ifem, say the words right now. Claim me. Better still, I invite you to come up to my penthouse on the top floor of the hotel. I invite you to claim my body. Make it yours forever." His voice acquired the deep gravelly tone that melted her insides. Tempting her.

Her clit throbbed, her body heated.

She pictured him spread on a massive bed in an enormous apartment, waiting for her to possess him.

A thrill pulsed through her with images. Of climbing him, taking his hardened length inside her, mouthing the oath, claiming him as hers, riding him to completion until they collapsed in a sweaty, panting heap.

She caught sight of the laptop she'd left on the desk last night. Remembered everything that had happened last night. And her spine stiffened. She really had to cut all ties with him.

"Nero, let me make this abundantly clear. I don't want to see you. I don't want to talk to you. I certainly don't want to claim you. So don't call me again and don't interfere with my affairs again."

She didn't wait for him to speak. She ended the conversation and blocked his number.

Afterwards, her travel agent called. She'd gotten a flight to Nigeria via Amsterdam. Twenty-four hours later, Ifeoma and her team were home.

• • ☙ • •

The two weeks since had been hectic, with preparations for the new school year. Then her personal assistant had resigned from her position last week, citing personal reasons. It turned out her husband got a position with a company abroad and was relocating the whole family. Her PA had been with her for the past five years. So it was hard to lose someone she relied on to help her in the running of Hillcrest School.

Her life as a principal was tough enough. So now, Ifeoma was trawling through the shortlist of CVs her outgoing PA had already filtered through the first round of interviews. Ifeoma would conduct the final review before selecting her replacement.

The car horn beeped, and the car slowed down as it approached the closed gates leading to her house in the exclusive estate. Jacaranda trees lined the avenue, their lavender in bloom. The air was scented with eucalyptus and damp earth following the recent rain. Aso Rock loomed in the shadowy distance.

The security team scanned the car and then pulled the barrier aside to let her chauffeured vehicle through into the cul-de-sac. Five detached mansions stood on both sides of the tarred road, a streetlamp outside each structure on the grassy pavement every so often. A low fence and hedges separated each house. Some had trees while other had flowering plant. Each front yard had space to park up to four cars. At the other end of the street was the playground, which included a basketball court and a kid's outdoor gym all within the estate perimeter walls.

Emeka Eze, husband to Ifeoma's former sister-in-law, Amaoge, Maddox's sister, had constructed the residences designed for families. They lived in the same estate, opposite Ifeoma, one house to the left, with their young daughter.

Ifeoma knew all the other families in the estate whose kids ranged from infants to young adults at university like her son, Abuchi. Although Abuchi was at the military equivalent, training as an officer and a soldier. Following in his father's footsteps. She was proud of the man her son was becoming.

The car pulled into her driveway, and the driver parked it under the carport. He came around and opened her door, took Ifeoma's briefcase. There was another car in the carport and Ifeoma recognised it. It was her brother's car. Her housekeeper had already called her to say she had visitors while she'd been heading home.

Ifeoma stepped out and walked towards the front door, which was already opened by the housekeeper.

"Welcome, ma," Florence the housekeeper said, taking her tote from the driver.

"Thank you. Where are my visitors?" she replied, her shoes clicking across the stone tiles.

"They are in the living room." Florence pointed at the door.

"Please get me a glass of water." Ifeoma headed toward the sitting room.

She entered the space to find her siblings sitting on the padded sofas, watching the big screen TV. There were cold drinks and tumblers on the low glass tables.

"Sista," her immediate younger sister, Nonye, stood with a smile, coming towards her.

"Da Ify," her youngest sibling and only brother Afam, also stood too, sounding even more cheerful.

Ifeoma's spine stiffened because their smiling faces did not deceive her. They were up to something and just wanted her to lower her guard.

Still, she embraced each of them individually and asked about their wellbeing as they all settled down on the sofas. She was the oldest of the three siblings. She always felt obligated and responsible to them.

Nonye was married with four children. Afam was also married and had two children.

Eventually, when they got all the pleasantries out of the way, she asked the question on her mind since her housekeeper informed her of the visitors.

"Nke a ụnụ abụọ biara ihu m na abalị a, ihe adịkwa mma?" *This one you two came to see me this night, is everything okay?*

"My sister, there's something we wish to discuss with you because it impacts all of us," her sister replied in Igbo.

Ifeoma glanced from one to the other, gaging their hopeful expressions. "Okay, tell me. What is it?"

"I will let Afam explain it because he knows it best," Nonye said.

They both turned in their brother's direction.

Afam shifted in his seat.

"Sister," he cleared his throat. "You know the economy has been difficult for everyone over the last few years. We're hoping things will improve soon. But in the meantime, Zequer Industries has hit hard times and we're talking to the banks about a loan to tide us over. However, they won't talk to us without collateral."

"I understand. Have you offered your house and Nonye's house as assets for the loan?" Her gaze flitted from her sister to brother.

Afam was the CEO of the company their father had founded. He'd taken over when their father passed. Nonye also worked for the same company and the two of them ran it.

"We're already maxed out on our properties," Nonye said. "They want extra assets. That's why we're here. We're hoping you will let us use this house as collateral."

"This house?" Ifeoma sat upright. "Asi. Not going to happen."

"Sis, this affects all of us. If we don't get the loan for the business, Zequer Industries will have to close and all the employees will lose their jobs. Have you forgotten? This is our father's legacy. A business he built with his sweat and blood. Nonye and I have been working hard to keep his legacy alive."

"And you get paid handsomely for it. I have shares in that company that I make barely anything from. It's your responsibility to keep the company afloat. Why do I have to give up my house?"

"Why are you even behaving as if you did anything to earn this house? Maddox gave it to you for free. Why can't you be generous for once?" her brother said snidely.

"Isi gini? Are you talking to me?" Ifeoma jumped up from the chair and stomped towards her brother, who stood and backed away. "Ara o na-agba gi?" Are you mad?

"Sista, calm down," Nonye interceded, standing between them.

"I should calm down. You're here, and he's saying nonsense to me. That I'm not generous. How many times has he come to beg for money and I've had to send him money? Since he started running the business, there's been one problem or the other. And he has the guts to say I'm not generous."

"Ifeoma, biko," Nonye pleaded. "This is serious this time. We're on the verge of losing everything. I've seen the numbers. We have some financiers looking to invest in Zequer. This loan will give us time to work things out and get the investment needed to put the business on a better footing. Please think about all the people who will lose their jobs if Zequer closes. All the families that will be affected. How do you think this will affect our family name and status within the Yadili? Your status as well."

This gave Ifeoma pause. The impact of Zequer closing will be massive and her family influence will drop if they make other Yadili jobless because of mismanagement. Their reputation will be in tatters. She could lose her position as enforcer for Ezenwanyi Ejiofor.

She puffed out a breath. "If I do this, then we need to bring in another CEO. Someone who can actually run the company well."

"Mba. Not happening," Afam shouted.

"That is my condition. Take it or leave it," she snapped.

"Okay. We'll consider it and put it to vote with the other shareholders," Nonye said.

Afam growled and stomped out of the house.

FOURTEEN

Three months later

Nero stepped out of the blacked-out SUV outside the premises of Zequer Industries headquarters. It was a ten-storey glass and concrete building in the commercial district of the FCT. High in the clear blue sky, the sun shone brightly while the sound of the city buzzed around them. Vehicles and pedestrians filled the busy adjacent road.

The building looked worn and could do with a fresh coat of paint and refurbishment. It had changed little since business partners and friends John Ezeilo and Victor Nzekwe commissioned the building thirty years ago.

A vortex of bittersweet memories swarmed Nero.

Back then, they named the business Ezequer Industries, a combination and play on both founders' surnames—Eze from Ezeilo and Zekwe from Nzekwe becoming Ezekwe branded as Ezequer. After his father's death, the Nzekwe family dropped the E and renamed the business as Zequer Industries.

Anger pulsed through Nero, and his hands balled into fists.

They'd removed his father's name as if he never existed, as if he hadn't been a crucial part of building the business.

Now, Nero was back to take back everything that was taken away from him and his family.

"Are you ready?" Kane Waziri, his local head of security, stood beside him on the left side of the forecourt. His brow was furrowed in concern as his gaze scanned the location.

Nero had recruited the man about a year ago after he started working for Rocha Maduka in Iguocha. They hadn't been utilising the man's full potential. He'd come highly recommended as a former military man and a security expert. When Nero made him an offer to head his security crew in Nigeria, Kane accepted it. He'd since hired the rest of the security team.

On Nero's right side was Lottie Bain, his deputy and right-hand person, who executed his plans in Nigeria in his absence. As his cousin, daughter of his father's sister, she was infuriated about what happened to his family and was eager for him to wreak revenge on his enemies. She'd been working with him, covertly, for years, to put his plans in motion.

She was also Yadili, although not affiliated with any clan.

This worked well for Nero, because he was intent on building his own clan and sitting at the head. Hence, he was employing associates on the periphery of the Yadili. Those not affiliated with any godfathers or godmothers. He was basically forming a clan of Yadili outcasts, just like himself.

Lottie and Kane were in his inner circle in Nigeria and had his back.

"Yes, we're ready," Nero said and strode towards the entrance of the building.

It was time to stop hiding and show his face to his enemies as he struck the blow to destroy their lives.

The security man opened the swinging door leading into the air-conditioned lobby. At the reception desk, the woman greeted them and signed them in before pointing them to the lifts in the lobby.

Although Nero knew about the security measures in the building or lack of them, he was still a little surprised there wasn't even a metal scanner in place. For sure, Kane had concealed weapons on him and had been allowed to walk through and head into the office building.

This was a serious breach in a country with insecurity problems.

Still, they left the lifts unimpeded. Then a plump woman in a black blouse and black and yellow print pencil skirt came towards them, heels clicking on the hard flooring.

"Good afternoon, I'm Nonye Nzekwe, the marketing director here at Zequer. You must be Mr Piedimonte." She stuck out her hand.

He recognised her, although she had changed in twenty-five years. It seemed she didn't recognise him. Her older sister hadn't recognised him when they'd met in Italy four months ago. It seemed their family had actually wiped his existence out of their minds. It only fuelled his anger. He couldn't wait to see their faces when the penny dropped. It would be worth all the years he planned covertly for his return. For now, he restrained himself.

"Yes, I'm Nero." He shook her hand firmly. "These are my associates, Lottie and Kane."

He stood aside as they exchanged greetings and handshakes.

"We're in the boardroom. This way, please." Nonye led the way down the corridor.

Nero followed her, Lottie and Kane taking up the rear. Behind them, two of his most trusted men follow, ready to bring hell with them if this meeting went south. They waited outside the doors.

Nonye ushered Nero, Lottie and Kane into a conference room with an oval wooden table and twenty padded wooden chairs around it. One long wall had the windows overlooking the busy freeway. The other three walls obscured the view of the offices. There were two doors on each end of the conference room.

At the far end, an elegantly dressed older woman sat at the head of the table. On her right was a man in a flamboyant two-piece suit made of multi-print fabric. He recognised them instantly and the simmering hatred sparked to life. The wife and son of the man who killed his parents.

Two bodyguards stood at the corners of the room.

He ignored them and fixed his gaze on the people he planned to destroy.

Kane was right to be worried.

Being face-to-face with this family made him want to put bullets in them.

But he controlled the pain and anger, something he'd mastered over the past two decades.

"This is my mother, Chief Mrs Nzekwe, the board chairperson, and my brother the CEO, Afam Nzekwe," Nonye introduced. "Mum, this is Nero Piedimonte from Italy, one of the new shareholders with his associates."

"Good afternoon," he greeted. This time, he didn't extend his hand or even move from his spot at the other end of the table. Because he wasn't sure he could shake hands with those two without doing something he would regret, considering the amount of rage he held towards them. Then again, emotions never got the best of him.

Not until—he cut off the thought.

"We're happy to welcome you to Zequer," Mrs Nzekwe said, looking at him with greedy, assessing eyes as if he was the goose who laid the golden egg.

"Thank you," he replied and settled into the top chair at the opposite end of the table.

Another woman sat near the middle of the table, back to the dividing wall. An open laptop stood on the table in front of her.

"We're waiting for the other shareholders," Nonye said, glancing at the tablet device in her hand. "Mr Bain, Mr Waziri and my sister Ifeoma Nzekwe."

His heart skipped a beat at the mention of Ifeoma's name. But he squashed the feeling like a pesky bug.

"In that case, you're only waiting for one because Mr Waziri and Mrs Bain are here." Nero waved at his companions, his expression deadpan.

"Oh. I didn't realise." Nonye frowned.

"I'm Mrs Okoro, the company secretary." The woman by the open laptop spoke up. "Do you have your share certificates for confirmation?"

"Of course." Lottie placed her briefcase on the table and pulled out the documents before handing them over.

"Thank you. I'm going to make some copies and return the originals." Mrs Okoro left the room.

"Please help yourselves to the refreshments." Nonye pointed at the table at the back with jugs of hot water and a selection of hot beverages as well as cold drinks.

Nero grabbed the green bottle of sparkling water and poured some into a glass. He took a slow sip as he watched Nonye walk over to murmur something in a low tone to her family on the other end.

Afam looked up sharply, his eyes narrowed suspiciously at Nero. Then he lowered his head and spoke, probably asking to clarify what Nonye told them.

Nero said nothing, didn't even flinch. He was a master at hiding his emotions. Some said he didn't have any feelings.

The company secretary returned and handed back the share certificates to Lottie.

"I want to see those," Mrs Nzekwe said and Mrs Okoro took the copies over to her. She surveyed the documents before speaking sharply. "How did this happen?"

"What's the matter?" Nero asked confidently, arms folded on the table.

"These documents say Mrs Bain and Mr Waziri own 10% shares each," she said.

"Yes, that's correct," Nero maintained his poker face.

"But this one says you, Mr Piedimonte, have 30% shares in Zequer."

"That's also correct."

Nero spent years acquiring the stakes through shell companies and proxies, and had only consolidated them recently.

"That will make you the largest shareholder on the board. That's impossible," Afam shouted.

Nero shrugged nonchalantly. He would wait to reveal that not only did he have the largest share, he had half the equity ownership when he combined Lottie's and Kane's shares.

"No! Not happening. You are not permitted to own that much equity," Afam continued ranting. "Mum, we have to do something."

The air was tense.

Before Nero could reply, the door at the far end opened and Ifeoma walked in. She wore a red blouse and a long black skirt that swirled around her ankles with a belt cinched her waist.

His pulse accelerated, and he became aware of the strong beating of his heart. His palms turned clammy and blood whooshed in his ears.

Damn. He hadn't seen her, hadn't been in the same room with her for four months, and his body missed hers. Going by his visceral reaction to her presence. But as usual, he locked down the feeling, using her family's reaction to his presence as a distraction.

Ifeoma was looking at the phone in her hand as she sashayed across the room.

"Good afternoon, everyone," she greeted as she pulled out a chair beside her sister. Then she looked in Nero's direction.

"Nero?" Her eyes widened in shock and she slumped into the chair as if her legs gave way. "What are you doing here?"

"Good to see you could join us, Ms Nzekwe." He purposely ignored her question and used her formal name. "Now that everyone is here, we can get on with the meeting."

"Sis, do you know Mr Piedimonte? He's a new shareholder," Nonye said.

"With 30% shares. How did that happen?" Afam grumbled.

Ifeoma gasped, her mouth dropping open as she stared at Nero. "Thirty percent?"

"Mr Piedimonte, I don't understand how you acquired those shares. But no one outside the Nzekwe family is permitted to have shares that large. It must be a mistake," Mrs Nzekwe said in a condescending tone, as if Nero had stolen the shares rather than paid for them.

Nero's anger boiled, although he maintained an inscrutable expression.

This was the exact proof that they ripped his father off. They wanted to keep the company in the Nzekwe family only.

Well, he was about to show them that the Ezeilo family wasn't wiped out. That he wasn't as soft as his father. That he was indeed more ruthless than they could imagine.

"Mrs Nzekwe, I believe you have more pressing issues than the legitimate shares I bought."

"What pressing issues?" she replied and laughed derisively

"Like the money you owe me."

"Owe you?"

"Yes, one hundred million dollars."

"What!"

"How!"

Everyone on that side of the table exclaimed.

Afam laughed snidely. "You must be mad. How did you come up with that?"

"The money you borrowed against your portfolio for the Damali deal."

The blood drained from Afam's face as the pieces tumbled into place in his brain.

He wasn't laughing now.

"How the fuck do you know about that?" His voice was low and threatening.

Nero scoffed and adjusted the cuffs of his shirtsleeves. "You borrowed one hundred million dollars from Premier Financial. Premier Financial is owned by Serpico Corporation, and Serpico Corporation is owned by Piedimonte Inc and Piedimonte Inc is owned by...?" He lifted his eyebrows.

"You?" Afam paled.

Smiling smugly, Nero clapped for him, showing him how to condescend properly. "Well done, Mr Nzekwe. Well done."

Afam's hands curled into fists on the desk.

The temperature in the room plummeted as the tension thickened.

"And now, I'm calling in that loan."

Afam's eyes narrowed. "You can't do that. There's a contract."

Leaning down, Nero placed two palms on the table and looked him square in the eyes as he delivered the fatal blow.

"Oh, I assure you I can, and I am doing it. Your desperation and greediness for money and your cockiness about the Damali deal made you overlook the full implications. For example, you didn't scrutinise the clause in the contract that says the financial institution has the discretion to pull the loan at any time." Nero straightened. "Well, ladies and gentlemen, that time is here. I'm pulling the loan."

"Bullshit!" Afam seethed. "I have the best lawyer in this city and he wouldn't have missed that clause."

Nero flashed his teeth in a wintry smile. "Again, you didn't account for what I can accomplish with a lot of money."

Afam's head almost exploded off his shoulders. "Money? You bought him?"

"Yes, for five million dollars. He didn't even hesitate to take my money."

Afam shared a look with his siblings like he didn't believe Nero.

"Don't bother looking for him," Nero continued. "He knows I'm at this meeting and is on his way abroad with his family. Be warned, he is under my protection now. Don't try to harm him or his family. Or else..."

Mrs Nzekwe looked like she was about to have a coronary attack. She struggled to breathe and Nonye passed her a glass of water. She muttered something inaudible in Igbo under her breath.

"But everything looked good on paper," Afam growled, and he shook his head.

"Too good, don't you think? Didn't your mother teach you that if something is too good to be true, it probably isn't good?" Nero said, taking a swipe at mother and son in one swoop.

Everyone at the opposite end of the table stared at him in horror. Things were about to get worse for them. He ignored their expressions and continued. "This also brings me to the other matter. You will all need to move out of your homes because the foreclosure letters are being issued on all the properties as we speak."

He delivered the words with a grin to drive the stake in deeper. He'd set them up from the start. From the moment his associates dangled the loan offer in front of them.

The bomb blew up in their faces, and audible gasps filled the air.

Afam jumped up and pounded the table in front of him. "You modafucker!"

Ready to raise their weapons, the bodyguards stepped forward, but Nero signalled for them to stop with the wave of a hand. Today wasn't about bullets. Financial ruin would have a greater effect. He would take everything from them.

When he'd destroyed their business and family, he would take Ifeoma too.

Surprising she hadn't spoken for a while. Just watching him with narrowed eyes, as if uncertain about what she heard, yet suspicious. She was like her mother in that sense. Condescending, yet unwilling to give away any emotions.

Afam seemed the dramatic one.

"You set me up," Afam fumed.

"Yes."

"You created a scam business opportunity to try to destroy me?"

"Afam. I'm not *trying* to destroy you. *I am* destroying you and your family." Venom dripped off every word. "By the way, no one forced you to sign on the dotted line. I dangled the Damali deal in front of your greedy, beady eyes, and you stuck your nose in like a filthy pig."

Nero started planning this the moment he found out what really happened to his parents over two decades ago. He decided the Nzekwe family needed to know what it felt like to lose everything. So, he formulated a plan to ruin them by forcing them into so much debt. He would force them into bankruptcy and make them lose the lifestyle they were accustomed to living.

It was never about marrying Ifeoma. But now he needed a wife, and she would be the goddamn cherry on top.

"Fraud will get you thrown in prison," Mrs Nzekwe sneered. "The Financial Crimes Commission doesn't take kindly to this kind of nonsense."

"Indeed," Nero scoffed. "Don't you worry about me. You need to be more worried about getting the FCC involved in your family affairs. What would they discover if they started digging?"

Did they really think Nero didn't come prepared for this fight? That he didn't know all their dirty little financial secrets? Of course, he'd covered any legal loopholes they might want to exploit.

"You have some balls on you," Ifeoma spoke, disdain dripping from her words. "You came all the way to Nigeria to threaten *my* family. Do you think you are still in Italy? Do you know where you are, at all?"

He ignored her and directed his gaze to Afam. "You have twenty-four hours to come up with the full one hundred million or face financial ruin."

Afam's nose flared as realisation dawned. Nero had him over a barrel. His eyes blazed with animosity as he slowly returned to his chair. He waited a moment before speaking. "What do you want?"

A smug smile curled Nero's lip. "Ifeoma will become my wife."

"O si gini?" Ifeoma turned her full glare at him, hostility rolling off her. "If you call my name again, you will regret it."

Nero chuckled without humour. She hadn't seen anything yet. This train was barrelling along the tracks and nothing could stop a score years of the hatred fuelling it.

Ignoring her threats, he maintained his gaze on her brother with a look of indifference. "Afam, I can make all your troubles disappear, just like that." He snapped his fingers. "You are the man of the house in your father's absence. You can play the father's role and give me your sister in marriage."

"Never!" Ifeoma countered.

Nero was doing it on purpose, ignoring her and talking to her brother in her presence. He was provoking and pissing her off. However, she'd started it by telling him never to speak to her. She'd even gone as far as blocking his phone number.

Payback was a bitch.

Then again, observing Ifeoma for the past years had shown she possessed a fierce heart and would not easily succumb to coercion.

"This is a boardroom, not a marketplace," Nero said sternly. "It would be good if everyone acted accordingly."

Ifeoma growled but said nothing. Nonye placed a hand on her arm and whispered in her ear, probably trying to calm her.

"Think about my offer," Nero continued. "Everything you own will be gone. But I'm offering you an alternative solution, a way out."

"For the price of my daughter," Mrs Nzekwe said.

"Arranged marriages have been around for as long as time. She will be provided for, and well taken care of," he said. "She will be under my protection and want for nothing."

Ifeoma said nothing. She glared at him, muscles on her neck straining, hands on the table clenching and unclenching.

Cornered, the shoulders sagged on the Nzekwe family members facing him. Only Ifeoma looked like she was ready to tear him to shreds.

"Mr Piedimonte, why are you doing this to us?" Nonye sounded deflated.

Finally, the question he'd been waiting for someone to ask.

"Your family destroyed mine."

"How? We've never met you before."

"Oh, but you have." The truth constricted his chest. "My parents named me Nebolisa Ezeilo and your father stole what belonged to my father and tried to wipe out my entire family. Although my parents died, my uncle rescued me and raised me abroad. Now, I'm back here with revenge on my mind."

FIFTEEN

"Nebolisa? This is you?" Afam asked, his gaze intent on Nero as recognition dawned.

"Yes, it is," Nero said. He'd thought his former friend would have recognised him earlier. But over twenty years was a very long time, a lifetime. And he'd changed, matured from the young adult they'd known.

Afam jerked back. He looked like he had seen a ghost. "I thought it was you when I first saw you. But you were supposed to be dead."

"So you wish," Nero bit out. They could blame their father's assassin for not completing the job because once he was done with them, they would wish he'd died with his parents.

Mrs Nzekwe scrutinised him as if not believing her eyes. "You mean you are John Ezeilo's son?"

"The one and only."

"Now, it makes sense." Ifeoma's expression changed as she made the realisation, emotions chasing across her features. She looked at Nero, shook her head, and turned away with a disappointed expression.

"Nebolisa, there are things you don't understand," Mrs Nzekwe said in a softened voice, probably trying to appease him.

Nero's muscles tensed. He hated that she'd used the name his parents had given him, considering she and her husband contributed to his parents' demise.

"I know that my father and your husband built this business," he bit out. "I know my parents are dead. I know that your family is living off my parents' sweat and blood. It doesn't take a genius to figure out."

"It's not that simple." Her voice hardened. For the first time, Nero saw the bitter hatred burning in her eyes.

Nero slammed his palm down, and the table rattled beneath it. "It is, and now I am here for retribution."

"Retribution for benefitting from our family business?" She said derisively and shook her head.

"No, it goes much deeper than that." Nero dragged his finger along the edge of the table as he stood and walked towards them slowly. "You need to pay for everything that happened."

"Then kill us all if you feel so much hatred."

He stopped behind Ifeoma, savouring the closeness to her. He fought the urge to touch her, to feel the warmth of her skin. She sat stiffly but didn't turn towards him.

"No. That would be too easy for you and less satisfying for me. You see, I want you alive and kicking so you can see me take everything from you." He leaned down and whispered into Ifeoma's ear. "I want you all to know how it feels to lose everything."

. . ⌘ . .

I feoma knew something was wrong before she walked into the Zequer boardroom this afternoon. Had carried the unshakeable niggling sensation for months. Yet could not pinpoint the reason she had been uneasy.

After her return from her travels during the long holiday, she'd focused her energy on preparations for the new school year. Aside from the initial hitch of losing her personal assistant and recruiting a replacement, things had been running smoothly. Sure, the country's current economic climate meant they'd lost a crop of students. Yet they'd gained new ones from parents who sent their children from abroad because it was cheaper to educate them in a private school here than in Europe.

The only major crisis had been with Zequer Industries needing a financial bailout, which her siblings had secured via a loan to keep the company running. Sure, they'd had to use their private homes as collateral with the financiers, but that was par for the course these days. Zequer Industries was their collective responsibility as a family, since it was their father's legacy and employed thousands of people.

However, Ifeoma had made one stipulation in the pre-loan agreement with her siblings. They would discuss hiring a new chief executive to run the business at the next board meeting.

Hence her arrival in the Zequer head office today for the meeting with the shareholders and non-executive directors. She was running slightly late because she'd had a meeting with prospective parents this morning, which had overrun.

As she got out of the lift on the top floor where the boardroom was located, her phone beeped with a message. Checking it, she walked towards the conference room. There were new emails, but nothing urgent.

A man stood at the entrance and opened the door to the conference room for her. She thanked him and walked in. The air-conditioned room was occupied. Her mother and siblings came into view first and sat—more like huddled—closest to her entry point. They were the major shareholders at Zequer with ten percent each and their mother with the larger share of twenty percent. Making the Nzekwe family equity in the business at fifty percent.

Ifeoma said her greetings and pulled out the seat next to Nonye. She usually sat with her family as a show of their solidarity to the other shareholders at the meeting.

As she lowered her body into the chair, her neck prickled with alertness, a survival instinct to search for danger. She glanced towards the other end of the room and her gaze connected with the last person on earth she expected to meet here.

"Nero?" she didn't even know when she said his name as her knees weakened and she descended into the chair faster than she intended. "What are you doing here?"

Other people sat beside him. Yet everything else faded away. Her vision and mind focused on him. A light-headedness overtook her.

His face was set, inscrutable. Just like the first night she'd met him at the hotel bar in Rome. The arched dark brows, the angular cheekbones, the full lips pressed together, the tight jawline, the ebony skin.

Damn! He was gorgeous, and he was here. There was no way she could forget that face, that body filling out the tailored suit like a cover model, no matter how much she tried.

"Good to see you could join us, Ms Nzekwe." His voice was icy, detached, a splash of freezing cold water on her skin, waking her from the brief daydream. He seemed to look through her, not at her, as if he didn't know her. Hadn't known her intimately, like no other man had done since the only one she'd once married.

What was going on?

The rest of the meeting degenerated. No other word for it.

Ifeoma sat in shock, trying to figure it out.

Her sister mentioned Nero was a shareholder. Okay, not a big deal in itself.

However, Afam then queried his share ownership of thirty percent.

"Thirty percent?" Ifeoma blurted out.

Now this was problematic, considering it meant Nero had more equity in the company than their mother. It made him the most prominent shareholder. No one outside the Nzekwe family was allowed that much stake in the business. How did this happen? Why wasn't it noticed earlier?

More to the point, why had Nero acquired this much stake in Zequer Industries? What game was he playing? Was this because of her?

She hadn't seen or spoken to him for four months. A part of her had been disappointed because he hadn't tried to contact her in any other way since. Meanwhile, he'd been buying shares in her family business.

The conversation in the boardroom went back and forth until Nero mentioned money.

"One hundred million dollars."

No way! Ifeoma sat upright, her muscles tensed in alertness.

It turned out the loan Afam had borrowed to keep Zequer Industries running had been financed by a company owned by Nero. The loan which they'd all put up their homes as collateral.

Now Nero was calling back the loan, telling them to pay back one hundred million dollars.

Initially, Ifeoma was too shocked to say anything. This was her brother's show as the chief executive officer of Zequer Industries.

However, as she watched Nero chew and spit out Afam, and threaten to destroy her family and their legacy, Ifeoma couldn't keep quiet any longer.

"You have some balls on you. You came all the way to Nigeria to threaten my family. Do you think you are still in Italy? Do you know where you are, at all?"

Nero didn't acknowledge her threat, didn't even look at her. It was like she wasn't in the room. Or she was a ghost. He'd been that way since her arrival.

He hadn't acknowledged her presence. At first, the shock of seeing him here had masked her mild annoyance at his infuriating behaviour. Now it was morphing into full-blown anger. Why was he ignoring her? How long would he pretend he didn't know her?

Her muscles quivered, and her heartbeat pounded in her ears.

Nero continued ignoring her, talking directly to her brother instead as if she wasn't here. "You have twenty-four hours to come up with the full one hundred million or face financial ruin."

Impossible. Where did he expect them to get that kind of money from?

But she suspected this wasn't just about money.

"What do you want?" Afam asked the question on her mind.

Nero's eyes sparkled with something she couldn't decipher. "Ifeoma will become my wife."

"What did he say?" she blurted in Igbo. "If you call my name again, you will regret it."

Ifeoma clenched her palms into fists to hide their trembling. Oh, she wanted to smack the smug smile off his face. He'd ignored her all afternoon as if she was an insignificant piece of lint. Now he dared to mention her name and wife in the same sentence.

The man laughed. He dared to laugh in her face, talking to Afam about giving her away in marriage. What goddamned century did he think they were in? Sure, there were some idiots who thought they could arrange marriages for their daughters in this country. But her father had never tried it with his children. Never mind her younger brother trying it, someone five years her junior.

"Never!" She ground her teeth.

Afam knew better than to negotiate marriage on her behalf. Knew better than to arrange anything for her. No one would dare make wedding plans without her permission. Not if they wanted a peaceful life.

"This is a boardroom, not a marketplace," Nero said sternly. "It would be good if everyone acted accordingly."

He didn't mention her name, but Ifeoma knew he'd said it because of her outburst. Her face flamed and she bit back her retort, fuming inside. The conversation revolved around an arranged marriage between her and Nero to stop him from destroying their family.

Then he dropped the most devastating bombshell.

He was Nebolisa Ezeilo, the son of her father's former business partner, John Ezeilo.

Ifeoma thought he'd died in the car crash that killed his parents decades ago. At least it was what she'd been told by her parents at the time. They'd mourned the tragic loss. Yet here he was.

And suddenly everything else made sense. Why he'd seemed vaguely familiar the first time she'd seen him. How he'd known so much about her in Rome. How he'd been able to get involved in their family business.

His father had been Yadili and Nero must have been initiated into the secret society by his father before his death. Hence his knowledge of some of their practices.

Still, there were unanswered questions. What really happened to his parents? How did he survive the crash? Why was he only showing up now?

"You need to pay for everything that happened." He seemed to answer her last silent question as he stood and strolled towards her.

Her pulse sped up. Did he also want revenge because she jilted him in Rome and blocked him from contacting her? Because she refused to complete the bonding ritual he started.

"Then kill us all if you feel so much hatred," her mother dared him.

Ifeoma stiffened. It probably wasn't a good idea to dare a man who was threatening to destroy their lives.

Nero stood behind Ifeoma. Her skin prickled, and she fought the urge to turn around.

Would he touch her? It had been so long since she had body contact with a lover, with him. She swallowed repeatedly, sitting stiff and upright.

"No. That would be too easy for you and less satisfying for me. You see, I want you alive and kicking so you can see me take everything from you. I want you all to know how it feels to lose everything." He leaned down and his breath whispered across her earlobe as he spoke. "Of course, I can be lenient if I get the trophy wife instead."

"Trophy wife? You're mad if you think I will agree to this blackmail." Ifeoma spat out in disgust. A heavy knot sat in her belly.

Why did Nero want her as his wife? Was it just to exact revenge on her family? To flex his delirious power over their lives?

"Then sit back and watch me rip your family to shreds." Nero moved away from her and she missed his heat instantly, the chest squeezing tight. "Remember, you have twenty-four hours. I'll see myself out."

He headed for the exit without even glancing back. One of his associates, the female one, slid a card across the table before following Nero and the other one out with their bodyguards.

"Shit," Ifeoma swore aloud in the silent aftermath of Nero's exit.

"What are we going to do?" Nonye asked, looking shell-shocked.

"I say we hire assassins to go and finish what Dad started twenty years ago," Afam said flippantly.

"Shut your mouth," Mum said in an irritated tone. "Mrs Okoro, thank you for your help. But please excuse us."

"Of course, Mrs Nzekwe," the company secretary who had been typing away earlier. She packed up her laptop and papers. "I will email you the draft of the minutes."

"Yes, thank you," Mum said. She waited for the woman to leave and the door shut behind her. "Afam, why would you talk about assassins in front of Mrs Okoro?"

"Mum, she understands it's a joke," her brother said defensively.

"A joke? Is this whole situation a joke to you?" Mum's irritation seeped through. "That Ezeilo boy walked in here and turned our lives upside down and you're making jokes."

"Well, he offered us a way out of the mess..." Afam trailed off.

Everyone turned in Ifeoma's direction and a tingling sensation crawled in her belly. "No one should look at me. I'm not getting married again."

"Didn't you hear him? We're going to lose everything. Where are we going to get one hundred million?"

The amount made Ifeoma sick. But... "How is it my responsibility?"

Her mother shook her head. "It doesn't matter whose responsibility. We're in this mess together. If you were still married to Maddox, you could have asked him for help to pay off the loan. But you didn't listen to me and you divorced him. Now he has remarried and we can no longer go to his family for help."

Her mother had returned to the old tune. Her disapproval of Ifeoma divorcing Maddox. Ifeoma's earlier annoyance returned, and she spoke without thinking.

"So, it's my fault. Last time I checked, I'm not your only daughter who got married. Why don't you go to Nonye's husband for help?"

"We all know her husband is not worth the manhood between his legs," Mum said snidely, a dig at Nonye's husband impregnating her four times, yet unable to take care of his family financially. Her sister was the one paying their household bills. Good thing her kids were at Hillcrest School, so they received scholarships via the bursary.

Nonye flinched at their mother's statement, looking hurt.

Ifeoma's chest constricted. She hadn't meant for her sister to catch a stray bullet. However, it wasn't fair that she seemed to be the one always targeted for shaming by their mother because she was divorced.

"Perhaps Nero will take a partial payment. We will have to take out the money from the company account. But it will mean we can't pay suppliers or staff in the short term," Nonye said.

"Not a good idea affecting your cash flow like that." Ifeoma knew how problematic it could get. "What about the money from the loan? Surely there should be a chunk of it still available. We can return it."

"That's not going to work," Afam said, shifting uncomfortably.

"Why?" Ifeoma asked.

"I invested most of it in a scheme I thought could earn us some returns. But the deal collapsed. It was a fraud."

"What? You were duped?"

"Unfortunately. But, sis, it won't matter if you marry Nebolisa."

"Typical. You lose the money and I get to bail you out again. Mum, you see why I say Afam should not be CEO of Zequer. I bet Nonye will make a better CEO."

"Why should Nonye be the CEO? Is it her children that will inherit Zequer Industries?" their mother retorted.

Ifeoma threw her hands in the air at the woman's misogyny. "Mum, at the rate Afam is going, there will be no Zequer Industries for anyone to inherit. You know what? I've had enough. I think it's time for us to let it go."

She pushed back the chair and stood.

"Ifeoma, biko," Nonye pleaded, tears in her eyes. "If Zequer goes down, I will be left with nothing. How will I sustain my family?"

"You can get another job. You're intelligent and brilliant at what you do?" Ifeoma replied.

"Which job? Where? At this my age? In this economy?" Nonye swiped the tears from her cheeks. "You don't know what it's like, trying to keep it together. Trying to juggle a career and a family when your spouse..." she trailed off. "Not to mention that my in-laws are nothing like yours."

Ifeoma stretched her hand out, but Nonye jerked back. "You've always had your life together as the firstborn. You married the military boy next door every other girl wanted, had the most supportive in-laws who continued taking care of you even after you divorced their son. So much so, they gifted you a house and a school to run. On top of that, you walk around with your nose up, looking down at the rest of us."

"No, I don't do that!" Ifeoma denied, unaware that her sister felt so strongly about things.

"Yes, you do. You think you are better than the rest of us. And Mum keeps reminding me that I didn't marry well enough. Then of course there is Afam who is honestly a wastrel—"

"Me, a wastrel?" Afam spat out. "It is your husband that is a wastrel."

"Afam, admit it. You gambled away most of the money in the name of 'investments'" Nonye did hand quotes. "You're the reason we're in this mess."

"Fuck you! In fact, fuck all of you." Her brother stormed out, slamming the door.

The Nzekwe women sat silently in the aftermath. Their mother looked lost for words. Nonye lowered her head to the table and started sobbing. Ifeoma returned to the chair she abandoned and wrapped an arm around her sister, trying to console her.

Her family was imploding.

Nero, what have you done?

More to the point, what was she going to do?

She couldn't sit back and watch him destroy her family.

SIXTEEN

Later in the evening, Ifeoma was going over the home ownership documents for her house. Sure, her generous in-laws had given her the house as a gift, but she'd transformed it into a home. It was the place she raised her son. It held so many memories.

Now she could lose it all because her brother was playing at CEO and haemorrhaging cash from Zequer like a haemophiliac.

One hundred million.

Her breath caught, and she grimaced, thinking about the huge amount of money.

Where could she find such an amount from?

There was the school coffer with all the newly paid fees. Yet she couldn't touch it. It would be irresponsible to dip into the school funds. She'd never done it before. Wouldn't try it now. She had the board of governors to account to never mind Ezenwanyi Ejiofor. If she mismanaged the funds, she would lose the school franchise and the Yadili sisterhood would reject her as an enforcer.

She couldn't risk her reputation for her family, regardless of how much she loved them.

"You have twenty-four hours to come up with the full one hundred million or face financial ruin."

Nero's words from earlier today flashed in her mind.

Her head spun, and the anger swelled for the man whom she'd spent a glorious time in Italy only a few months ago. It could morph into dark hatred, considering what he was trying to do to her family.

He was going to take everything from her family unless she married him.

All seemed lost.

However, she hadn't attained her position in life or as a Yadili enforcer by being a pushover. Wasn't about to roll over and play good little wifey to anyone. Even if it was the man who'd awakened her sexuality in Italy months ago.

She'd been stupid to let her guard down to a flirtatious, handsome man because she'd been abroad. She should have known she was never far from the Yadili, who were everywhere.

She'd allowed Nero into her body and he'd dared to claim it as his. She should have known he would unleash havoc on her life.

He'd dared to set her brother up. Sure, Afam was a fool and irresponsible. But Nero had set him up, had duped him into falling into a deep hole of debt. A debt that would cripple the entire Nzekwe family and cost thousands of their employees their jobs.

She felt blindsided and betrayed. By Afam and Nero.

Now she had to step up and clean up the mess, offer herself as the sacrificial lamb to satisfy arrogant, irresponsible, vengeful male egos.

Hatred rattled her bones, grew and morphed into a giant monster. Every muscle in her body coiled with tight, unrestrained anger.

So, Nero Piedimonte or Nebolisa Ezeilo was a man who always got what he wanted, when he wanted it. And now he wanted Ifeoma.

A bark of sharp laughter escaped as she paced the bedroom.

Many men had wanted her, had tried to get her. And where were they now? They all ran and hid from her, eventually.

Nero should have asked questions about her before he came on this quest.

Someone should have warned him to be careful about what he wished for.

He'd once told her he wasn't intimidated by her, that he could handle her.

But the Cruel King of Italy was about to meet the Agbara Nwanyi of Umudike.

And he was about to learn that this lioness bites back, hard.

She grabbed her phone and made the call. It rang several times before Nkoli answered it.

"Ify, kedu?" Nkoli said on the other end. She sounded out of breath.

"I have a situation. Can you talk?" Ifeoma replied.

"Sure, just give me a second." There was rattling on the other end, then silence. "Okay. What's up?"

Did her friend have someone in the house with her? Nkoli broke up with Lorenzo after she found out Lorenzo had intentionally brought Nero to the bar the night he met Ifeoma in Italy. He'd admitted the whole thing had been pre-arranged, down to Ifeoma's accommodation at the hotel.

"Sorry if I called at a bad time. Do you have company? I can call later."

"No. I was doing a workout. It's okay. What is the situation?"

"Nero is in Nigeria."

"What? Are you okay?"

"No. I saw him today. He came to a shareholders' meeting at Zequer. It turns out he now owns thirty percent shares, more than any other single individual, more than any members of my family."

"What? How did that happen?"

"I don't know. But that is not the biggest problem. You remember a few months ago, Nonye and Afam convinced me to put up my house as collateral for a loan for a Zequer business project?"

"Yes?"

"Guess who financed the loan? ... a company owned by Nero."

"No!"

"And now he's calling in the loan. One hundred million dollars. In twenty-four hours."

"Isi gini? That's not possible, na."

"Tell me about it. Turns out most of the money is lost because Afam blew it in one of his stupid frivolous schemes and got duped. So, we can't even give back some of the money."

"Mba nu. Not Afam again. But surely there has to be a legal agreement. Nero can't just call in a loan, especially if the debt repayment schedule has been honoured."

"Yes. But apparently, Afam's lawyer was working for Nero and messed up the contract. So, we don't have a legal footing."

"Ha. But why is Nero doing this? Why is he targeting your family? It can't be because you jilted him in Italy."

"No. You won't believe this, but he is the son of my father's former business partner. His parents died years ago, and we all thought Nero died with them. It turns out he was living in Italy all this while. He claims my father killed his parents and now he's back for revenge."

"Revenge, kwa. So, getting close to you in Rome was revenge? Ifeoma, that man fooled me, us. Him and Lorenzo fooled us both."

"I know."

"What are you going to do? Where will you find one hundred million? You know I would help out if I could. But I work for an NGO and we're under a lot of scrutiny. Every cent spent is co-signed and accounted for. I would have asked Lorenzo, but I haven't spoken to him in months."

"I understand. But there would be no point in asking Lorenzo anyway, since he is in bed with Nero."

"True. Can you ask Maddox? Maybe Ezenwanyi?"

"No! Never. I can't go begging the Ejiofors for anything now that Maddox is remarried. I would rather let Zequer go down in flames than do that. Mba."

"Okay. Can you take a loan from the school account?"

"No. I won't touch it. My principles aside, I feel it is a trap Nero has set up. He knows it's the only other option for me to raise funds. The minute I dip into it, he's going to know somehow, and he's going to use it against me. No. it's not an option I will consider."

"So, what are you going to do? No one will give you a loan when you're already in debt for a hundred million."

"True. But Nero offered us a way out."

"How?"

"He says if I agree to be his wife, he will write off the loan and let my family be."

"He said that?"

"Yep."

"Nah wah. This man has a serious obsession with you. Did you date him when we were young or something?"

"Me date him, kwa? No. I never had anything to do with him. I barely even remember him. He's not my age mate now. He is Afam's age mate and his friend. You know how I felt about Afam and his friends in those days. They were immature boys who took their parents' cars out for joy rides to impress girls. All they did was piss me off. In fact, come to think of it. I think I remember telling Nero, Nebolisa—that's the name he used back then—off because he couldn't speak in

Igbo then and only spoke English. I called him an efulefu. After that, I never saw him again."

"Ha, Ify. You must have bruised the poor boy's ego. You know teenage boys. Maybe he was trying to impress you with all the English and you crushed his spirit."

"I bruised his ego back then, and now he's back for more? He's tearing my family apart because he couldn't handle a little criticism as a young man. Well, he's in for a world of pain because I will tear him to shreds for what he's doing."

"What are you saying? Are you going to marry him?"

"Oh, he's going to get his trophy wife. But I can't guarantee he will survive marriage to me. I need you to pool our Italian Yadili resources. I want to know everything there is to know about Nero Piedimonte. We already know Lorenzo is his uncle and business partner at Piedimonte Holdings. But I want a deep dive into his personal life and what he's been doing over the past twenty-five years. I want to know his business connections and associates. Most importantly, I want to know his enemies. The enemy of my enemy could very well become my friend, and I want to leverage that information when I get it."

"Are you sure about this?"

"Nkoli, did you not hear what I said?" Ifeoma said in her hard, enforcer tone. "The man came into a meeting and threatened to destroy my family and everything my father built. He might have the upper hand now, but it won't be for long. He is just digging his own grave. So, get me the information and tell the investigators that it's of utmost urgency. We're meeting with Nero again tomorrow and I want to read his dossier before then. Can you get it done?"

"Agbara nwanyi, your wish is my command. I will send the file to you as soon as I get it," Nkoli said haltingly, probably shocked at Ifeoma's tone.

"Good." Ifeoma puffed out air. She'd pulled rank on her friend. But these were desperate times. She said in a softer voice, "Thank you for your help. I need to make a few other calls. I'll speak to you tomorrow."

"Sure. Have a good night." Her friend hung up.

Ifeoma puffed out another sigh before ringing her sister's number.

"Hello," Nonye answered. She sounded sniffly and stressed, probably crying again.

"Are you okay?" Ifeoma asked.

"I'm fine." She sniffed again.

"Are the kids okay?"

"Yes, they are in bed."

"And Frank?"

"He's not home yet."

"At this time?" Ifeoma glanced at the clock on her phone. Past midnight.

Nonye said nothing.

Ifeoma waited a beat before saying. "I called to ask you to reconvene the board meeting for tomorrow. I mean this afternoon. I have a solution that will satisfy everyone."

"Really? Including Mr Piedimonte?" Nonye sounded hopeful and warmth filled Ifeoma's chest. She really had to sort this, especially for her sister.

"Yes. I don't want you to lose any sleep over this. Everything will be okay. I promise," she said.

"That is such a relief. Thank you so much," Nonye said, sounding upbeat.

"You're welcome. Have a good night."

"Good night, sis."

Ifeoma sat on her bed after the call ended.

It seemed she now had a hit-list of errant men to bring to their knees and educate.

Her brother, Afam.

Her brother-in-law, Frank.

And the man who would soon be her husband, Nero.

SEVENTEEN

Nero waited in the back seat of the blacked-out SUV parked in the forecourt of the famous brand hotel. It wasn't his hotel. However, it provided a vantage point to watch the visitors in and out of the Zequer Industries HQ, which was on the other side of the freeway running through the business district.

An hour ago, he'd walked out of the building following his devastating input into the shareholder meeting where he'd left a shell-shocked Nzekwe family.

It had been of the utmost interest for him to watch Ifeoma's reaction when he'd delivered the news of her father's involvement in the deaths of his parents.

It seemed she'd been unaware of the extent of their crimes. Then again, perhaps she'd become adept at putting up a façade.

Nero's father had been a visionary entrepreneur, keen to expand the business beyond the regional base. He'd fallen out with his business partner on the best way forward. In the end, they'd killed him and tried to grow the business, but it had never really reached its full potential.

Partly because Nero had blocked any international expansion attempts.

And mostly because the current CEO was running the company into the ground with no one's interference.

Nonye seemed to have a good head on her shoulders, but her brother and mother were hindrances to her success.

This was the reason Nero had penetrated their midst and gained so many shares. There was no proper corporate oversight because Afam hadn't wanted anyone looking into his affairs and his embezzlement of Zequer's finances.

Now the fox was in the henhouse.

Ifeoma had been busy running Hillcrest School to pay any attention to what was going on with their family business.

Thinking about her made him clench his teeth. Pain shot through his jaw.

It was hard watching her from afar, as she got on with her life over the past four months, as if he didn't exist. Somehow, her inner glow had faded and her passion had dimmed. The fun-loving, passionate woman was gone, replaced by an automaton who seemed solely focused on work.

There was a man sniffing around her like a dog, a man she played tennis with regularly at the sports club. But luckily for both of them, they hadn't extended the games into the bedroom. Otherwise, the first order of business when Nero arrived in Nigeria would have been murder.

Because Ifeoma belonged to him, whether she liked it or not.

And soon she would become his wife. She had no other option. He'd ensured it. There was no way for her to raise one hundred million in twenty-four hours.

Afam had lost a good chunk of the money.

Of course, Ifeoma could dip into the school funds. It would be like jumping from the frying pan into the fire. So much worse.

If she tried it, Nero would receive an instant alert. He had spies in her school community and at the bank.

No, she would become his wife. He would reignite her passion and feel her hellfire sear his skin.

Inside the SUV, there was no sound except for the steady thrum of his heartbeat in his ears as he waited. Kane was with him in the front seat with the driver. Lottie had gone home. There was no need for her tonight.

Ifeoma, like the rest of her family, must have figured out there was no other option but marriage to him. Afam had already stormed out of the premises and driven out like a man with the devil on his tail.

Nero lived to witness the moment someone realised their fate. It had become an addiction to him. That split second, when they understood everything had changed, was charged with so much power and retribution, so intoxicating.

His own came when he'd been a boy of eighteen, and it shaped him into the man he was today.

The sky had darkened when Ifeoma exited the building. She stepped out, looking lost in thought. The wind fluttered the hem of her skirt as she walked towards her car. The driver held the door as she slid into the back.

When they pulled away, Kane manoeuvred the SUV and joined the traffic behind them and followed her through the glittering streets of the FCT.

Several kilometres down the road, the Toyota Landcruiser stopped at a supermarket. Kane parked up and followed her discretely inside. When they came out, he reported that she'd bought a bottle of wine.

A small smile played on Nero's lips, but quickly vanished.

Another ten minutes' drive and they arrived at the estate where she lived. The heavens opened and there was a downpour. Heavy drops thrummed on the roof of the SUV. Nero couldn't follow her in the car because the security on the estate was top-notch. They needed an invitation from a resident to get past the heavily armed security.

Kane parked the car on the other side of the road and they watched Ifeoma's car get through the checkpoint into the estate. It stopped outside her house. She didn't have an umbrella when she stepped onto the drenched driveway. The driver brought one to cover her, and she sent him away.

She stood under the rain, tipped her head back so the raindrops splattered her face and clothes.

Nero wondered why she hadn't gone inside. But she stood there for a good minute, twirling in the rain, soaking her hair and clothes. There was no one else on the private street lit by ribbons of light from the streetlamp. Even her driver had gone inside the house with her briefcase.

The light caught her face and Nero glimpsed a smile on her moistened lips.

Something kicked inside his chest at the display of happiness.

Then she laughed, and although he couldn't hear it, he felt it inside his bones, inside his dark soul. He couldn't look away. Mesmerised, he wanted to join her in the rain. To feel her wet lips against his. His fingers curled around the door handle and he fought the urge to leave the car.

But as suddenly as the rain started, it stopped.

Ifeoma ceased twirling and turned toward Nero's car. For a second, his heart thumped hard. Her smile was gone. Could she see him?

Impossible. He sat several hundred metres away in a blacked-out vehicle. She didn't have x-ray vision.

Then she turned, walked into the house, disappearing from sight.

The spell on Nero shattered, and he took in shallow breaths, wondering what just came over him.

· · ⚘ · ·

The next morning, Nonye called Nero, inviting him back to Zequer headquarters for another shareholder's meeting. For most of the day, Nero could barely contain his anticipation. He couldn't remember the last time he was excited about attending any corporate meetings.

Even the thrill of attending the first shareholder meeting yesterday, knowing what he was about to unleash, hadn't been on the same level.

He hadn't received any alerts about large funds being withdrawn from the Hillcrest accounts. So, the Nzekwes still had no way of returning his one hundred million.

However, several searches across different databases for his name were brought to his attention. Someone had scoured online networks searching for information about him over the past few hours.

No one else would have authorised the searches but Ifeoma.

A smile played on his lips.

She was trying to find dirt on him. Something she could leverage.

His woman had fight.

His dick hardened at the thought.

This was exactly how he wanted her. To come at him, swinging.

Still, he remained unaffected. There was nothing she would find that he hadn't put out there to be found. One of the perks of investing in media houses was that he could control the narrative about him in the media.

The question became what she would do with any information she received about him. How would she act?

He couldn't wait to find out.

He left his hotel with the same entourage as yesterday and headed to Zequer headquarters.

"I just got a message from the team I sent ahead. The Zequer building has increased security personnel today," Kane reported while they were on the way. "What do you want to do?"

It seemed the Nzekwes had learned not to let just anyone walk into their building. But he wasn't deterred.

"Stay on course," Nero instructed.

Kane nodded, passing the information along. Afterwards, he said, "We might be unable to take weapons into the building if they have scanners."

"Is it possible they've installed scanners in under twenty-four hours?"

"It's highly improbable. But Ifeoma has military connections through her former in-laws, so it's possible."

The mention of Ifeoma's in-laws made anger boil inside Nero, but he said nothing.

They arrived at the Zequer building, and as reported, new security personnel swarmed the place. Nero had to verify his identity before the car could enter the premises, following a scan for explosive devices.

Kane left his weapons in the car because, surprisingly, there was an airport-style security arch installed in the lobby. It seemed Ifeoma had pulled her military connections, after all. Had she contacted her ex-husband?

Nero's hands balled into fists. He contained his annoyance as he went through the harassment of being searched and scanned before he could walk into the lifts.

But the biggest shock didn't happen until he stepped into the boardroom.

Ifeoma was already there. She sat at the head of the table where her mother had been yesterday.

Beside her were her sister Nonye and a woman he recognised from the dossier provided about Ifeoma's in-laws—Maddox's new wife, Zoe Himba. Behind them was another recent addition, also someone flagged in the dossier, Zoe's enforcer, Xandra.

All members of the local Yadili sisterhood. All people he'd been warned to keep in sight and not provoke.

Ifeoma's mother and brother sat together towards the middle of the table. But from the setup, this was purely Ifeoma's show.

"Welcome, Mr Piedimonte and co. It's good you could join us," Ifeoma greeted in the same snide tone he'd used yesterday to address her.

Adrenaline rushed through him as he stepped up to the table and made a realisation.

He'd stepped into the lioness's den and woken the matriarch. She was roaring.

He couldn't suppress the thrill that went through him. He would welcome the bite.

EIGHTEEN

Ifeoma knew the moment Nero arrived at the Zequer headquarters for the shareholders' follow-up meeting.

Her head of security called her as soon as his SUV pulled up at the security barrier. They'd verified the occupants of the vehicle and had called her to confirm that she wanted them to enter the premises before allowing them through.

She'd spent last night making arrangements for today.

After she spoke to her sister, she'd called her ex-husband's new wife, Zoe Himba. As much as she could never ask the Ejiofors for money to pay back the loan Afam had borrowed, she needed Zoe's expertise as a lawyer.

Since Nero had gone to the effort of corrupting the Nzekwe family lawyer, Ifeoma couldn't trust that he hadn't corrupted her lawyer too. She'd needed to hire someone neutral, someone who could step up at short notice, someone incorruptible by Nero. Zoe was it.

She understood the importance of the Yadili sisterhood, of protecting family.

During the brief conversation last night, she hadn't gone into details. Simply explained the situation in the board-room yesterday and that she needed a lawyer to ensure any new agreements were binding. Zoe had agreed to help. She'd requested a copy of the loan agreement which Nonye emailed her.

Ifeoma had asked Zoe to keep their conversation con-fidential and not discuss it with anyone, including her hus-band, Maddox. Zoe was bound by the attorney-client code of conduct. But even more important, she was bound by Yadili sisterhood laws to not divulge Ifeoma's secrets.

Once the call ended, Ifeoma called her chief of security and instructed him to double the security presence at Ze-quer for the day. She'd also told him to install an airport style security checkpoint in the reception area to ensure no one entered the building with weapons.

This morning, Nonye sent a memo to all the staff, telling them the building will close early, and all staff were told to work from home. Those in the building would depart by noon. The board meeting was scheduled to start at two o'clock, giving the security team time to clear the building.

Ifeoma wasn't sure what stunt Nero would pull during the meeting. But she wasn't about to risk the lives of the Ze-quer employees. Best to be safe than sorry.

At one o'clock, Ifeoma arrived at the premises, pleased to see the increased and tightened protection. When the driver pulled into a spot in the car park, she stayed in the vehicle with the engine running and the AC on.

Zoe was on her way. They had spoken on the phone earlier and she would be here soon.

Five minutes later, Ifeoma's phone rang, and she answered it.

"Three new arrivals in one vehicle," Adiele, her security chief, said on the phone. "Zoe Himba, Xandra and Agatha."

"Let them through," Ifeoma commanded.

"Understood." The man hung up.

Seconds later, a car pulled into the parking space beside Ifeoma's SUV and Zoe stepped out. The grey power suit and stilettos showcased her slender figure and round hips, her hair cascading in waves around her shoulders and back.

For a moment, Ifeoma felt a twinge in her chest. Maddox's new wife was beautiful and always looked great. If Maddox had a type, Zoe was it.

Ifeoma had once had the same silhouette, but motherhood had changed her body. Her breasts weren't so pert, and a scar ran across her stomach from hip to hip.

"Madam, they are here," her driver Okwudili said, snapping her out of her melancholy.

"Let's go," she said. She waited as he came around and opened her door and she climbed out. He took her leather tote.

Zoe turned in her direction as she walked over.

"Ifeoma, hi. How are you?" Zoe said.

"I'm fine. Thank you for doing this at short notice." Ifeoma extended her hand for a shake.

Hugging was out of the question because they were not friends. But there was mutual respect. And they were Yadili sisters. Maybe with time, they would become friends. But they were not there yet. Ifeoma still felt raw about losing Maddox to another woman.

"There's no need to thank me. I owe you for what you did for Maddox when he was abducted." Zoe shook her hand firmly.

"I didn't do it for you," Ifeoma said honestly. Maddox might be her ex, but he was also Abuchi's father. She wouldn't have allowed her son to become fatherless if she could help it.

"I know. But I owe you regardless."

The woman understood Ifeoma's perspective, one reason Ifeoma respected her.

"I get it. Good to see you two here, Xandra and Agatha." She acknowledged the other women.

She had also requested their presence. Xandra's reputation was enough to put fear in any man's heart. Ifeoma needed Nero to be afraid. In fact, terrified. Agatha was Zoe's chief of security. She would come upstairs with them while Ifeoma's chief of security stayed down here to coordinate the rest of the operation.

"You're welcome," Xandra replied, and Agatha nodded.

"Shall we go in?" Ifeoma said.

"Of course. Lead the way." Zoe waved her on.

They entered the building, Zoe a step behind Ifeoma, Agatha and Xandra at the rear.

"Welcome," the big and tall Adiele greeted them. "Please remove any items in your pockets and put your items in the basket with your bags and any electronic devices."

They all went through the motion of putting their items in the plastic containers going along the conveyor belt through the scanner. Then each individual walked under the electronic scanning arch. Xandra and Agatha had weapons, which they picked up at the other end and put in the body holsters.

This was the reason Ifeoma waited for them to arrive, because they would be the only people allowed with weapons in the boardroom.

Afterwards, they boarded the lift to the top floor. When she stepped out of the lift, Ifeoma headed straight to her brother's office. She didn't bother knocking and pushed the door open.

Afam and their mother were already there. She'd requested for them to be here at one-thirty this afternoon for a brief family meeting before the board meeting.

"Ah, Ifeoma. This is my office. Can't you knock?" Afam grumbled as she walked in.

"Good afternoon, Mother," Ifeoma ignored his childish behaviour.

"Afternoon." Her mother eyed her. "I thought you said we were having a family meeting. Who are these people?"

"I'm sure you remember Zoe. She is Maddox's wife," she said as Zoe came into the office to stand beside her.

"Good afternoon," Zoe greeted.

"Good afternoon," her mother replied, frowning. "I don't understand. Is she here to represent the Ejiofors? Are they giving us the money to pay back the loan?"

"No. Zoe is here as the new Zequer lawyer, since the last one was a traitor and quit," Ifeoma said.

"What? You can't appoint a lawyer for Zequer without authorisation," Afam shouted.

"I authorised it," Nonye walked in, joining the women standing in front of Afam and their mother.

"You? You have no right. I'm the CEO." Afam jumped up from the chair behind his desk.

"Yes, that's the other thing." Ifeoma pulled out the envelope from her tote and put it on his desk. "Read it. Sign it."

"What is it?" he tore the envelope and pulled out the sheet of A4 paper with a typed letter. "This says I'm resigning as CEO due to ill health. I'm not signing it."

He tossed it on the desk.

"What? Let me see that." Mother grabbed the paper and read it. "Ifeoma, you did this to your brother? This is wicked."

"Wicked? Wicked is embezzling money from company funds and depriving thousands of people of their jobs and livelihood. Listen, I'm not here to argue about this. Afam has a choice—resign willingly. Otherwise, when we go into the boardroom, the first item on the agenda will be the termination of his contract."

"What?" Afam cried.

"You forget I have double vote. You will never get my vote on this." Mother glared at her.

"Oh, but you forget. You are no longer the majority shareholder. Nero is, and he will soon be my husband. Trust me. He will not vote against me. This is in the bag. So, what will it be? The clock is ticking."

NINETEEN

"Asi! You lie! Nebolisa is not your husband yet," Mother ranted. "And if he is to become your husband, he has to accept that Zequer is Afam's inheritance. Afam has to remain CEO." She tore the paper in her hand into shreds.

"Exactly! I'm not going anywhere," Afam grinned cockily and returned to his armchair.

Ifeoma glanced at her wristwatch. She didn't have time for her brother's delusion or her mother's ingrained misogyny. That they all stood as shareholders didn't seem to mean anything to them. They'll soon learn the hard way.

"With that same logic, Zequer is also Mr Piedimonte's inheritance," Nonye chimed in, saying what was on Ifeoma's mind.

"Mechie onu gi. Shut up!" Mother barked.

"Nonye, is it because you have a job at Zequer that you have a mouth to talk," Afam blustered.

"As if you could run this place without me," Nonye retorted.

Ifeoma smiled. It seemed her sister had regained some of her self-esteem around their mother. Nonye usually wasn't this outspoken at family meetings.

Then again, Ifeoma hadn't invested herself so much in Zequer and their family issues in so many years. Perhaps her stepping up had given her sister the confidence to confront Afam for his failures.

"What did you say?" Afam glared at Nonye.

"I don't have time for your childish bickering today." Ifeoma swivelled towards the door. "I have a board meeting to chair."

"What?" her mother shouted.

But Ifeoma didn't stay to listen to the rest of her rant. She headed down the corridor, followed by Zoe, Nonye, Xandra and Agatha. The offices were empty. Security had cleared the floor out, along with the rest of the building. Management granted the staff the rest of the day off work.

When they entered the boardroom, Ifeoma shut the door and beckoned them to come closer.

"We potentially have two different hostile groups this afternoon," she said in a low voice. "The first group includes Afam and my mother. They are fairly predictable, but I don't want to be caught unawares. Nonye, do you know if Afam keeps any weapons in his office?"

"Yes, there is a gun in his safe," her sister replied.

"Xandra and Agatha, before he enters the boardroom, I want you to search him and disarm him. Mother will not be armed because she believes it's the man's job to protect her," Ifeoma instructed. She was back in enforcer mode.

"Plus, she thinks her tongue is weapon enough," Nonye commented, shaking her head.

Ifeoma couldn't help the wry smile because this was true of her mother. Her tongue had been injuring members of this family for years.

Xandra nodded.

"Where do you want me?" Zoe asked.

"I will be at the head of the table," Ifeoma replied. "Nonye, will sit on my right side, while you will be on the left. After my mother and brother are seated, Xandra will stand behind us to observe those two. Nero and his crew will be searched and disarmed downstairs. When they enter the boardroom, Agatha will stand behind them to monitor them. Treat both groups as hostiles and use non-lethal actions to take them down if necessary. They need to know that I mean business. Understood?"

"Your wish is our command, Agbara nwanyi!" the women chorused, acknowledging her as enforcer and the most senior Yadili in their midst.

Agatha and Xandra went to stand outside the door while the rest went to sit.

Ifeoma settled at the head of the table spot, usually reserved for her mother as chairperson of the board. Nonye sat immediately to her right while Zoe sat on the left.

Her phone rang, and she answered it. Adiele informed her that Nero had arrived with his crew.

"Search them thoroughly before letting them upstairs," she instructed and hung up.

Nero wouldn't be pleased, but she didn't care. She had to take his arrogance down a few pegs. He needed to learn some humility.

She pulled out her tablet device, scanning through the dossier Nkoli sent her this morning about Nero. She'd read through it already, but there was no harm in going through it again. The investigators had done a brilliant job considering the short notice. It wasn't a complete view of the man, yet it gave her several nuggets of information she could leverage.

They'd dug up a birth certificate from the local registry in Turin, where he'd been born. He'd been named Nebolisa Nero Ezeilo to Lucy Piedimonte, his mother, and John Ezeilo, his father. He'd spent his early years in Italy while his father had been a student and then worked for a few years. Later, they relocated to Nigeria, where he lived until his late teens, when everyone assumed he'd died with his parents.

However, Nero Piedimonte resurfaced in Italy but never used the Ezeilo surname again, or even his given name of Nebolisa. He didn't interact with the Nigerian or Yadili community in Italy. His biography said his Piedimonte grandmother and his uncle Lorenzo adopted and raised him. Hence the reason his profile didn't alert the Yadili community until recently. If he had Yadili contacts in Italy, then they kept his secrets until now.

The sound of her brother's arrival at the boardroom door distracted her, and she lifted her head.

"Get out of my way. I have a board meeting to attend," Afam shouted.

"Please wait, sir. We need to search you." Agatha spoke.

"Search me? Mum, are you hearing this?"

"Young ladies, move out of the way. This is Afamefuna Nzekwe, the CEO of Zequer Industries," her mother said.

"Madam, we need to search him. It's our job."

"Then you are sacked immediately. Move—" A body thudded against the wall, making it vibrate. "Ow!"

"Ewo! You people want to kill my son. Ifeoma!" Her mother appeared inside the doorway, screaming. "Ifeoma, you're sitting there calmly while your thugs are manhandling your brother. What kind of wicked person are you, eh? Tell them to leave my son alone."

"Mother, come and sit down. No amount of shouting will stop them from doing their job," she replied.

Meanwhile, she could hear Afam panting loudly outside. Xandra and Agatha must have restrained him and were searching him.

"Hehn!" Mother didn't budge from the doorway. "Were nu nwayọọ! Take it easy. This is a grown man you're manhandling like this. Somebody's husband."

Eventually Afam appeared at the doorway looking dishevelled and righting his clothes. He shook off mother's reaching hands and glared at Ifeoma as he stomped over.

"Ifeoma, you will not get away with this. I swear it." He touched the carpet with his forefinger, tapped it to his tongue and raised it to the sky.

Xandra followed him and blocked him from reaching Ifeoma.

Ifeoma sat upright and looked him straight in the eyes. "Afamefuna, you stood in front of me, Agbara Nwanyi, and invoked the Sky and Mother Earth to bear witness to your threat. I don't blame you. It is our mother who gives you impetus to behave like a spoilt child. And I handle unruly children every day. So, I will treat you like the disruptive child you are. Sit down, shut up and pay attention. The adults in the room have business to handle."

Afam's mouth dropped open. "Mum—"

"I said, sit down!" Ifeoma raised her voice. "The same goes for you, Mother."

"You're in my chair," Mother grumbled.

"Xandra, pull out chairs for them since they seem to be confused about where to sit," Ifeoma instructed.

Xandra pulled out two chairs in the middle section of the table. Mother and Afam glared at her as they settled next to each other. Xandra walked to stand behind Ifeoma. There was a bulge in her jacket pocket. Probably the weapon she'd taken from Afam. Agatha stepped back outside the door.

Ifeoma opened her email and sent out the updated agenda and minutes from the last meeting to all the attendees.

Soon after, footsteps announced new arrivals. Then Nero appeared at the doorway with Ms Bain and Mr Waziri. There were no bodyguards with them this time.

He wore a two-piece navy suit that clung to his defined muscles as he strode in. Her heart rate kicked up and her mouth moistened. Damn, she'd forgotten how effortlessly he oozed power and mystery.

He wore the inscrutable expression, however, the clenched fists gave away his irritation. Ifeoma would bet he didn't have an easy ride at the security screening in the foyer. And she wasn't about to make his life any easier.

She tilted her chin up and spoke in a snooty tone. "Welcome, Mr Piedimonte and co. It's good you could join us."

For a moment, his lips parted, and he held her gaze with steady eyes, his pupils appearing larger as he walked to the chair opposite hers.

Was that adoration in his expression? Nah, it couldn't be.

He pulled out the chair and sat down. When he looked up again, his face was expressionless.

Yes, this was more like it. The enigmatic Nero.

Except he wasn't so mysterious anymore because she had a dossier on him.

"Good of you to invite me back today," Nero said in a slow, hard tone, the voice rumbling like she remembered. She hadn't realised how much she'd missed listening to him talk until yesterday. She shook off the arousal as he continued. "But I see there are some changes and unfamiliar faces. I would like to be introduced."

That wasn't quite the response she'd expected, but it made sense to make him aware of the changes.

"Yes, your presence at yesterday's meeting triggered some changes within the structure of the board of directors. If you check your email, you will see the updated agenda and minutes from the last meeting. For starters, Mrs Okoro will not be taking the minutes this afternoon." She didn't want Mrs Okoro in danger in case things deteriorated at the meeting. Also, there were certain things pertaining to her private life she didn't want Mrs Okoro to know, although the woman had signed a non-disclosure agreement.

"We have set up an electronic voice recorder with automatic voice recognition to record the minutes which will also be transcribed into text and available as a document for you to review afterwards," she continued as the others fiddled with their phones to read the agenda. "Do you have any objections to the electronic voice recorder, Mr Piedimonte?"

"No." he replied.

"Mr Waziri?"

"No."

"Ms Bain?"

"No."

"Good. You have all given consent to be audio recorded," Ifeoma said. "Next, let it be noted that I, Ifeoma Nzekwe, will chair this meeting today. If you have any objections, state your name for the recording."

"I am Mrs Obiageli Nzekwe, major shareholder at Zequer Industries and I object," her mother said.

"I am Afamefuna Nzekwe, CEO and major shareholder of Zequer Industries, and I object too," her brother said.

"Do we have any other objections?" Ifeoma asked, looking around the table. Her gaze landed on Nero, who was scrutinising her, and she swallowed.

No one replied.

"The three-count objections have been noted. But the majority of seven carry the vote and I will chair this meeting. Thank you."

Ifeoma breathed a little easier that she'd sailed through the first challenge of chairing the meeting. It was a litmus test of how Nero and his crew would behave for the rest of the afternoon. Nero, Lottie Bain and Kane Waziri were a voting bloc. Whatever Nero accepted, the rest would accept. When he objected, they would object.

Although she'd sounded confident earlier about Nero voting to oust Afam as CEO, it had been more bravado than reality. Nero was still an unpredictable element.

"Next I would like to introduce you to my attorney, Ms Himba—" she tapped the left side where the lawyer sat "—who I have retained to ensure any agreement reached between us is fair and legal."

"I am Zoe Himba of Himba and Associates. It's good to meet you," Zoe said.

"Same here," Mr Piedimonte replied. "This is also a good time to formally introduce my associates here."

"I am Mrs Lottie Bain, Mr Piedimonte's lawyer. I'm a Zequer Industries shareholder."

"And I'm Kane Waziri, Mr Piedimonte's chief of security. I too am a shareholder."

Mother gasped, staring at Nero and co as if they'd sprouted horns.

The introductions only proved what Ifeoma already knew. Nero had used his associates to gain large shareholdings in Zequer to avoid triggering regulatory and Nzekwe scrutiny.

"Also present are Xandra and Agatha, who are acting purely as security for this occasion and are not shareholders," Ifeoma kept her tone even. "I will let my sister introduce herself."

"I am Nonye Nzekwe, the Director of Marketing and shareholder of Zequer Industries."

"Good. With the introductions out of the way, we can move on to the next item on the agenda. The termination of the contract of employment for the current CEO, Afamefu-na Nzekwe."

TWENTY

"Before we get to vote, I need to understand why this has been raised for the board," Nero spoke after Ifeoma's pronouncement. He had to admit he had underestimated her.

His woman was a lioness, a queen.

It was probably the reason for his past infatuation with her as a teenager. She'd been his best friend's older sister. She'd walked around like a powerful goddess, superior to mere mortals like him. He'd wanted her, yearned for the day he could claim her as his.

Now some of the old feelings returned. He could barely conceal his admiration as his mouth dried out and his nerve endings tingled.

This meeting was a thousand times more organised than the one he'd walked into yesterday. It had been obvious from the moment they arrived at Zequer headquarters how many things had changed from the increase in security. But he hadn't realised how far-reaching.

After Afam's incompetence and Mrs Nzekwe's flailing, Ifeoma had stepped up and taken charge, instigating a bloodless coup to take over as chairperson. And it seemed she wasn't done.

She wanted to oust her brother as CEO. But who would she install as a replacement?

Perhaps her sister was the obvious choice if she wanted to keep it in-house. No one else in the executive team was qualified.

"Very well," Ifeoma said and glanced at the tablet device in front of her. "If you examine Addendum A attached to the meeting agenda, you will see a summary report of fund withdrawals from the Zequer business accounts into the personal accounts of the CEO going back several years—"

"And so?" Afam interrupted rudely. "The accountant is aware. Those are loans taken against future earnings."

"A quick audit revealed these withdrawals were not authorised and there is no evidence of any repayments in recent years," Ifeoma continued as if her brother hadn't spoken and a smile tugged Nero's lips, but he didn't let it bloom. "A quick review of the annual financial reports has shown a steady decline in profits and dividends for Zequer shareholders. Projections for the current year show a potential loss. At best, this indicates irresponsible mismanagement by the current CEO and, at worst, it is gross misconduct and embezzlement of company funds. Either way, as members of the board, we owe it to ourselves to ensure the executive team is capable of running a profitable and sustainable company."

Ifeoma paused as if to let it sink into their minds while Afam's mouth bobbed open like a stunned fish. It was interesting watching Ifeoma take her brother to the cleaners. However, suspicion knotted his stomach. Nero wasn't buying the whole house-clearing gimmick. Was it for his benefit? Why the sudden need for change? The rot had been occurring for several years.

"I'm curious why you feel the sudden need to change the executive leadership now," Nero said in a harsh voice as he narrowed his eyes. "You have sat on this board and each year you allowed your brother to embezzle company funds. The fact that you knew it was happening and allowed it to happen indicates that the Nzekwe family colluded to defraud Zequer Industries and the shareholders. You should all be investigated by the Financial Crimes Commission for embezzlement and conspiracy to defraud the company."

Ifeoma's eyes widened, and Nonye's breath hitched. Afam and their mother sat smugly, knowing they were the major culprits. They would obviously go down and take the others down with them.

Nero smelled blood in the water like a shark and continued. "Oh, were you not expecting me to talk about the elephant in the room? That the Nzekwe family has been defrauding other shareholders for years. Never mind how they defrauded my family twenty-five years ago."

Ifeoma opened her mouth to speak, but Zoe tapped her hand and leaned sideways to whisper something in her ear Nero couldn't hear. Nonye leaned in and the three women huddled and spoke in low voices for a few seconds, while Nonye showed them something on her tablet.

Then they straightened, and the lawyer spoke, "Mr Pied-imonte, you are correct to point out the grievous nature of the financial irregularities in the company accounts. However, we have evidence in the form of a trail of emails which prove my clients Ifeoma Nzekwe and Nonye Nzekwe individually and jointly were unaware of the irregularities in financial transactions until recently, when they discovered the CEO had conspired with the accountant to defraud Zequer. Immediately they found out they organised this board meeting to rectify the problem and raise a vote of no confidence in the CEO Afamefuna Nzekwe and the former board chairperson, Mrs Obiageli Nzekwe."

Damn. Was Ifeoma really willing to sacrifice her mother and brother to save the company, or was that more bluffing? She would soon find out that Nero called every bluff.

"So, are your clients willing to submit all the evidence they have to the financial crimes investigators?" Nero asked, keeping his stern gaze on Ifeoma.

She didn't blink. "Yes, if—"

"No!" Mrs Nzekwe cut in. "That's not necessary. Afam is resigning as the CEO of Zequer with immediate effect."

"Mum?" Afam jerked back, glowering at his mother.

"This is the best option for now." She patted his hand, but he withdrew it.

"How is it the best option that they are conspiring to kick me out of the company my father handed down to me?" he said.

The man was truly infantile. Nero couldn't believe they'd once been friends. If he was honest, he probably only hung out with Afam because he wanted the chance to see Ifeoma at their house. It seemed the man had never fully grown up.

"Would you rather take your chances with the vote of no confidence your sister proposed? The numbers don't look good for you." Surely the man could do the simple arithmetic.

Afam glowered some more, but he gradually deflated as the realisation hit—he was outnumbered. "Fine. I resign as CEO. Let me see who else you think can run this company and make money for it in the current economy."

Ifeoma pulled out a sheet of paper from the stack in an envelope and slid it across the table. "Read it and sign it."

It seemed Ifeoma had come prepared with a resignation letter for her brother.

The fluttering sensation returned to Nero's stomach.

Afam muttered something under his breath as he scribbled on the dotted line before he shoved the letter across the table.

"Let it be noted that the board accepts the resignation letter for the CEO and he is to step down with immediate effect," Ifeoma said.

"So noted," Nero concurred.

"With that out of the way," Ifeoma said. "We can move on to the next item on the agenda—the appointment of an interim CEO while the board searches for a permanent replacement."

Nero could guess who she wanted to appoint as CEO, but he asked anyway, "Who do you have in mind?"

"Actually, I have two people I want to propose to the board."

"Two?" Did she want them to choose between the candidates?

"Yes, I propose to have two interim CEOs and I will explain. The first person is Nonye Nzekwe—"

"What?" Afam grumbled as expected.

"Me?" Nonye's eyes widened and her mouth dropped open as she stared at her sister. It seemed she hadn't been expecting her name to be put forward as a candidate. "Is that why you asked for my resume?"

"Yes," Ifeoma replied with a smile. "And I've attached the resume as Addendum B on the agenda. I believe Nonye has the appropriate qualifications to be the CEO in waiting. During her tenure as Marketing Director, Zequer's profile has been raised both nationally and internationally. However, I think there are areas where her leadership skills need improvement. Therefore, I'm recommending a second interim CEO to work with her as her mentor for a year to prepare her to take on the role full time."

"And who do you have in mind?" Nero asked. Whoever else she was introducing would have to be thoroughly vetted.

"I recommend you, Mr Piedimonte," she said.

Stunned, Nero went perfectly still, his muscles freezing. He must have misheard her because sounds seemed muffled in his ears. "What did you say?"

"I put forward Mr Piedimonte as the second CEO and mentor to Nonye Nzekwe."

"No way—"

"Shut up!"

He'd had enough of Afam's whining already.

Nero glanced up at Ifeoma. It seemed she'd shouted at her brother to shut up, too. Her lips were curled in a smile for the first time since they'd reunited yesterday. Unexpected euphoria buzzed through him. Instantly everything else faded, and they were back in the Brazilian restaurant in Rome and she was carefree and laughing at his jokes.

The urge to reach across and pull her up for an intimate dance pulsed through him. But she was sitting so far away. Suddenly he was back in the boardroom surrounded by other people, reminded he was in a professional setting and Ifeoma had placed herself firmly in the enemy's camp.

He coughed to clear his throat before speaking. "Ms Nzekwe, you were saying something about me mentoring your sister as CEO. Why on earth would I want to do that? I already have another business to run."

"I'm aware of that. This is why I'm recommending you work with her on a part-time basis. Your track record as a CEO speaks for itself, and you are the best person to help guide Nonye in the right direction as a CEO. And before you say it, I'm not the right person to do it. Skills required to run as school are not quite the same required to run Zequer. While I can provide oversight and scrutiny as board chairperson, I do not have the necessary skills to take Zequer through the next phase as a profitable business. Nonye had the qualifications for success. Mr Piedimonte has the talent for making money. The two of you are what Zequer needs."

"What does Nonye think about it?" he asked, a frown marring his features. She made valid points, but this wasn't going exactly as he planned.

"I'm pleasantly surprised and willing to work with you to make Zequer a success," Nonye said with a smile. "What do you say, Mr Piedimonte?"

"I'm still not convinced about what is in it for me. Why should I help your family business?" *When I came to destroy it*, he omitted to add.

Ifeoma's proposal made sense to the entrepreneur in him. He could see the potential to make money. However, decades of anger and plotting vengeance would not go away readily. He might be a shareholder, but his primary aim was to destroy the Nzekwe family. Rebuilding their business was out of the question. Unless...

"Mr Piedimonte, are you not a Zequer Industries shareholder?" Ifeoma replied, eyeing him as if he was a student who had missed the point of the lesson. "If so, then I must re-educate you on the responsibility. By the calculations, you own the largest shares in this company. If I include the shares owned by your associates, Piedimonte and co have equal share ownership in Zequer as the Nzekwe family because it is fifty-fifty split."

Nero stiffened as heat flashed across his cheeks. She was talking to him like he was a recalcitrant child.

"I don't care about that," he retorted.

"Really? You don't care that you spent hundreds of millions buying shares only to watch the share values drop to nothing? Is that how much you hate the Nzekwes that you are willing to lose so much money as long as you take us down?"

"I—" he opened his mouth to tell her to go to hell, but Lottie cut him off with a hand on his arm.

She leaned in and whispered in his ear. "Mind the recording."

He nodded, puffed out a breath, and leaned back.

Ifeoma glared at him before speaking again. "And if you hate the Nzekwe family so much that you're willing to destroy us, are you also willing to see thousands of innocent employees lose their jobs?"

"That is on your brother and your family. Not my doing!"

"Yes, it's not your doing. But you have to opportunity to step in and save thousands of jobs, to become a hero to the people."

He gave a bark of humourless laughter as he sneered. "You really haven't learned anything about me. I am not a hero. Now let's stop this bullshit and get to the reason I came back here today. Where is my hundred million? Your time is up."

Ifeoma glared at him some more and shook her head. "I really hoped you were a reasonable human. But since you won't listen to reason, I have to ask, is this what the great iconic designer and entrepreneur John Ezeilo would have wanted for his son?"

All the bottled-up rage over the last two decades pulsed through Nero and he shoved his chair back as he stood, making it topple over.

"Don't you dare speak my father's name? You have no right." His entire body vibrated as he stomped towards Ifeoma, his vision tunnelled. He couldn't see past his anger at the Nzekwe family whenever any of them spoke his father's name, considering what they did to the man. Everything else that happened earlier today had already caused him annoyance.

Xandra blocked his path, standing in front of him midway down the side of the long table.

"I'm not trying to disrespect your father, who is with his ancestors," Ifeoma continued in a sombre tone. "But are you honouring his legacy with your actions? Will he be proud of you, knowing you could have saved the company he founded, but you didn't?"

"Ifeoma, I'm warning you!" There was pounding in his ears and his throat dried from his rushed breathing.

The urge to retaliate, to inflict pain, to see blood flow pounded inside him. Yet when he looked up at his attacker, all he saw was the face of the woman of his dreams.

Instead, he stood still with pain in his jaw from his clenched teeth.

"Well, if you won't do it for your father. Then will you do it for your daughter? Make Lucia proud," Ifeoma said in a condescending tone, as if she was losing patience with him.

She was playing hardball, determined to rip him open, to cut him, to shred and press all his buttons.

But this was the last straw. Mentioning his daughter was a veiled threat. He wasn't stupid enough to miss it. It seemed Ifeoma really was like the rest of her family, not caring who she used as long as she gained the upper hand.

He swivelled, not looking at her as he returned to his position at the other end of the table.

"For the record," he said in a harsh tone. "Your time for coming up with alternative arrangements for the load is over. I am officially issuing the order to my lawyer to commence repossession of all the assets listed on the loan guarantee schedule. The houses, vehicles, machinery, computers and all other items listed as collateral. I want them recovered and sold at auction to raise the fund to cover the cost of the original loan."

Ifeoma blinked rapidly, as everyone sat silently in obvious shock.

"Mr Piedimonte, the minutes from yesterday's meeting said you offered an alternative repayment method for the loan," Zoe said.

"That option is no longer available. I've withdrawn it," he said.

"What? You said you wanted me as your wife," Ifeoma's voice warbled with emotion.

"I did. But now I don't want you as my wife anymore," he injected venom into his words.

She flinched as if he'd slapped her. Her mouth opened, but no words formed.

He'd hurt her, but he couldn't take the words back. She'd targeted the one person he would do anything to protect. The one innocent person in his life. His daughter. He couldn't let it go unpunished.

TWENTY-ONE

I feoma sat motionless with shock and disbelief at Nero's words. Did he really mean it? Did he not want her anymore? Or was he just lashing out because she had provoked him?

She knew the moment he stood on the precipice. When she'd mentioned his father's name and he'd lost his temper. The only other time she'd seen him lose his temper was at the beach in Italy, when she'd called him a liar.

He was usually so composed and controlled.

And he'd been that way through the meeting, helping her oust her mother and brother from decision-making positions.

Even when she'd suggested making Nonye the CEO, he hadn't objected.

It was when she'd recommended him to work with Nonye he'd pushed back.

At first, she'd thought it was part of their game. He'd won some and lost others.

Then she'd gotten annoyed with him because he'd said he wasn't a hero.

What did he think being Yadili entailed, anyway? It was about putting community before individual interests. The foundation of the organisation rested on those principles. One could never attain elevated status without showing acts of selflessness.

Helping to rebuild Zequer would have been the perfect opportunity for Nero to be recognised and welcomed back into the Yadili fold.

Of course, there would have been something in it for her. She was a titled woman and as such needed to be matched with a titled man. Nero as he stood was at the bottom level even with his millions in the bank. Unless he did something to benefit his community with his millions.

So, she'd become frustrated with his stubborn behaviour and had mentioned his father because it was a trigger for him during the meeting yesterday.

As predicted, he'd reacted and stomped towards her. Yet he hadn't caved in. Running out of options, she'd mentioned his eleven-year-old daughter.

And he'd shut down and recalled the full loan.

In hindsight, it had been a mistake to push him this far. She probably would have reacted the same way if the shoe was on the other foot and he'd mentioned Abuchi.

However, she hadn't expected him to withdraw the offer of marriage. That was a personal attack designed to hurt her alone.

She'd jerked back as pain ripped through her, her throat constricting.

"Mr Piedimonte, yesterday you gave the Nzekwe family twenty-four hours to make a decision," Zoe spoke up. "By my wristwatch, the time is not up yet. You cannot change the terms that were agreed before the duration elapses. Or we will see you in court. Ask you attorney for verification."

Nero frowned and glanced at Lottie Bain, who nodded. He took his time righting his chair, which had fallen over before lowering his body back into it.

Thank goodness for Zoe. Ifeoma exhaled a breath, but the relief was short-lived.

"Hian, Ifeoma. Did you not boast that Nebolisa will soon be your husband?" Her mother laughed derisively, cutting into her thoughts. "Pride comes before a fall. Ihu gọ nu ya. Your first husband rejected you. This one is not even your husband yet, and he's rejected you. Eme i na-eko, na-eko. Let's see how any man will marry you."

Her mother dusted her hands as if distancing herself from Ifeoma. If her mother knew anything, it was how to kick a person when they were down.

Ifeoma's stomach hardened as an old wound reopened. She fought to stay upright. To not bend over and collapse her body posture with the crushing weight of hurt and loss.

Her lungs constricted, making it hard to breathe, making her eyes water. She tipped her head down, pretending to look at her tablet, to hide the overwhelming emotions.

"Chairperson, clear the room. I want to speak with you alone." Nero's voice was like a whip, sharp and cutting.

She blinked, lifting her head to meet his gaze. "What?"

"Clear the room," he ordered.

Her first instinct was to pushback. But she was also aware this could be a reprieve since the clock was ticking. There was no time for pride.

"Everyone, take a convenience break. We will reconvene in—" she turned to Zoe "How long before the deadline?"

"Thirty minutes."

"Good. We will reconvene in fifteen minutes."

Ifeoma and Nero stayed in their seats as activities bustled around them. Wood scuffed the carpet as chairs were pushed back. Conversations and footsteps faded as the others left the boardroom and shut the doors.

Silence descended for a few seconds as they watched each other. Suddenly aware they were the only two people in the space, her heart raced, blood rushing in her ears.

The silence was unnerving, especially after the heated debate and the words of anger. This was her chance to make her case. To convince him that saving Zequer was good for him and for everyone. Success was a form of vengeance, wasn't it?

She swallowed, cleared her throat to speak. "Why did you want everyone out?"

He blinked, breaking the intensity of his stare. "You needed time to compose yourself."

Her mouth dropped open. He'd sent everyone out because of her? To give her time to compose herself. He'd seen her distress and yet hadn't capitalised on it in front of the others like her mother had done.

"Why?" she asked, confused by his actions. He was the one who started all this. He threatened her family and then withdrew the offer of marriage.

"It doesn't matter now." He shook his head and pushed back his chair, ready to stand.

"Nero, wait, please," she blurted out. She couldn't let him leave. Everyone else was depending on her to reach an agreement with him. She couldn't let them down.

No time like the present. She stood and walked towards him.

She would do whatever it took to win him back to her side even if it meant begging, something she'd never done to any other man, not even her ex-husband.

. . ⁂ . .

Nero sat immobilised as he watched Ifeoma approach him. Today she was in a V-neck, knee-length multi-print wraparound dress with ties around the side. She'd worn it with a grey blazer which now hung over the chair she'd been sitting on.

Walking away from a woman had never been difficult for him. And it shouldn't be with Ifeoma. Yet a heavy weight had crushed his chest when he'd told her he was no longer interested in marrying her.

She leaned her hips against the table beside him and caught his wrist in her soft hand.

His flesh burned at the contact, sparks shooting down his arm. It annoyed him.

This unwavering attraction he held for her had to be because it had been months since he fucked any woman. Months since he fucked her. She was the last woman he'd touched intimately.

She'd run away after their night together, blocked him from contacting her. Yet here he was, burning from her simple touch.

"Don't." The one word was filled with the emotions she roused. A growl rumbled from his chest as he pulled his hand away from her.

Instead of cowering like every other person around him when he was angry, she notched her chin up. "You are a hero."

"I'm not," he countered, looking away.

"But you saved my face. You didn't want others to see my distress."

"That doesn't make me a hero."

"In my book it does, especially when I know you're angry at me." She placed her hand on his chest against his erratic heartbeat.

"Fuck!" he swore aloud, unable to control his reaction to her touch.

For a second, he imagined a life without the rage and vengeance he'd carried for decades. A life full of freedom and endless possibilities with her by his side.

Yet, it was a life based on the dreams of a teenage boy. A life with no coherence to reality.

Even when she looked at him with those eyes full of hope.

Yet the hope was for him to free her family. Not because she wanted him..

He pushed off the chair and backed away, needing space to think clearly. "Ifeoma, what do you want from me?"

"I want..." she started walking toward him. "I want to say I'm sorry."

Okay, this was a surprise.

"I'm sorry for mentioning your daughter in our negotiations. I shouldn't have."

His anger resurrected, and he snatched her hand, tugged her close until she collided with his chest.

"You're only saying that because you think I will offer you marriage again if you apologise," he said in a low, growling tone in her ear. "But we both know you don't want to get married. And I will not have a sacrificial lamb in my marital bed."

He released her.

Her eyes flashed with fire as she scowled.

"You don't know what I want," her voice crackled with violence and she poked his chest with the heel of her palm. "I am no sacrificial lamb."

His teeth clenched as his dick hardened. The combination of everything nearly driving him insane—her attitude, her proximity, her scent. "Is that not what you're doing? Sacrificing yourself to save your family?"

"I'm not sacrificing myself. You're not man enough to survive marriage to me." A spark ignited in her frosty eyes.

An answering flame sparked inside him, searing through his principles and any integrity he had left. He turned into her, slamming her against the wall. Then his hand was on her nape, gripping it, tilting her head up as he claimed her mouth, crushing her lips with his, his tongue invading her sweet, warm depth. Damn, it felt good to taste her again, even if it was rough.

He wanted her shaken and scared, to run from him like she'd done before.

She didn't fight back, didn't push him away. Only made a rasping sound in her throat and gripped his neck with her palms.

"Is this man enough for you?" he asked, lifting his head as she panted, her eyes heavy-lidded.

Ifeoma liked it rough, loved the sensual power he wielded over her. Even though she had no submissive bone in her body. Even when she fought back in every other situation. But when she was in his arms, she revelled in his firm embrace. In the feel of him.

But he shouldn't be doing this. This was a trap. He released her nape.

She didn't let go of him.

"Show me how much of a man you are," she said in a husky voice.

Yes, it was definitely a trap. She was a lifetime of temptation.

"Ifeoma—"

"Show me!"

He scooped her into his arms, swivelled, and carried her to the table, sitting her on the edge. Nudging her knees apart, he hiked up her dress and settled in the warmth radiating between her thighs. He gripped her nape again, tilted her head to expose her neck and went to town with his teeth on her delicate throat.

She moaned aloud, arching her body against his, leaning on her arms. He trailed his bites, tormented her as he de-

scend to the deep dip of her cleavage. Her smell was intoxicating. She writhed, rubbing against him.

Electricity bit into his skin and he slipped his fingers
up her thigh and under the lace fabric of her undies. Met
slick warm flesh, and he slid into her channel, gathered her
juices and trailed it around her clit. He brushed the bundle
of nerves and she bucked in his arm. He did it again and
again, pressing, teasing, circling before entering her slit with
curved fingers and brushing her sweet spot.

"Oh," she cried again and again, arching, writing, panting for breath. He took her to the edge but withdrew before
she could fly.

He loved seeing her like this. Could barely control his
throbbing erection. Could barely stop himself from sinking
into her. But she'd been insolent, gone too far, threatened his
daughter. She needed to be punished. He needed it before
they could start afresh.

"Nero, I need..." she trailed off.

"I know what you need," he replied, pushing her bra
aside to suck on her nipple, making her keen.

"Tell me you won't block my number again," he ordered.

"What?" she sounded confused as she blinked her eyes
open.

He tugged her clit hard and demanded again. "Tell me
you won't block my number again."

"I won't. I won't." She panted.

"Tell me you won't run away again."

"I won't run away. Nero, come on." She growled at him
with that fierce expression.

He smiled as he leaned up, his hand still grazing her clit.

"Tell me you will marry me."

Her lashes fluttered open, and she stared at him incredulously. "Are you proposing?"

"I am. What is your answer?"

He pumped fingers inside her as he pressed down on her clit.

She tilted her head back and yelled, "Yes!" as her body shuddered and shuddered with her orgasm.

He held her in his arms, staring into her blinking bewildered eyes as she slumped against him.

TWENTY-TWO

Ifeoma didn't want to come down from the warm glow of the euphoric climax or detach herself from Nero's hardness. It had been so long since she was in his embrace. Since he was inside her. She would give anything to feel his hardness inside her, to chase the pleasure and completion together.

However, a tapping sound on the door brought a cold splash of reality and she stiffened.

"Give us a minute!" Nero called out.

Heat rushed at Ifeoma's face that there were people waiting outside who'd heard her in the throes of climax. Mortified, she shoved at Nero's chest. "What did we do?"

"We did what lovers do?" He didn't release her, tidying up her dress instead.

"And they probably heard us. My family is out there." She pushed off the table, standing on wobbly legs. She'd forgotten his orgasms left her limbs feeling like cooked noodles.

"I'm your fiancé and I'm right here." He cupped her cheeks with both palms and kissed her lips lightly.

"You are." A smile bloomed on her face. She was engaged. Surprisingly, the prospect of wedding Nero didn't trouble her. They would talk later when they had time to discuss in depth. But for now, they were engaged and hopefully, it meant Zequer wasn't lost.

"Ifem, there's nothing to be ashamed about what we did. You are my fiancée, and I find you very desirable." He brushed his hand over her hair, tidying the loose strands.

His words filled her chest with joyful warmth. The stress of the past day melted away. It was wonderful to have him looking at her with the softened gaze and talking to her with such respect.

He glanced at his wristwatch. "We've got a few minutes. Use the ladies to freshen up."

"Good idea." She rushed over and grabbed her tote and blazer.

He waited at the door, opened and held it for her. She stepped into the hallway and no one was in the immediate vicinity. Agatha and Xandra stood near the entrance to the staff kitchen at the end of the hall as she walked past to the ladies. They must have ensured the corridor was clear of any eavesdroppers.

Ifeoma was more than grateful for the Yadili sisterhood because they'd stepped up and watched her back today. She would never forget it.

In the ladies, she used the WC, washed her hands afterwards and tidied her appearance. Thankfully, her dress wasn't too creased or stained. But she wore the blazer over it in case there was any stain. She brushed her hair and re-pinned it with the grip away from her face.

As she walked back to the boardroom, Agatha and Xandra were standing at the doors.

"Everyone is back inside," Xandra said and opened the door.

"Thank you," Ifeoma said as she entered the room.

There was a low hum of conversations in the different huddles—Nero in his seat at the other end, with Lottie and Kane. Mother and Afam were in the middle section, while Nonye and Zoe were in the former seats. They quietened as Ifeoma took her seat. Xandra and Agatha came inside and closed the doors, returning to their positions on opposite ends of the room.

Nonye and Zoe leaned into Ifeoma and Nonye asked, "Are you okay?"

"Yes, I'm okay." Ifeoma looked at her and nodded. "Restart the recording."

Nonye pressed the button for the automated voice recorder.

"Ladies and gentlemen, welcome back. I would like to draw your attention back to the last item we were discussing before we went on a break," Ifeoma said.

"Chairperson, pardon my interruption," Nero said, looking up and meeting her gaze. "I would like to make a brief statement about the issue of the interim CEO."

"Yes, go ahead."

"You made some valid points earlier. My father, John Ezeilo, was proud of his contributions to Zequer Industries. He designed products to enhance people's lives. I would like to do what I can to celebrate his legacy. With that in mind, I would like to accept the nomination for the position of interim CEO. I'm happy for my name to be put forward to a vote by this board."

There were cheers and smiles around the table, except for Mother and Afam.

For Ifeoma, this was an unexpected win, considering the fight Nero had put up earlier.

"Thank you, Mr Piedimonte," she said, smiling at him. "With that in mind, I would like to put this to a vote. All those in favour of Nero Piedimonte working alongside Nonye Nzekwe as the interim CEO for the next year, please say, aye."

Everyone voted them through except the usual suspects—Afam and Mother.

Ifeoma didn't care. "Now, we move onto the issue of the loan repayment. Unfortunately, due to the financial irregularities instigated by the outgoing CEO, we are unable to return the loan within the twenty-four-hour period as stipulated. However, during the break, I came to an agreement with Mr Piedimonte. At this point, I would like to invite him to clarify his position on this matter for the board."

"Thank you. Yes, Ifeoma and I have come to a satisfactory arrangement. During the break I proposed to her, and she accepted to be my wife."

There were more smiles and cheers and congratulations.

"Wait. Does it mean the loan is forgiven?" Afam asked.

"It means the loan is back on its original repayment cycle. As the new CEOs, Nonye and I will ensure the money is invested in Zequer Industries and not spent frivolously," Nero said.

"But Afam lost a sizeable chunk of that money," Ifeoma said.

"How are we going to recover it?" Nonye asked.

"I will ensure the amount lost is recovered," Nero said, meeting Ifeoma's gaze.

She nodded. He was being extremely generous, and it was simply because she'd accepted his proposal.

Did he have feelings for her? Perhaps Nkoli was right when she'd said he must have had an infatuation for her as a teenager. Perhaps he carried the same feelings.

This had to be the reason he'd initiated the bonding ritual in Rome.

Then again, there was the vendetta he held against her family. Would he let it all go once they were wedded?

She'd managed to convince him to help rebuild Zequer, but it didn't mean he would let go of his vendetta.

Maybe as his wife, she would become the new focus of his hatred.

Her heart lurched in her chest and nausea rose in her throat.

She really couldn't marry another man who would walk away from her.

She cleared her throat.

"Is there any other item for discussion before I close this meeting?" she asked, getting her mind back to business.

"Nothing from me," Nero said,

Everyone else shook their head.

"In that case, we will reconvene in three months to review progress with Zequer's new executive team," Ifeoma said.

"Sounds good," Nonye said, and Nero nodded.

"Afam will clear his office immediately within the next hour and hand in his passes. He is not allowed into this building until the next board meeting."

"Ifeoma, you are stupid if you think you can kick me out." Afam jumped up.

"I'm the one kicking you out because you're in my office," Nero said in a harsh voice as he straightened to his full height. "And don't ever call my fiancée nasty names again. You won't like what I will do if you do. That goes for you too, Mrs Nzekwe."

Afam's mouth opened and closed at Nero's threat, and Mother glowered.

"Thank you, everyone. Here ends the meeting," Ifeoma concluded.

Afam and Mother got up and stormed out together.

"Xandra, please make sure my brother leaves the building within the hour," Ifeoma said.

"Understood." Xandra walked out to follow her instructions.

Nero came over. "I have a few phone calls to make. Is there an office I can use?"

"Yes, sure. I'll show you," Nonye said.

"Thanks. Ifem, are you hanging around for a bit?" He stepped up to Ifeoma, beaming a smile.

Ifeoma stood, too. "No. I'm heading back to Hillcrest shortly."

"Okay, I'll speak to you later?" he asked.

She nodded, and he pulled her into his embrace and pressed a kiss to her forehead.

"Later. Drive safe."

"Thank you."

He stepped back and followed Nonye out.

She missed his warmth and hardness immediately. Emotions clogged her throat.

She was at risk of falling for Nero and he would break her heart for sure.

TWENTY-THREE

The next day, the ringing phone woke Ifeoma. The sky was grey outside the drawn curtains of her bedroom and birds were chirping in the trees in her garden. She set the air conditioner to stop before dawn, so she would wake from the rising temperature and listen to the songbirds.

She leaned across the bed and grabbed it from the night-stand. The caller ID showed 'Nero'.

She sat upright, her heart rate picking up a notch. She'd unblocked his number yesterday after the board meeting. He'd gone to make some calls, and she'd chatted briefly with Zoe and Nonye about the outcome of the meeting. Soon afterwards, she'd left to head back to Hillcrest to grab any paperwork needing her attention. She'd worked late, gone home and had been in bed when Nero called to wish her good night.

Now he was calling again. She would bet he wanted to be the first to wish her good morning. Just like he'd done in Rome.

A smile crept on her face as she answered the call. "Good morning."

"Ifem, you beat me to it. Good morning," he sounded amused.

Her smile bloomed. "I didn't know we were in competition for saying good morning."

He chuckled. "We're not. Only teasing you. Did you sleep well?"

"Actually, I did. It's great to not worry about Zequer anymore, knowing it's in good hands."

"You think my hands are good?" His voice deepened. He wasn't referring to his business skills.

A warm shiver went down her spine at his innuendo. She remembered what he did with his hands to her body yesterday.

"You have amazing hands," she sounded breathless.

"Ifem, you're killing me. I can't wait to put my hands on you." He coughed. "When can I see you?"

She swallowed. "I'm at the sports club to play tennis this morning. But I'm free this afternoon."

Well, she still had Hillcrest work to catch up on, but she wanted to see him. They needed to talk.

"Oh good. I have a video call with Lucia this morning. Then maybe we can meet for lunch."

She remembered Lucia was his daughter. One of the people they needed to discuss. She needed to understand his relationship with his daughter's mother.

"Oh, I eat lunch at the sports club after tennis. Do you mind meeting me there? It's members only, but I will send you a code you can use for entry."

"Not a problem. I will meet you there around noon."

"Okay. I'll send you the address."

"Great. I look forward to it, Ifem."

"See you later."

"Bye." He hung up.

She padded out of bed and across the bedroom into the ensuite bathroom with a sizzle in her bones. She was excited and looking forward to seeing Nero again. This time purely for pleasure and not business. If their whirlwind affair in Rome was anything to go by, then it would be a thrilling day.

She carried out her daily routine. Brushed her teeth, dressed in a robe, she went downstairs to eat breakfast prepared by her housekeeper. Then she returned upstairs, showered, dressed in her tennis gear—sports undies, t-shirt, skort and tennis shoes. Then she packed her sports bag with her change of clothes for after tennis.

Playing tennis was a Saturday routine and also her opportunity to socialise outside work. She started playing more regularly when her son became an older teenager and her weekends became free.

She drove herself to the leisure centre and parked in the car park. Her chauffeur had the weekends off because he deserved a break like everyone else. He had a young family and needed to spend time with them before they grew up and left home. He worked long hours when he was with her, arriving early to wash the car and then staying with her all day until she returned home at night every day of the week. So, he earned his days off. Also, she believed all her employees should have a work-life balance. Even the domestic staff.

"Ify!" someone called out as she grabbed her bag and shut the car door.

She swivelled and saw her tennis partner walking towards her with a grin on his face.

"Mike, good morning," she greeted and headed towards the entrance.

"Morning. How are you?" he asked, walking beside her with his gym bag strapped on his shoulder.

"I'm good. You?"

"I'm good too. You remember my niece's wedding is coming up in two weeks. I can't wait to spend the entire weekend with you in Opal City." He winked at her as he swiped his membership card at the electronic barrier.

Her heart kicked in her chest. "What? Whose wedding?"

"My niece, remember? You promised to go with me as my plus one." He grinned as he walked through the turnstile.

Shit. "Yes, I remember." She muttered and tapped her card on the reader.

"I'm going to change. I'll see you at the court." He walked off.

Shit. Shit. Adrenaline shot through her with heart palpitations as she walked through the barrier.

She'd forgotten the wedding she'd agreed to attend with Mike months ago. It had been after the news of Maddox's remarriage and in one reckless moment when Mike had asked her to accompany him on the trip to Opal City, she'd agreed.

It had been before she'd gone to Italy and met Nero. Before Nero began a bonding ritual with her and she accepted a marriage proposal from him.

Could she attend a wedding as Mike's plus one?

Her relationship with Mike was platonic. Mike was a widower who'd lost his wife to cancer. He was older than her with kids slightly older than Abuchi. He was good company, and they got on well together. They met once a week and played tennis together. Afterwards, they hung out with friends at the club and ate lunch. Then they would go back to their separate homes until the next Saturday.

So, attending the wedding with him was harmless. However, she needed to inform him of the change in her relationship status. She was now engaged.

She collected the locker key and towels from the receptionist, walked to the changing room and put her bag in a storage and locked it. Taking her reusable water bottle, she headed for the gym. She liked to warm up on the treadmill before playing tennis.

Afterwards, she took her racket and walked over to the outdoor tennis court. They'd pre-booked the court for their doubles' match. Mike was already there, chatting to their opponents, Mr and Mrs Aminu.

They all exchanged greetings as they prepared to get on court. She really needed to talk to Mike, but she couldn't do it here just before the game. She would wait until they finished.

"I hope I'm not too late for the game."

Ifeoma recognised the deep, rumbling voice instantly and swivelled.

Nero strode towards her dressed in tennis gear, t-shirt, shorts and shoes and carrying a tennis racket.

"Nero, what are you doing here?" she exclaimed.

"I came to play tennis with you." He stepped up to her, lowered his head, and kissed her on the lips.

She was too stunned to react, but he moved back after the brief kiss. "I thought you had a call with your daughter."

"That didn't go too well. But we'll talk about it later. Will you introduce me to your friends?" He placed his hand on the small of her back and swivelled them to face the rest.

Mike's eyes narrowed, and the couple stared at them curiously.

"Nero, this is Mike Nnamede, my tennis partner, and the couple are Mr and Mrs Aminu. We all play tennis every Saturday. Guys, this is Nero, my fiancé," she introduced.

"You are engaged?" Mrs Aminu beamed a smile at her, stepping forward to hug her.

"Congratulations," her husband shook Nero's hand.

"Thank you," Nero said.

Mike didn't shake his hand, though. "Ifeoma, you're engaged, and you hid it from me."

"I was going to tell you after the game," she replied.

"Enjoy your tennis game with your new partner." He grabbed his racket and stormed off.

"I hope you know how to play, because Ifeoma doesn't like losing." Mr Aminu winked and went to the other side with his wife.

Nero stepped up to Ifeoma and said in a low voice. "I'm a very possessive lover and also very competitive."

He kissed her on the lips and she couldn't help chuckling. "You don't say."

TWENTY-FOUR

After showering and dressing in fresh clothes, Ifeoma left the changing and walked to the restaurant. She felt exhilarated. The tennis game had been intense and fun.

She hadn't expected Nero to show up for it. But like he'd said, he was intensely competitive, and they'd beaten the Aminus. She hadn't even known Nero could play tennis until today. But he seemed to be the perfect match and was as driven as her to win the game. The Aminus were also competitive and good-natured. They had been graceful in defeat and looked forward to the rematch next week.

It was a shame that Mike stormed out. It seemed he was expecting more from her. More than she could have ever given him. He'd always been a platonic friend. Nothing more. She was glad he'd found out about her engagement and she didn't have to sit through lunch trying to explain why she couldn't attend his niece's wedding.

She spotted Nero sitting at a table at the back when she entered the restaurant. Her heart rate kicked up a notch. He'd changed from his sports gear into a black shirt and navy trousers. The wet, dark curls on his head flopped on his forehead. This was the most obvious sign of his mixed heritage because his skin was darker than hers.

The man was full of surprises and charm when he wanted to be. To be honest, since their encounter in Rome, she'd thought about him daily, although she'd refused to acknowledge it.

Now he was in Nigeria and her heart cheered each time she saw him because he was always laser focused on her. She loved the attention he gave. It had been too long since she felt the butterflies fluttering in her belly.

The restaurant was atmospheric, and there were flickering candles in little decorative pots on the tables. Mr and Mrs Aminu sat at a different table and she waved at them as she went past. She usually ate lunch with them and Mike on Saturdays. But it seemed they were giving her and Nero space today.

Nero rose from his seat and waited as she approached. He waved at the waiter and put his thumb up. The background music changed to 'All My Life' by K-Ci and JoJo. Was that Nero's doing? Was it for her?

"Ifem," he greeted and opened his arms, beaming a smile.

With a giddy grin on her face, she stepped into his embrace, feeling the warmth of his arms around her. She couldn't help it. She loved the attention he paid to her. "You know Nigerians are not about public displays, right?"

He leaned back with a twinkle in his eyes. "It's a good thing I'm Italian then."

She giggled, shaking her head as she turned toward the table.

There was a bouquet of tied red roses standing in a black and gold box alongside a bottle of champagne in an ice bucket.

"What's all these?" she waved at the items on the table as her chest drummed.

"For you. We got engaged, remember?" He came around to hold the chair for her to sit on, and she lowered her body into it.

"It's for me?" Her heart raced. She couldn't remember the last time anyone bought her flowers. It must have been twenty years ago.

He went around and settled into the chair opposite hers. "I didn't get to give them to you yesterday when I proposed. But better late than never."

"Indeed." Warmth radiated through her chest and adrenaline flushed through her. She reached for his hand across the table and squeezed it. "Thank you."

"You're welcome, but I'm not done yet." He turned to reach into the blazer hanging over the back of the chair and pulled out a small box.

"No way." She squealed and leaned back, palms to the sides of her face.

"Yes way." He opened the black box and the gold ring with a huge orange sapphire surrounded by a cluster of diamonds glimmered in the velvet lining.

"That is one huge rock," she commented, too flabbergasted to fully comprehend what he was doing.

"You are worth more to me. Your hand, please." He reached with his left hand, holding the ring in the right.

She lowered her left hand and could barely contain her elation as he slipped the ring onto her fourth finger. Clapping erupted around them. She glanced around as people shouted 'Congratulations!' at them. They said their 'thank you' and it quietened down.

She lifted her hand and the dazzling ring caught the light. "It's beautiful."

"Not as beautiful as you." He held her gaze, making her forget that yesterday they'd been arguing about the company their fathers founded and he'd threatened to destroy her family.

A waiter arrived and offered to open the bottle of champagne. She nodded, and he popped the cap before pouring the light gold liquid into the crystal flutes.

The interlude gave her time to think.

Nero seemed genuine with all the fuss he'd made with his proposal, and she enjoyed his company. Yet, a niggle of doubt about his true purpose lingered. What about his plan for vengeance on her family? Was all forgiven?

When the waiter left, Nero raised his glass, and she picked hers and raised it.

"To us and a grand future together," he said and tipped a drop over the side of the table onto the floor. It was an offering to Mother Earth, seeking her blessing for their union. Sure, they were in the restaurant and the floor had stone tiles. Still, it was symbolic and powerful and the best indicator of how serious he was about their union. He would not do this otherwise.

Some of her doubts receded, and she raised her glass and said, "Ise!"

He smiled as he took a sip and so did she, letting the effervescent liquid bubble on her tongue.

"What is—" she started to ask, but the waiter arrived to take their orders.

She ordered the seafood Asaro served with steamed spinach. Nero ordered the Fish Nsala served with steamed plantain.

A frisson of surprise went through her because he ordered a local meal when he could have chosen a European option like pasta. She waited for the waiter to walk away before asking, "You eat Nsala?"

"Of course I eat Nsala. It used to be my father's favourite dish. I remember being in the kitchen while my paternal grandmother taught my mother how to cook it," he said in a flat monotone voice. His eyes developed a distant, empty stare telegraphing his sorrow.

The people he mentioned had been important to him. Yet, none of them were alive today. She remembered his grandmother had died years before his parents died. The Nzekwe family attended the funeral.

The trauma he endured fuelled his need for revenge, driving him to lash out at the Nzekwe family. It was evident in his eyes, and it resonated deep within her bones.

An ache bloomed in her throat. She wished she could alleviate the emotional pain he felt at all the people he'd lost.

Reaching across the table, she took his hands in hers again. She softened her voice, allowing her emotions to seep through. "I haven't said this to you before and I should. You lost your family in a short period and I can only imagine how traumatic it was for you witnessing it so young. Ndo, biko dibee. Ka obi kaa gi." *Sorry, please be consoled. May your heart be strengthened.*

He tipped his head forward, nodding before lifting it to meet her gaze as he blinked several times. His eyes were bright and glassy, and she squeezed his hands in sympathy.

Wait. He might not have grasped her words of consolation. "Oh, I'm sorry. I'm not sure if you understood all the Igbo phrases."

"Ifem, aghọta m." A small smile played on his lips. "It means a lot to hear you acknowledge my loss. Daalụ. But today is about celebrating our future together. It should be a joyous occasion. So enough of the melancholy."

He lifted his champagne flute and took a sip, prompting her to do the same.

"Talking about our future," she kept her voice low and leaned towards him. "In Rome, you mentioned Yadili, but you don't attend the meetings in Italy. You know I can't marry you if you're not a full-fledged adult member."

"I know. I plan to retake the oath."

"Oh. Good. But who will you pledge under?"

"No one. I'm going to become the godfather."

"What? You can't attain that level in status without exceeding the criteria for acts of service to the community."

"I reckon saving Zequer Industries and all the jobs should get me on the way there. I looked at the figures and

Zequer can't afford to pay two CEO salaries. So, my work there will be unpaid. I would rather invest the money in product design and development and upgrading our production processes."

"That is definitely an act of service to the community. But what about your team? You only have two that I can identify so far. It's nowhere near the size of other godfathers."

"Ifem, hasn't anyone ever told you? It's not the size that matters, it's what you do with it."

He winked, and she giggled, shaking her head.

The waiter returned with their meals and left and they settled to eating. He ate with as much gusto as he'd eaten the Italian meals in Rome.

"Back to the topic of the future. If we get married—" she started.

"Not if, when we get married," he interrupted.

"You're very confident," she said, giggling.

"Ifem, I proposed, you accepted and our ancestors bore witness. Of course, I'm confident."

"Which brings me back to the question I was going to ask. You live in Italy, I live here. How are we going to stay married with a long-distance relationship? Out of sight is out of mind."

"First of all," he put his cutlery down. "Absence makes the heart grow fonder. Secondly, I'm pretty much in Nigeria for the next year because of Zequer. The work I do for Piedimonte I can do from anywhere in the world as long as I have a phone, a laptop and internet connection. Thirdly and most importantly—" he crooked his forefinger for her to come closer as he leaned forward. The corners of his lips curled up and his breath whispered on her face when he spoke. "I will follow you to the end of the earth."

The promise made her breath hitch and emotions clogged her throat. No one had ever said that to her. Not even her former husband.

His warm mouth descended on her, and his palm cupped her nape. She placed her hand on his arm, anchoring herself to him.

Just like that, he reawakened her desire for him. He was a lighter to her fuel and their combination was combustible. They were in a busy restaurant, but she didn't care. Only craved him, his heat, this madness he evoked. Because this turbulence she felt in his presence that shook her to the core and turned her into a purely passionate woman had to be madness.

He tugged her bottom lip and grazed his thumb on her skin as he pulled back. "I want you."

"Then let's go." They hadn't made love since Rome four months ago. Yesterday's session in the boardroom had been an interlude, an appetiser. She wanted the full main course. All of him.

"But you haven't finished your lunch."

"Lunch is overrated."

He frowned. "I don't want to rush you."

"Nero, I need you. Please." She couldn't believe she was begging, but she was overwhelmed by the urge to reconnect with him at a deeper level.

There were anecdotes about the bonding ritual creating urges within the partners to have sex. She had no lived experience because she and Maddox hadn't been bonded in that manner.

"Okay. Let me settle the bill," he said, his eyes sparkling with heat.

TWENTY-FIVE

"So now we've agreed we're staying together. Where are we going to live?" Nero said as he waited for the waiter to bring the bill. "Should we house-hunt for a new home? Somewhere big enough for your son and my daughter to have their rooms with extra guest rooms."

His question brought an extra dimension to their upcoming marriage. They had children who would become stepchildren. The thought of having a stepdaughter excited her. However, the idea of moving house didn't. She loved her home. Was he one of those men who liked to put his stamp on everything? This could prove to be a sticking point for them.

"I don't want to move house. I live in a six-bed house with a guest annex already. There's room for our kids and guests. We don't need to move," she said.

He frowned. "Your ex bought that house. We can buy a new one, bigger and better, and make our home in it."

Her eyebrows rose because he knew this level of detail about her. Then again, he knew so much about her already when they met in Rome.

Still, his stance annoyed her. "Nero, let me be clear. I'm not moving house. My house holds so many memories of me and my son. I'm not ready to let go of them."

The waiter brought the bill, interrupting them. Nero pulled his card and inserted it into the POS machine and entered his pin code. Afterwards, the waiter gave him the receipt and Nero thanked him.

He rubbed his knuckles on his forehead. "Ifeoma, do you want us to live together or not?"

"Of course I do," she replied flippantly.

"And your current house is where you want us to live?"

"Yes. As I said, it's big enough to accommodate all of us."

"Then, so be it. Let's go home." He stood and lifted his gym bag, then he reached for hers. "You can carry the flowers."

She lifted the bouquet in the box and followed him out of the restaurant, a little concerned he'd accepted her demand about living in her house.

As they stepped outside the tropical sun high in the sky, she asked, "Are you really okay with moving into my house?"

He halted, making her stop. "Ifeoma, in case you haven't figured it out, I came from Italy to Nigeria to be with you. I don't care where we live as long as we live in it together."

"Okay," she said in a breathy voice, lost for words at his declaration. He came to Nigeria because of her. To be with her.

He reached out, lifted her hand, and kissed her fingertips.

Her stomach clenched. All it took was a touch and a look from him and she was melting like butter on a hot pan.

She couldn't wait to get him alone. All the pent-up energy, all the emotion and passion of the past two days since she saw him again were driving her insane.

A shiny black SUV pulled up in front of them and two men climbed out, cutting into her lust haze.

"Ifem, these are my personal bodyguards, Lucas and Max." Nero handed over the bag.

"Good afternoon, ma," they greeted with a nod and put the bag in the boot of the SUV.

"Afternoon," she replied, and handed over the flowers. They put it on the front seat and strapped the box in with the seat belt.

"Give Max your car keys. He'll drive your car," Nero said, taking her free hand.

"I can drive." She frowned.

"I know. But you're coming with me." He guided her towards the back seat of the SUV.

"Okay." She handed her key bunch to the bodyguard. "Wait. Let me show you where my car is."

"I know where it is, Ma," he said and walked off.

She frowned as she climbed into the SUV. Nero slid in beside her and shut the door as Lucas started the ignition.

"How does Max know my car or where I'm parked?" she asked as the car started moving.

"I reassigned him to your security yesterday after we got engaged. He's been following you ever since. So, he knows your car and where you live." He put his hand on her thigh.

"What?" She frowned. "You've had men following me?"

"Guarding you."

"I have my own personal guard."

"You have a driver who moonlights as a guard five days a week. He goes home every night."

"My estate is well guarded. I don't need him at night." Her voice rose.

"You came to the sports club today by yourself."

"Well, apparently not because you had someone following me all along." She glared at him.

"Ifeoma, think about it. You had to borrow your ex-husband's new wife's security crew just to have a show of strength yesterday. I know you have Adiele, but you only use him on a contract basis because he looks after the estate security."

She opened her mouth, closed it and opened it again. "That's because I don't need full-time security. I've never needed it in the past."

"Only because your ex-husband was watching your back," he replied in a sharp tone. "It's not his job anymore. It's mine. You have me now."

"But—"

"Ifeoma, I let you choose where we're going to live. You must let me choose how to protect you. Relationships are about give and take. You will not win every argument."

She rolled her eyes heavenward. "I know that. But I still don't understand why I need security twenty-four-seven."

"You're with me now and I'm an influential man. It also means I have powerful enemies."

"In Italy, maybe."

"The people who killed my parents are in this country and still out there."

The statement sobered her. "You think they want to kill you?"

"They tried once. They would try again and could use you to get to me. I don't want you to get hurt," his voice deepened and sounded concerned.

The thought of people being after him and trying to hurt him rattled her.

Honestly, she'd always taken her security for granted. Never had to face a threat to her life, or a loved one's. However, Maddox's recent abduction and near-death experience had been a wake-up call. She didn't want anything like that to happen to Nero.

"Okay. Increase the security until we figure out who killed your parents," she said.

"Good. That's settled. We'll stop at my hotel so I can pack my things before we head to yours," he said, reaching for her hand and holding it.

"What? You're moving in today?"

"Yes. I don't see the point in waiting."

"But you could move your things tomorrow." She wanted them to get to bed as quickly as possible. She was looking forward to some bed-quaking sex.

"I don't want us to make love in my hotel room. Maybe I still haven't gotten over your response from the last time we did it in a hotel room. I have a fear I will wake up and find you've snuck out in the middle of the night." He chuckled.

"Then let's go to my house. I won't be sneaking out." She teased.

"I agree. Since I'm going there as your partner, I might as well take my things, so I don't have to go back to get my luggage," he said.

"Makes sense." She smiled.

"Don't worry. I promise to make love to you thoroughly tonight." He smirked.

"You better. For making me wait so long." She warned.

But he didn't keep her long when they reached the hotel, which wasn't far from the sports club. She stayed in the running SUV with Lucas while he went into the lobby with Max, who had pulled up in the car park beside them. Ten minutes later, Nero climbed back into the back seat of the SUV with her. His luggage was now in the boot of her car.

"Let's go home," he said, leaning across and kissing her on the lips, his tongue sweeping in. This was the intense man she'd met in Rome. The one who'd given her adventure and passion for a day. The one who'd claimed her body and was halfway to claiming her heart.

Excitement pulsed through her as she responded, brushing her palm over the hair on his chin. He was coming home with her. Her home would become his, at least in this country.

They would have multiple homes, commuting between Italy and Nigeria. It didn't seem so daunting at this moment when he held her in his arms. When he kissed her with the promise of what was to come.

"Nero Piedimonte," she said his name reverently.

"Yes, that's me," he replied, grinning as he leaned back.

"I missed you," she whispered honestly before she could think better of it.

"Ifem, I missed you more. Don't run from me again." He cupped her cheek and stared into her eyes, his full of heat.

The drive to the estate didn't seem to take long. They arrived mid-afternoon. At the security checkpoint, they lowered the windows so the guards could check and confirm their identities.

"This is my fiancé, Nero Piedimonte. He and the driver, Lucas, will be staying in my house. Behind us in my car is Max, who will also be staying at my house," she said.

All new residents and guests to the estate had to be checked in so the security team would know their identities.

The guards scanned the cars and let them in. Lucas drove down the quiet street and pulled into her driveway. Max pulled in with her car and parked beside Nero's SUV. They really knew her residence. She hadn't needed to give directions.

Her stomach became unsettled as Nero stepped out of the vehicle and came around to open her door.

Did Nero like the place so far? Although she'd fought him to keep the place and he'd agreed, she wanted him to fall in love with the place like she had when she'd first moved in.

The estate showcased incredible maintenance, with functioning streetlamps and manicured public spaces. Mature trees, hedges and flowering plants beautified the area.

There was the children's play area and basketball court as well.

"What do you think about the estate?" she asked after she stepped out.

"It looks good so far." He smiled. "Shall we go inside?"

"Of course." The housekeeper wasn't working this afternoon, so she had to open the door herself. She unlocked it and walked in, turning on the air-conditioning units as the bodyguards brought in the luggage.

"Do you have room for Lucas and Max to stay?" Nero asked.

"Yes. The annex has two bedrooms. My live-in housekeeper stays in one. They can have the other," she replied.

Her usually quiet house was now filled with a bustling energy as the men carried in the luggage and closed the front door.

"This way." She walked up the stairs and Nero followed her.

The bodyguards brought the baggage, and she showed them where to put them in the master bedroom, a space she had never shared with anyone. For one crazy moment, she panicked. What was she doing? Was she seriously considering living with a man again? Perhaps Nero should stay in a different room. Many married couples had separate bedrooms.

"What's on your mind?" Nero asked when the men returned downstairs. He must have seen a frown on her face, because he stared at her with intensity.

She shook her head and walked into her bedroom. "It's nothing. There is a his-and-hers closet and an ensuite bathroom in here."

"Ifem, you know I will punish you when you lie to me. Lies are not a good way to start a marriage. Something was bothering you. Tell me." He got into her personal space, clasping her neck.

"Fine. I just panicked, okay? I haven't lived with anyone else in twenty years except my son and domestic staff. I don't know how I will cope with having you in my house, in my bedroom. In my life. What happens if I get fed up? What if you get annoyed and leave?"

"We'll work through it. Remember, I will have to commute between two countries for a while. So, there will be periods when you will get some breathing space if you need it. But I will always come back to you. I won't give up on you. So don't give up on us."

His words were the reassurance she needed to quell the panic, and she smiled. "Thank you."

"No need." He waved her off. "I should say you have a beautiful house. I love the potted plants and marble floors. I especially love this bedroom with the four-poster king-size bed."

"Of course you do," she laughed.

He stood tall, hands in the pockets of his navy trousers, exuding control and power. An enigma, all his own. He was younger, handsome, virile.

And he wanted her. Was this even real? Sometimes she wanted to pinch herself.

Did women her age get a second chance to fall in love? Yet she would swear she was getting a do-over at love with a man who seemed to have eyes only for her.

As if he'd been waiting so long for her, he leaned in and kissed her, tongue sweeping through her open mouth. He grabbed her nape to position her where he wanted her. There was a ferociousness to their exchange as he plundered her depths.

Her body tingled with remembrance and awakening. She craved him. His kiss, his touch, all of him.

"Ifem, I want you naked," he purred with urgency.

Her hands tugged at the ties and he pulled the dress apart, letting it drop around her ankles. She stood in her black lace bra and matching high-waist knickers. It covered her scar, and she didn't feel so self-conscious. It had been four months since he saw her naked and called her beautiful.

His eyes darkened as his gaze scanned her body. He grabbed a cushion from the ottoman and tossed it on the floor. Then he placed his hands on her shoulders and pushed her onto her knees. Her heartbeat became erratic, anticipation flooding her body with adrenaline. She knew what he wanted, wanted the same. It had been so long since she did this.

She wanted to give him pleasure. Just like he'd given her several times without asking for any in return. He was her lover and could be gentle. Yet he was also fierce, and she loved every aspect of him.

He lowered his body, kneeling on the carpet in front of her. He grabbed her thighs, shoving them apart. His fingers grazed her crotch over her lace knickers.

She gasped, rocking her hips involuntarily, seeking more pressure. He withdrew his hand, and she groaned.

"Ifem, we're starting a new life together. Yet you lied to me earlier. We can't have lies between us in our marriage. So, you will be punished. You understand?" He straightened and looked impossibly tall from this angle.

"And what happens if you lie to me?" she asked, eyeing him as her heart raced.

"I promise to never lie to you or cheat on you henceforth. But if, for whatever reason, I break my promise, then punish me."

"Fair enough. And what is my punishment this time?"

She closed her eyes and held her breath. She'd played these games with her ex, so she knew what to expect. The sound of movement made her lashes flutter open.

He walked around her, surveying her body as if trying to figure out how to punish her. "There will be no climaxing for you until I give you permission."

He took his jacket off and threw it on the ottoman. He undid buttons and cufflinks of his shirt and tugged the shirt out of the trousers. With his eyes locked onto hers, he unzipped his trousers and pulled out the dark, throbbing erection.

Damn, he was so fucking hot as he stroked it. His gaze locked on hers. He stroked himself and her core clenched, juices soaking her panties.

Kicking off his shoes, he dropped his trousers, giving her a full view of his thick, veiny, engorged dick. Precum gathered at the tip and dripped onto the carpet.

He was magnificent and her mouth watered with the urge to taste him.

"Rachaa amụ m."

It took her a couple of seconds to comprehend the command because she wasn't expecting him to speak in Igbo.

He grabbed her head, tugging it back so their gazes met.

"Do you need me to translate?" He smirked.

"No." Her cheeks heated because she was more fluent in the language.

She opened her mouth, leaned in, and flicked her tongue around the bulbous tip. He tasted of musk and man. Her insides melted.

"Open your mouth wider." His dark eyes held hers as he fed her his hard length and she took him deep into her throat.

His gaze softened, and he hissed in approval, gently massaging her scalp. "Ifem, that's it. Take all of me."

He pushed deeper, making her gag as she struggled to take his length and breadth.

"Ifem, you're doing so well." He rocked his hips slowly, and she closed her eyes. As he showered her with words of encouragement, her confidence soared, and she relaxed in his company as they settled into a smooth rhythm.

"Stand up."

She glanced up and the wildness she witnessed in his eyes turned her inside out. This man was showing himself. He was coming undone, losing control.

He reached for her, helping her up and unhooking her bra at the same time. Then he was on his knees, tugging her knickers off. She was too far gone to consider what he thought about her scar or wobbly belly.

He leaned in, parted her labia, and swiped his tongue around her clit. She moaned, and he pulled away.

"Don't stop," she griped, unable to control her response to him. This was torture.

"No orgasm, remember?"

"Grrr." She growled.

He chuckled. "Get on the bed on your hands and knees."

She hesitated, sulking.

"The longer you take to obey me, the longer it takes for you to get your climax."

"It better be worth it," she grumbled and climbed onto the bed on all fours, spreading her thighs so he got a full view of her pussy and ass.

He groaned aloud, and his gaze burned into her back. "This is the most erotic sight ever. You are my living, breathing, wet dream."

"Wow," she muttered, her body trembling. Goosebump covered her skin as he caressed her thighs and ass cheeks. She pushed her face into the mattress and tried to control her breathing. Needing to be fucked, she moved her knees apart.

He obliged the invitation, tugged her to the edge of the bed so he stood directly behind her and his dick rubbed her bum. Her body throbbed, her craving increasing, her blood whooshing in her ears.

He leaned forward and squeezed her breast with one hand while the other swept the hair off one shoulder. He alternated between sucking and nipping her neck and shoulder while tugging her nipple and kneading her breast. The weight of his body forced her towards the mattress.

He was in control of her body, making her pant and drip wetness, her body galloping towards climax, yet he wasn't inside her.

He moved from her back, and she missed his weight. But then his breath whispered on her bum, where he placed a tender kiss. His tongue brushed over her slick entrance and she shivered. Damn. It felt good. She wriggled, but he held her in place with large hands and did it again.

She moaned into the mattress. "Nero."

"Ifem." His voice was husky.

She turned her head to look back at him. His dick was rock hard and leaking.

"I need you. Please." She couldn't take for much longer without having his solidity inside her.

He licked her one more time before straightening. Then his cockhead was at her slit and he was slamming in, just as his thumb penetrated her puckered hole.

Her grip on the bedsheet tightened as she cried out, her eyes rolling back.

Her knees buckled, making him slip out, leaving her breathless.

She panted as he yanked her up and slid back in. He got harder and faster, going deeper with each slam, claiming her like no one had ever claimed before. Burying her head on the mattress, she moaned with each pump of his hips. She struggled to hear, to talk, she could only feel. Feel his hardness, his rhythm, their oneness. The wildness. The way he loved her.

Emotions reached a part of her she'd kept locked away for so long. It sent her over the edge. Nothing could stop her from crying out with the world-rocking orgasm which ripped through her body.

As she clenched around him, he seemed to lose control and started snapping his hips as he fucked her hard, holding her up tightly. The sounds of their skin slapping together echoed around the room.

"Fuck!" he murmured, slamming in deep and holding.

His dick jerked and twitched inside her as he filled her with his release. He thrust slowly until he emptied himself deep inside of her.

She was exhausted, sated, slick with perspiration and their mixed juices.

He settled his weight on her, turning her head to face him.

"Ifeomalicham." *My beautiful thing*, he started in a guttural voice. "You don't know how much I've missed you."

His lips claimed hers and the last of her reservations vanished.

"Di m ọma, I missed you too," she whimpered into his mouth.

"It's so exhilarating to hear it from you, considering I waited more than half my life for you," he whispered.

Her throat clogged and her eyes filled with tears. "I'm glad you came for me."

TWENTY-SIX

Monday morning, Nero woke Ifeoma with his face buried between her thighs, lighting her body with a dawn orgasm before seeking completion inside her. Afterwards, while Nero went to the bathroom, she stretched languorously, reluctant to get out of bed and prepare for work for the first time since she could remember.

She'd never wanted to stay in bed and do nothing but just curled up with her lover. By now, she should have dressed and started making her way to the school. Instead, she emailed her PA and the deputy headteacher, informing them she would be in later. They understood she had ongoing family issues because of the problems at Zequer. Her deputy was competent and could handle situations in her absence.

Nero had been nothing but considerate and passionate all weekend.

After their first lovemaking session in this house, he'd pulled out of her achy body. As she'd winced at the loss of his body heat and weight, he'd scooped her up and carried her into the bathroom. He'd sat her on the WC as he'd run the bath. She'd sat there speechless as he'd repeated the routine he'd attempted for their first time in Rome. He'd filled the warm running water with bath crystals. Once it was ready, he'd carried her into the enormous tub, lowering their bodies into the soothing water.

She'd done nothing but cling to him tightly, her emotions raw. This kind of attention she'd thought she'd lost forever at the end of her previous marriage. Never thought she would meet someone who would care for her this intimately again.

He sat with her back against his chest and he took his time, rubbing her skin with the soft sponge and massaging any tense muscles. They didn't speak. Words were unnecessary. His non-sexual actions spoke volumes. They were loving, caring, everything she thought she would never have again. In his arms, she felt welcomed and sheltered.

The feeling carried through the rest of the weekend.

She'd woken Sunday morning to breakfast in bed. Nero had made frittata with red peppers, cherry tomatoes, and cheese from her fridge. Served it on a tray with a cup of coffee.

They'd pottered around, making plans for the wedding. They applied online for a special marriage license, which allowed them to get married after seven days' notice. Nero didn't want to wait too long. Surprisingly, neither did she. The holiday season was a few weeks away. They would have the civil ceremony at the FCT registry at the earliest date available. Then they would travel to Umudike for the Igbankwu and wedding party for their family and friends during the festival week at the end of the calendar year. They would spend the rest of the festivities in his hometown, which wasn't far from hers.

This meant they needed to talk to their children. Ifeoma had called Abuchi on Sunday evening. He was in Lori Osa with his father for the weekend. Her son was happy for her and looked forward to meeting Nero. Maddox, however, sounded sceptical about her getting married so soon after meeting a man. She'd wanted to remind him he'd married Zoe within months of meeting her. Still, she didn't bother. She was no longer his concern.

She'd been more concerned about Nero who'd tried to contact his daughter Lucia several times but couldn't get through. He'd said Lucia had a phone, but it seemed switched off. Lucia attended an international boarding school but sometimes came home during the weekends, outside school breaks. He'd called his baby mama, Alina, but the woman's number was out of reach.

Pacing the living room, he'd made a few other phone calls and later found out Alina travelled with Lucia to Qatar. He assumed they must be mid-flight. That was why he couldn't reach them. Alina sometimes travelled to Dubai, so he wasn't surprised about her travelling to Doha.

Still, he'd been annoyed because Alina had taken his daughter out of Turin without informing him beforehand. He'd explained his tumultuous relationship with his baby mama. He'd agreed to share accommodation with Alina because she'd threatened to do a late abortion if he hadn't agreed for her to move in with him. Alina had attempted to extort him over the years using their daughter. Now, he counted down the days until Lucia's thirteenth birthday, when he could finally evict Alina from his home.

Despite feeling irked to the core, she had accepted his reasons for sharing his Turin home with another woman. He was protecting his vulnerable daughter. She, as his wife, would have to bear his sacrifice with him. Bear his pain with him. The life of a child depended on it. Although she hadn't met Lucia, she felt an affinity to the girl through Nero.

A ringing phone jarred her from her thoughts and she glanced at the bedside cabinet where two phones sat side-by-side. Nero's and hers.

"Nero, honey," she called out, sitting up. "Your phone is ringing."

"Ifem, answer it for me," he replied. It sounded like he was in the shower as the sprinkling stopped briefly.

She hesitated because she was unused to answering other people's phones. Even her son didn't let her pick his device. This showed the level of trust Nero held for her and his own self-assurance. He opened all aspects of his life to her. And had exceeded all her expectation. What more could she ask of him?

She grabbed the phone and swiped to answer. Before she could say anything, there was a barrage of Italian words coming at her from what sounded like a hysterical woman on the other end.

"Slow down. I can't understand a word you're saying," she said in between the Italian rambling coming at her.

"Who is this?" the woman asked with an attitude in heavily accented English.

Ifeoma's hackles rose. She had zero tolerance for a bad attitude. "I should ask you?"

"I want to talk to Nero. I'm Alina, his girlfriend," the woman said in a snotty tone.

And I'm his wife, Ifeoma wanted to retort, but she bit her tongue. Nero had been trying to contact the woman for a few days. She didn't want the woman to hang up in anger and prevent Nero from finding out about Lucia.

However, she didn't want to listen to the woman's nasally whining. She got off the bed, her silk negligee sliding against the cotton sheet, and walked across the bedroom rug before opening the bathroom door.

Nero was getting out of the shower cubicle in his naked glory, his body glistening with the water drops. Yet all she felt was annoyance instead of the usual arousal.

She shoved the phone at his chest. "Your girlfriend is on the phone."

He frowned, taking the phone. "My girlfriend?"

"Alina." She turned and walked back into the bedroom.

Behind her, he broke into a string of Italian sentences. He didn't shut the bathroom door.

She sat on the bed and listened. She understood a word or two. But his tone sounded angry. He wasn't happy with whatever Alina was telling him. There was silence for a few seconds before he walked into the bedroom, a black towel around his hips.

He wore the inscrutable expression. It was his battle face. The mask he wore when he had a new challenge to conquer.

"What happened?" she asked.

"I need to go to the airport to pick Alina," he said, walking into the closet.

"She's here? Why?" She followed him and stood at the door while he chose his clothes from his half of the built-in wardrobe and drawers.

"Yes, she's here and I don't know why? You witnessed me trying to contact her yesterday. I didn't know where she was and now she's in Nigeria. She must have caught a flight from Doha."

"What the hell!" Ifeoma swore and returned to sit on the bed.

This would put their whole getting to know each other plan on hold, with his baby mama in the picture. Never mind her wedding plan.

Nero was supposed to be doing a 'soft' introduction to the Zequer senior management team today. This was another plan out of the window.

Nero walked into the bedroom, tucking his shirt into his trousers. He approached her, tilting his head as he studied her face. Then he cupped her bare shoulders.

"Ifem, Alina is not my girlfriend. She never was," he said, as if he just remembered what she'd said when she'd handed him the phone. "We had a one-night stand. She got pregnant. I accepted my responsibility as a father. She's nothing to me more than my daughter's mother. That's it."

"I know. I only referred to her as your girlfriend because that's how she introduced herself on the phone. I didn't believe her, anyway." She buttoned his shirt.

He let out a breath, closing his eyes before kissing her briefly. "Thank you. I'll pick her up and take her to the hotel I stayed in. I don't think I'll be able to get to Zequer until early afternoon. I need to make sure Lucia is okay."

"That's understandable. I'll call Nonye and let her know the situation. But if Lucia is with Alina, I'm not comfortable with them staying at a hotel. You can pick them and bring them here."

"Here? You want Alina in your house?"

"First of all. It's our house now. Our home. Secondly, your guests are my guests. Finally, I like to keep my enemies closer."

"I don't know. Alina can be aggravating and manipulative. She's like an invasive parasite. I don't want her coming between us."

"If you're spending more time with her out there rather than in here with me, she would be getting between us."

He sighed. "Okay. I'll bring them here."

"I'll speak to Florence, the housekeeper, to prepare Lucia's room and another one for her mother. I will work from home today to make sure Lucia settles well."

"Ifem, thank you again. Hopefully, they'll only be here a few days, so Lucia can return to school." He hugged her and pressed a kiss to her forehead. "Got to run. I'll be back as soon as possible."

· · ⚓ · ·

Two hours later, Ifeoma was dressed and downstairs, working on the laptop at the dining table. She'd made several phone calls, been in two video conferences already.

Nero had called about an hour ago to say he'd picked Alina and Lucia from the airport, and they were on their way back. They would be here any minute.

The housekeeping team had cleaned and prepared the rooms. Now they were cooking the meal for their guests. Ifeoma had instructed for the to keep it simple and prepare Italian dishes so Lucia could eat the meal.

The car horn beeped outside. She glanced out of the window as Nero's black SUV pulled into the driveway.

"Florence, please open the door. They are here."

Ifeoma scraped a hand over her hair and patted down her clothes in agitation. She would meet Nero's daughter for the first time. She hoped to make a good impression on the young girl. Lucia was precious to Nero and, therefore, important to Ifeoma. She would care for the child like her own.

"Yes, Ma," the housekeeper walked across the foyer towards the front door.

Then Ifeoma heard the lock click and the hinges squeak. Footsteps and conversations entered the house.

"In here."

She straightened from the chair and turned towards the entrance when she heard Nero's voice ushering the others in. He appeared at the door, holding a young girl's hand. She had straight dark hair and olive skin, a shade darker than the woman standing behind them.

"Hi, honey, welcome back." Ifeoma stepped forward as Nero kissed her on both cheeks.

"Thank you. This is my daughter. Lucia say hello to Aunty Ify," he introduced.

"Good afternoon, Aunty Ify," the girl said with confident English.

"Good afternoon, Lucia. It's nice to meet you." Ifeoma hugged her.

"And this is Alina." Nero indicated the girl's mother.

"Welcome," Ifeoma said.

"Thank you." Alina eyed her balefully as she walked into the living room. Then she broke into a string of Italian sentences.

"Alina, don't be rude," Nero warned. "You're a guest here. The people in this house speak English. You should too."

"Sorry." Alina shrugged and looked around the place with her nose wrinkled. "I was just saying that I hope the bathroom is clean. It's been a long flight and I need to freshen up."

Did this woman just imply her house was a dump? Ifeoma fought to control her temper and glanced at Nero.

He looked apologetic, his lips downturned. "Florence, please show our guests to the bedrooms. Lucia, I'll be up in a moment to see you."

He kissed her on the forehead.

"Okay, Papà." Lucia followed her mother and the housekeeper up the stairs.

"Did that woman just ask if my bathroom was clean? I want to strangle her." Ifeoma asked in a harsh whisper as soon as the others were out of earshot.

"Ifem, I'm sorry. I told you she wasn't an easy person to live with." He pulled her into a tight hug. "I'm going to send her back to Italy as soon as possible. I'm concerned about Lucia who is missing school. But from my conversation with

Alina in the car, she is insisting she will stay for as long as I'm in Nigeria."

"She wants to stay here for the next year." She leaned back, searching his face.

"That's what she says. But knowing her, I'll be surprised if she lasts a month here."

"Yeah. Not if she carries on like that."

Ifeoma wasn't looking forward to having Alina in her house for more than a few days. However, it was Lucia that was on her mind.

"I have a solution for Lucia if you're concerned about her schooling. She can enrol at Hillcrest at least for the year while you're here. There is no reason she should go back to Italy since you're here. Especially when her mother is so erratic."

"You think she'll fit in?" His forehead furrowed.

"Hillcrest is an international school. We have students from across the world. Children of expatriates and those sent here from abroad by their parents who want them to school in Nigeria. She can be a day boarder and commute from here to school daily if you prefer that option."

"Yes, it's given me food for thought. I will consider it. Let me go see Lucia," he said and headed upstairs.

Ifeoma's heart squeezed tight. It was obvious to see Nero's love for his daughter and his quest to be there for her. She would do whatever she could to keep father and daughter together. Regardless of the baby mama drama.

TWENTY-SEVEN

At the sound of the bell announcing the end of the school day, Ifeoma left her office and walked along the corridor as students left the classrooms and headed outside.

Many of them would end up in the boarding houses on the school grounds because, as full-time boarders, they lived there during the school term. However, half of the student population were classed as flexi-boarders, students who came to school from their homes outside the school premises daily, but could also board for up to ten days annually. They could arrive to school at seven in the morning and stay until eight at night, using the facilities, including the boarding houses. Their meals were provided here, too.

"Bye, Ms Nzekwe," the students greeted as they went past her.

She smiled and bid them goodbye by name, proud that she could identify each student by their face, especially the older teens who'd been in the school since age ten.

She knew the star students, and the academically challenged, the athletes and the creatively minded. Her job was to provide a safe environment where all of them could flourish. And she loved doing it. Loved seeing them transition from awkward pre-pubescent kids to confident teenagers ready to face the challenges of new adulthood.

Ifeoma stood by a window on the top floor and glanced down at the car park below. Cars came around the one-way system, picked up students and headed towards the exit. She spotted the car that was supposed to pick Lucia. It was parked in a parking spot. But there was no Lucia. She was probably at the boarding house where she could stay until 8pm tonight.

So much had happened in the past month since Nero and Ifeoma got together. For one thing, they got married in secret. On her birthday, they'd both gone to the registry office in the middle of the workday, dressed in their work clothes. Kane, Lottie and Nonye were there as witnesses and swore to keep the secret until Nero and Ifeoma announced it publicly. They'd said their vows, signed the papers and kissed before returning to their jobs. It was her favourite birthday to date.

Since then, making love with Nero had taken on a different meaning, as they were no longer just cohabiting but a married couple. They made their decisions jointly, and one of the major decisions they'd made was about keeping Lucia at Hillcrest School if she adjusted well.

The first day Lucia started school, Ifeoma had wanted to take her to the school in her vehicle. Lucia had complained because she didn't want to arrive at school on the first day in the principal's car. So, her father had dropped her off. However, since the school was in a different part of the city from Zequer headquarters, it meant Nero had been late at the office. The same thing happened after school. Lucia didn't want to travel back to the house in Ifeoma's car. So, Nero sent his driver to pick her up and take her home.

However, the arrangement wasn't sustainable. Nero bought a third car and assigned a driver and security to take Lucia to and from school. Alina was supposed to accompany her daughter, but she was never out of bed to ensure Lucia got to school on time. So, the responsibility fell on Nero and Ifeoma.

Ifeoma walked into one of the Year 7 tutor rooms. The woman was tidying up, putting away books into the allocated cubicles. "There you are, Mrs Adewale."

"Ms Nzekwe, good afternoon." The teacher straightened. She was the year group leader.

"Afternoon. Anything I should know about Lucia Piedimonte. How has she settled in?" Ifeoma asked. She was interested both as the principal of the school but also as a guardian and potential parent of the child. It was important to do all she could to support Lucia with adjusting to school since she started two weeks ago.

"Lucia has settled in quite well?"

This surprised Ifeoma, considering the girl had displayed some challenging behaviours for the past fortnight—isolating herself, mood swings and tantrums.

"Really?" she asked.

"Yes. The first week was a little touch-and-go. But we buddied her with Bianca, who seems to have a wonderful influence on her. There's been a significant improvement this week. She seems to have made friends with Bianca and some of the other students. She is participating in classes and her attitude is improving."

"That's good to know," Ifeoma said. She was concerned about Lucia's ability or not to settle in Hillcrest and had thought perhaps she needed to return to her old school in Italy. "I would be glad if you could send me the updated report for me to discuss with her father."

"Yes, I will send it to you this evening."

"Thank you."

Ifeoma left the room and walked back to the administrative block which held her office. Sitting in a chair at the reception area were Lucia and Bianca, giggling and fiddling with their phones.

"Lucia, is everything okay?" Ifeoma said as she approached them. "The driver is waiting to take you home."

The girls stopped giggling and stood.

"Good afternoon. We're fine, Ms Nzekwe," Bianca said, smiling.

"Good afternoon, Ms," Lucia said, her smile tentative. "Is it okay for Bianca to come over to the house?"

"Oh." Ifeoma glanced from one girl to the other. "When?"

"This weekend," Lucia said expectantly.

Ifeoma's first response was negative. She was already feeling claustrophobic with a full house. More people than she'd ever had staying in her house for the first time in decades—Nero, Lucia and Alina, Florence and the security team. Did she really want to add an extra pre-teen girl when one of them was proving a handful?

Ifeoma was stressed already, running a school and planning a wedding. Nero was overworked, juggling two high-powered jobs. She'd been hoping they would get downtime this weekend and time for themselves. A game of tennis, lunch and, who knew, some lovemaking.

Alina was erratic, going out partying and coming home drunk almost daily and neglecting her child. It was no wonder Lucia was having mood swings.

Ifeoma and Nero made time for her every day. Ifeoma helped with her homework. The three of them shared dinner when Nero came home from work. He liked to be home before Lucia went to bed.

"Lucia, did you ask your mother?" she asked.

Lucia's face fell, and Ifeoma felt her chest squeeze tight. "Yes, and she said no. I was hoping you would let Bianca visit, since it's your house."

Ifeoma's jaw tightened. Alina hadn't bothered to ask her. Still, she didn't want to be one of the people disappointing the girl. So, she said. "We have to get permission from Bianca's parents first."

"I messaged my mother, and she said you should call her," Bianca said. She was a full-time boarder and only went home during the holidays.

"She messaged you?" Ifeoma asked.

Bianca nodded.

"Okay. I'll call her. If she says yes, then Bianca can spend the weekend with us," Ifeoma said.

"Yes!" the girls cheered, celebrating already.

Warmth filled Ifeoma's chest, seeing Lucia look so happy. She headed back to her office to call Bianca's parent. Guess there would be no downtime for her this weekend.

. . ⚓ . .

Ifeoma spent the weekend chaperoning two early-adolescent girls.

After getting verbal agreement from Bianca's mother on the phone, Ifeoma had called Nero to inform him about Lucia's request to have her friend visit over the weekend. They'd discussed the pros and cons and had agreed it would be best for Lucia to form deep friendships quick to help her settle. Then she'd called Florence to let her prepare for another house guest. Thankfully, the housekeeper agreed to work the weekend too.

She left the office, shared the good news with the girls, and they rushed back to Bianca's dormitory to pack her things for the visit.

For the first time since Lucia started at Hillcrest School, she went home in Ifeoma's car that night rather than in the designated vehicle. Ifeoma had insisted she had to travel with Bianca because she was Bianca's guardian for the weekend. Lucia hadn't minded, supposedly because her friend was in the car.

However, when they arrived home, Alina showed little interest in Lucia's friend. As usual, she went out that evening, supposedly meeting friends. Ifeoma had to clear the house of alcohol after Alina's first week because she'd spent all day drinking and getting belligerent. Of course, since there were no drinks in the house, she had to go to bars to get some.

On Saturday, Alina was still in bed when the girls woke up and ate the breakfast Florence made. Then, Ifeoma and Nero took them to the sports club where they swam in the swimming pool, then sat by the poolside. Later, they showered, dressed and ate lunch before going to the cinema.

It was wonderful having Nero with her. They spent the time like a date and it gave them a view of their future as a family. During the outing, Nero revealed his intention to apply for sole custody of Lucia. Ifeoma agreed with him. They would provide a stable home environment for his daughter without Alina's toxic influence. Perhaps one day Lucia would feel at home enough to call her mother. For now, she would provide a loving home and safety for her.

Exhaustion caught up with Ifeoma and Nero by the end of the day. After the girls went to sleep, Ifeoma showered and crawled into bed.

Sunday morning, Nero woke her with a vibrating bullet on her clit and her first orgasm of the day before sliding inside her from behind. She bit the pillows to stop from waking everybody else with her moans of multiple ecstasy. He cleaned her up, and she fell back asleep.

By the time she woke again, showered and dressed, Nero was downstairs with the girls, eating brunch. It seemed everyone else had a late start, too.

They pottered around before Ifeoma and Lucia had to go drop Bianca off at the school premises that afternoon.

When they returned, Nero was standing in the living room. Ifeoma knew instantly something was off, although he kept his tone light when he spoke. "Lucia, stay down here and watch some TV. I need to talk to your Aunty Ify."

"Okay, Papa," Lucia said and settled on the sofa, grabbing the TV remote.

Nero took Ifeoma's hand and led her upstairs. He didn't speak until they got into the bedroom.

"What's going on?" she asked as soon as the door shut.

"Alina's brother, Mitja, is here," he said.

She stiffened. "What do you mean? Here, where?"

"Here, in the city. He arrived with two of his goons this morning from Italy via Doha," he said, running his hand over the back of his neck.

"This morning? And you're just telling me?" This wasn't good.

"I didn't know he was coming. I only found out after you left to drop off Bianca. I didn't want to tell you while you were in the car with Lucia." He sat on the bed.

"Okay. Back up. I need to understand what's going on. How did you find out? Most importantly, why is he here?" She sat on the settee, giving him her full attention.

This wasn't a pleasure trip for the Mitja person and could have dire implications for all of them.

"Well, you know I had Kane double the security around us," he started, leaning forward, arms on thighs. "Then Alina arrived with Lucia and we got the extra team guarding her on the school runs. Well, Alina is basically on a car share and uses the same car whenever she goes out. So, the team monitors her and gives me a report of where she goes and who she meets. We know she spent last night in a hotel. This morning, three white men arrived at the hotel and went to her suite. I was sent photographs."

He pulled out his phone and flicked the screen a few times before handing Ifeoma the gadget. "That guy in the pinstripes is Mitja. The other two are his goons."

Someone captured the photo in the hotel's foyer as the men arrived at the check-in counter.

"If you swipe through, you will see one with Alina hugging Mitja," Nero continued.

She swiped the screen and the next phone showed Alina approaching the men with a smile. Another swipe and she was hugging the Mitja person.

"So, Alina invited her brother to Nigeria. This can't be good."

"It's not. Mitja is a lowlife who dabbles in everything from human to drug trafficking. To make it worse, his uncle is Tommaso Conti, the head of one of the biggest mafia families in Italy. Don Conti is one of the investors at Piedimonte Financials."

Ifeoma understood the implications. Piedimonte Financials laundered money for mafia bosses. No wonder Nero had cash to throw around. However, it also meant he was in bed with the devil and these people could turn on him at any moment.

"So, he's basically mafia and now he's in our city." She handed the phone back and straightened. It was her turn to pace. "Does he really think he can show up here and we'll suddenly be quaking in our boots?"

"I thought the same thing, too. But he must be getting help locally. I've told Kane to find out who his connection is here. Alina hasn't been here long enough to raise reliable manpower. Someone else is involved."

"You're right. Someone will have to supply him with firearms and other items locally. Since Alina didn't inform you of the brother's arrival, I think whatever they're planning will be executed within twenty-four to forty-eight hours. Any later than that, they will know you are more likely to find out about Mitja's presence by then."

"I agree. They are counting on the element of surprise. But we have home turf advantage. Luckily, the hotel they're using is the one I stayed in. I already established a working relationship because the owners are interested in selling. We have eyes in the CCTV room and the public area. Also, Kane booked the room opposite the one Alina stayed in, so they can see who's coming in and out. The plan is to intercept their local fixer and courier, and seize any weapons being delivered."

"That's a good plan. But you know what? I can't shake the feeling that Afam is behind this."

"Afam? Your brother?"

"Yes. Think about it. Alina still hasn't told you why she came to Nigeria. She knew you were coming here before you left. Then, all of a sudden, when we got engaged, she packed her bags and boarded a plane to get here. The only person who could have told her is Afam or my mother. They knew you had a daughter because I mentioned Lucia during the board meeting—" A fact she now regretted. "—Now when Lucia is finally settling in, her uncle shows up, just a few weeks to our traditional marriage ceremony. We haven't discussed our nuptials with Alina, but I bet she knows and is trying very hard to stop it. And my brother could be helping her."

He stood and strode to her. "She can try all she wants, but she can't stop it. We're already husband and wife, Mrs Piedimonte."

He stroked a thumb against her cheek before tipping her chin up and kissing her lips briefly, making her tingle all over.

"True," she said in a breathy voice, trying to keep her wits. "So, what are we going to do about Alina and her brother?"

"I'm going to ship them back to Italy together," he said.

"But won't that cause problems with Don Conti?" she wondered if they'd bitten off more than they could chew.

"Lorenzo will handle Don Conti. He isn't the head of Piedimonte cartel for nothing."

Ifeoma's mouth dropped open. She hadn't known this. "Lorenzo is a mafia don?"

"Yes. It's not advertised, for obvious reasons. But how do you think I've been protected for so long in Italy? It's because of his influence and I'm his blood."

TWENTY-EIGHT

"Goodness! That's it!" Ifeoma jumped up from the chair where she'd been sitting, watching the livestream video sent by the surveillance team. They were photographing every arrival at the hotel where Mitja was staying so they could identify the local contact.

Kane had called in his old team from when he was part of the Death Squad, a special forces team linked to the Secret Service, which had been disbanded years ago. However, the team still performed assassinations as a rogue group.

"What is it?" Nero was sitting beside her as they looked at the images on the electronic tablet.

"That man. That's Frank. Nonye's husband."

"What?" Nero had still not met the man, although he worked with Nonye five days a week. The man hadn't been to the Zequer building. At least not to Nero's knowledge.

"That is Frank." She pointed at the man getting out of the vehicle from the last image just downloaded. It was dark, and the premises were lit with spotlights. "Tell the team to detain him immediately. He's probably not alone and he will be armed."

Nero didn't hesitate, trusting Ifeoma's instincts. He lifted his phone and called Kane, who answered right away, putting it on speakerphone. "The courier is here. Intercept the man in the blue tunic set who just came out of the red Beemer. Search him, his companion and his car and let me know what you find instantly."

"Target one Blue Tunic. Target two Black T-shirt with DG letters dragging a black suitcase. Intercept both now!" Kane ordered his men through his comms piece while Nero was still on the phone.

He waved for Ifeoma to sit down and watch the unfolding action.

On the tablet screen, armed men in balaclavas melted out of the shadows. They moved with stealth and precision, surrounding the two new arrivals at the hotel car park as they pulled out a suitcase from the boot of the car. Outnumbered six-to-two, the men tried to fight but were subdued quickly, restrained and searched. The livestream didn't have audio, but aggressive stances and jerky movements showed an argument going on.

"The man says his name is Frank Mbaka, and he's a businessman who has come to the hotel for a business meeting," one of the security men relayed.

Nero met Ifeoma's gaze and she shrug in an 'I told you so' manner.

"Search the suitcase," Nero reiterated, and Kane passed it along.

The men on screen forced the man in the blue tunic to unlock the suitcase. There were gasps on the speakerphone.

"The suitcase is full of semi-automatic assault rifles, handguns, and ammunition. Also, hunting knifes and knuckledusters," someone said.

"That's Mitja's favourite weapon," Nero said. "He likes to get up close and personal." He stood and gave more instructions to Kane. "Keep the men and weapons secure. I'm on my way."

"Done," Kane replied before the line went dead.

"I'm going with you," Ifeoma said and stood, too.

"But Lucia will be here alone." Nero worried about a sneak attack while he was out dealing with the Italian mob.

"She won't be alone. Florence is here with security. But I can take her to Amaoge's house. She'll be safe there too."

Ifeoma's former sister-in-law lived opposite them on the estate with her husband and child. They'd all been introduced weeks ago. Still...

"No. That would be too disruptive for Lucia. Just tell Adiele to lockdown the estate. No one goes in or out except residents. And he shouldn't allow any members of the Nzekwe family in."

"Okay." She pulled her phone from her pocket and made the call while he went into the closet to change his clothes.

When he came out, Ifeoma was on the phone, her expression sombre. His heart dropped. Something was wrong.

"Yes, Ezenwanyi. I understand. Have a good night," she said before ending the call.

"What's the matter?" He stepped up to her, searching her face for clues.

She sighed and blinked several times. "Adiele is locking down the estate, and I spoke to Florence. She is happy to stay with Lucia and get her to bed."

"But you were talking to your former mother-in-law," he probed.

"She is also my godmother."

"And?"

"And she said we need to complete the bonding ritual."

"What? Now?"

"Yes. Now. You haven't retaken your oath as Yadili and you have no powerbase. You're vulnerable without my protection."

He understood what she was saying. In the Yadili the husbands and brothers offered physical security but it was the women—the mothers and wives—who provided the mystical protection. The feminine bond gave a power boost unlike any other.

"But I have your protection, don't I? We're married," he said. Their legal vows and union should provide automatic covering, like insurance.

"Yes, you have some. But it's nowhere near enough. You started a spiritual thread with the bonding ritual. Right now, the thread is untethered and floating because it's uncompleted. It means you can't fully utilise my powers because there's leakage, like a dripping faucet, which in the long run will drain me faster. Also, others can latch onto an unanchored thread, cut it, destroy it. Destroy you. I will not lose my husband because I was afraid to love again. To love you."

She blinked, but he saw the tears gathered in her shiny eyes. She was laying herself bare to him, something he wouldn't have imagined months ago when he'd seen her in Rome. But the last month with her, she'd opened up and allowed him into her home, her life, and finally it seemed she was letting him into her heart.

The ultimate trophy. The one he'd coveted since he was a teenage boy. Her heart.

His chest tightened, and he leaned forward and pressed a kiss to her cheek, tasting her salty tears. "Ifem, I'm not going anywhere."

"Then, let's ensure it." She shoved him and he sat on the bed. "Undo your buckle."

Damn, she was fierce when she wanted something. He obeyed, reaching for his belt as she stepped out of her shoes and tugged her trousers and knickers down. His heart raced, warm blood pumping south, filling his dick at the sight of her naked thighs. He pushed his jeans and briefs down his knees, freeing his already hardening length. The anticipation of being inside her was enough to flip him from nought to sixty in a heartbeat.

She knelt in front of him, wrapped her fingers around his turgid length, and squeezed gently. His breath hitched, and he held it as she lowered her head, taking him into her mouth.

"If—em," he groaned, out of breath as his head rolled back and he settled on his elbows, letting her go to work on him. This was her show.

Heat flooded his body along with the tingling nerves as her tongue and lips licked and sucked him. The base of his spine tingled, and instead of chasing the impending orgasm, he reached for her head and tugged her off him. He crushed her lips with his, tasting himself and her power.

She rose and pushed him until his back hit the mattress, breaking the kiss. He panted as she climbed onto his lap. Then her body sank onto his as she took his throbbing dick deep inside her warm, wet channel.

"Oh!" they moaned in unison as she bottomed out before rising, only to sink down on him. Head tilted back, she set a fast pace, riding him like a goddess on a wild beast. He lost himself to her rhythm, gripping her hips, undulating with her, chasing the impending orgasm.

"You are so fucking beautiful," he said in a guttural voice.

She looked down at him, the passion in her gaze matching the fierceness inside him. "Nebolisa, I claim your body with my heart."

"Let our soul flames ignite, twinned for eternity," they completed in unison.

"Dim!" she cried out as her climax rippled around his dick, her expression blissful.

"Ifem!" Colours exploded temporarily in his vision as he slammed into her one last time, pumping his release into her body.

Wrapping his arms around her, he collapsed onto the bed, taking her with him. She lay on top of him as they caught their breaths, both of them still partially clothed.

He lifted his head, palmed the back of hers, and kissed her with the remaining embers of his passion.

"I love you," he whispered, knowing this had been true for the past two decades and would remain so for the rest of his life.

"I love you too." She pressed her lips to hers, holding for a couple of beats. "Now, you have my full protection. I've got your back, always."

"Good." He grinned, kissing her fiercely. Then he lifted his head and said, "Let's go to war."

TWENTY-NINE

Forty minutes later, Nero and Ifeoma reached a safe house where the security team had taken Frank Mbaka and his associate for further questioning. In an isolated rural neighbourhood on the outskirts of the FCT, sparsely scattered buildings surrounded it because the area was still underdeveloped.

Nero was calm on the drive over, although fury simmered in his veins. He was skilled at concealing his emotions, adept at maintaining a calm facade. Yet with the ones he loved, it took very little to trigger him, and he became overprotective.

This was a trauma response due to the way his parents died. Now, he would do anything to shield the people he loved. Knowing Mitja had come to Nigeria to hurt his family—Ifeoma, him, perhaps Lucia—had him on hyperalert. He couldn't let this go until everyone involved met their consequences.

Death. There was no other option. He needed to remind the underworld who he was. He was King Loathing, after all.

Kane met them outside as they left the vehicle. "Mr Mbaka is inside. This way."

Nero followed him into the newly built house powered by solar electricity. "What's the update on the Italians?"

"They are still in the suite waiting for the courier to arrive," Kane said and stopped at the entrance to what appeared to be the living room. The walls and floor had a grey plaster, but there was no paint or furniture.

Nero stepped in, followed by Ifeoma as the two bound men turned in their direction.

"What's going...?" Frank spoke, but trailed off as his eyes widened. "Ifeoma?"

The sound of his wife's name on the man's lips set off Nero's rage. How dare he say her name when he'd colluded to attack her? Who knew what Mitja had planned for those weapons?

Without thinking, he stormed across the room, swung his fist, and connected to the man's face. Next, the man was flat on the cold floor, groaning and his broken nose bleeding while Nero stood over him, ready to commit murder.

"Bring me one of those hunting knives," he ordered.

"Nero," Ifeoma's soft cautionary tone made him suck in a breath.

He glanced at her. Her expression showed she knew his thoughts, knew he was ready to bury everyone involved in the conspiracy to attack them six-feet-under.

But they needed answers before every last one of them was dispatched to their ancestors. And this was her brother-in-law. She had Nonye to worry about.

He bent down, grabbed the man by the back collar, and hoisted him to his feet. "Ifeoma is the one asking the questions. Every word out of your mouth better be the truth or I will cut you open right here."

Frank's Adam's apple bobbed as he swallowed.

"Say yes, if you understand me!" Nero ordered.

"Yes, I understand." He swallowed again, sweat beading his hairline.

"Good," Ifeoma said, stepping closer. "Tell me why you're selling arms to men who came to Nigeria to kill me."

"What?" His gazed bounced from Ifeoma to Nero. "No—"

"I told you to tell the truth." Nero slammed him against the wall and the man hissed in pain, probably with a dislocated shoulder because of his arms bound behind him.

"Listen, I'm not lying." Frank was sweating profusely. "Afam sent me."

Nero stiffened.

"Did you say Afam? My brother?" Ifeoma asked.

Frank blinked several times. "Yes. Afam came to see me a few days ago and told me he needed to source some ammunition for his business partners coming into the country in a few days. He gave me a list of what they needed. It included a car and a local driver who they needed for twenty-four hours, maybe two days. When I confirmed that I'd acquired the items, he told me where to deliver it. I was on my way to the drop off at the hotel before these guys grabbed us."

"Are you saying my brother sent you to drop off the weapons and you don't know who the buyers are?"

"Yes. He said they were white, from Italy. Room 313. They would be here only for two or three days. I don't know them or what they want to do with the weapons. I swear."

Nero glanced at Ifeoma, who shook her head. "And if tomorrow you hear that those men have killed me and your wife—"

"Nonye? Never! No one is killing her. The gods forbid it!" Frank said with vehemence.

This gave Nero pause. The man sounded like he cared for his wife.

Ifeoma jerked back. "Wait. Are you really saying you don't know that Afam is trying to wipe out everyone involved in ousting him as Chief Executive? The same position your wife currently occupies at Zequer. If he gets rid of me, Nero and Nonye are next."

Frank's eyes widened as the penny dropped. "Mba nu. I know I've been a lousy husband and Nonye is currently barely talking to me. We haven't discussed Zequer, although I'm happy she got the CEO position. She works too hard for that business. She deserves to run it."

"Hmmm," Ifeoma murmured, sounding unconvinced.

"Look. You don't have to believe me. I owe Afam no loyalties. Him and your mother have treated me as inconsequential since I married your sister. Like I was something they scraped off the bottom of their shoes. I was stupid. I let it get to me, let it come between me and my wife. But believe me, I love Nonye. I want the chance to make her happy again. If it means I kill Afam myself, I will."

"Afam is mine to handle," Nero said. "But there is something else you can do to prove whose side you're on."

"Name it. Anything," Frank said.

"Call Afam. Tell him you couldn't make the delivery because there was an incident at the hotel." Nero turned to his security chief. "Kane, can some of your men pose as law enforcement around the hotel? Make it look like they are hunting for fugitives?"

"Yes, no problem," Kane replied.

Of course, knowing those men were law enforcement once upon a time will help them pull it off.

Nero turned back to Frank. "Tell Afam police were there so you couldn't drop off the weapons. Tell him you left the vehicle and the keys are under the wheel. They can drive the car and come pick up the weapons from you here. The car has SATNAV, right?"

"Yes, but what about the driver? They wanted a driver?" He glanced at the other bound man in the corner.

"The driver had to leave because of the police. You will find another driver, but not tonight. But they need to pick up the weapons tonight, otherwise it'll be gone by the morning," Nero clarified.

"Okay. I'll do it. I'll call him." Frank nodded.

"Good," Ifeoma said. "Kane, you sure your team can handle this?"

"Of course," the man replied confidently. "It'll be done."

He went out to make the arrangements.

One of his team helped Frank pull out his phone. He held it to his ear as Frank spoke on the phone to Afam. Afam wasn't happy about the change in plans. He said he would call back.

In the meantime, Nero walked to another room and discussed with Kane about how to bring Afam and Mrs Nzekwe to the safe house. Kane said the men at the hotel would be redirected to pick up Afam and his mother once the Italians were on the way to the safe house.

Thirty minutes later, Afam called back. He got confirmation there was a police presence at the hotel and the Italian men had found the car and keys all right. They were ready to pick up the weapons.

Kane passed over a piece of paper with an address for Frank to relay to Afam. It was a different location from here. They didn't want this location compromised.

Frank passed it on, and Afam confirmed the men were on their way. They would call Frank in case they needed further directions.

After the phone call, Nero turned to head out with Kane to the ambush point, but Ifeoma didn't move. "Are you coming?"

They didn't tell Frank, but there will be an ambush team waiting to intercept the Italians before they could reach the safe house.

"No. I need a word with my brother-in-law," Ifeoma said ominously.

He nodded and kissed her on the forehead. "Be safe."

"You too," she said.

He walked out into the night and got into the front seat of the SUV with Kane driving. The ambush team was already in situ about four kilometres away.

When Kane reached a safe spot away from the ambush team, he parked by the side of the road and killed the engine. The area was rural farmland surrounding the road. At this time of the night, close to midnight, cars were intermittent.

They sat in the car's silence, waiting for a message from the trailing car following the Italians when they arrived.

"When this is all over, I will need a break," Kane broke the silence.

"Oh. Is everything okay with you?" Nero turned to study the man's side profile.

Kane had been working tirelessly since Nero arrived in Nigeria a little over a month ago. The man definitely deserved some downtime. But Nero knew little about his personal life.

"I'm okay. But my woman ... she's ... we're having a baby," Kane announced.

"Wow. That's wonderful. Congratulations." Nero patted his shoulder. "But I didn't know you had someone. How come I haven't met her? Is she in the FCT?"

"No. She's not in Nigeria at the moment." He scrubbed a palm over his head, looking frustrated.

"Where?"

"In London. I want to be with her. To protect her. But she's so far away."

"Then bring her home."

"I can't. We're not official. Her father is Yadili and won't approve."

"Fuck her father. If you want her as much as you seem to do, go claim her. You know I've got your back. Don't wait twenty-five years like I did."

"Yeah. The twenty-five years wait still has me puzzled. But you're half-Italian. You guys make a mountain out of a molehill." In the semi-darkness, his lips curled upwards at the corners.

"And Nigerians don't?" Nero quipped as they both chuckled. He believed he could count Kane as a friend because they had a lot in common. One was their loss of close family members so young. The other was their existence on the Yadili periphery. They were like outcasts in a brotherhood of Igbo indigenes with their mixed heritages.

"Target two minutes away," the comms device crackled, cutting into their moment of humour.

Nero's heart rate picked up. This was it. The showdown with Alina's brother.

"None of them walk away from that vehicle," Nero said.

"Absolutely," Kane replied as a beam of headlights appeared in the distance.

"Thirty seconds," the voice on the comms said.

Then shadows moved, getting into position to intercept the oncoming vehicle. Then a blaze of semiautomatic gunfire erupted. The driver must have been hit because the vehicle screeched, veered all over the road and crashed into the verge.

As quickly as it started, the gunfire stopped. Kane and Nero left their car and walked toward the ambushed vehicle now surrounded by balaclava-wearing gunmen.

"What's the status?" Kane asked.

"All dead or on the way," someone said and pointed at the open back door. "This one is still breathing."

Nero walked around and stood at the door. He raised his phone and turned on the torch, lighting up the interior of the vehicle.

Mitja was sitting in the back seat coughing up blood. He turned his head slowly towards Nero.

"Who?" his word was garbled as he coughed again.

Nero turned the light towards his face so he could see the face of the person who ended him.

Mitja's eyes widened, and then he exhaled for the last time.

Nero walked back to the car, feeling lighter. Some of his rage subsided. One problem was out of the way. But there was still Ifeoma's family.

By the time Kane got into the vehicle with him, the ambushed one was ablaze. He turned the car around and headed to the safe house to pick Ifeoma.

When he got inside, Frank looked pale and in agony, slumped against the wall and floor. There was a bandage around his left hand, which he was holding with his right.

"What happened to him?" Nero asked as Ifeoma approached.

"I took his little finger as a warning for the distress he caused my sister. He will go home and beg her forgiveness," she said.

Nero shook his head at Frank. The man really should have known better than to cross Ifeoma. He placed his arm around his wife and walked out with her before climbing into the backseat of the vehicle. Once the doors shut and it was just the two of them with the humming air-conditioner, he spoke.

"Mitja and his goons are gone. The car burned, IDs destroyed, along with tattoos. Since they checked into the hotel with false IDs, it will make it even more difficult for the bodies to be identified. This will buy Lorenzo time to handle Don Conti."

"Good." She turned to meet his gaze, her expression concerned. "What about Alina? Was she in the car?"

"No. She was at the hotel. She will be arrested and sent to jail. But she won't survive her first night, an overdose."

"Are you sure?" she reached out, placed a palm on his thigh.

He covered it with his. "I'm sure. She is toxic to Lucia. She brought her brother here to hurt you. Anyone who wishes you and Lucia harm dies. Which brings me to your brother and mother. They're on their way over here."

"Good." She nodded.

"Are you sure?" he repeated her earlier question.

"Of course. You said it. Anyone who intends harm to us dies. There's no quibbling about it," she said vehemently.

Still, he knew it must be hard for her to cope with it. He could end Alina and Mitja because he felt no familial connections to them. His relationship with Alina as co-parents was accidental, not one he would have chosen. Perhaps she saw her relationship with Afam and their mother as accidental, too. However, she shared blood with them and they'd been in each other's lives longer than Alina had been in his.

"Okay," he said and pulled her closer, wrapping his arms around her, hoping to convey his sympathy for her situation. "I wouldn't have brought them here. But I need answers."

She swallowed, and when she spoke, her voice was husky. "So do I."

"If at any point when they get here, you want to leave the room. Just go."

"I will, if I need it."

They said nothing for a while. He just held her in his arms, giving comfort.

Two vehicles arrived and the bound, gagged and blindfolded Afam and his mother were dragged out and into the house.

Nero waited a beat before moving back. "Are you ready?"

They left the car and walked into the building. He held onto her hand, and surprisingly, she didn't let go.

The hostages were sitting on the hard concrete. It couldn't be comfortable for Mrs Nzekwe.

"Remove the blindfolds and the gag," Ifeoma ordered.

Two hooded men came forward and carried out her order.

Her mother blinked several times, trying to adjust to the sudden change in lighting.

Afam recovered quicker, and his eyes went wide. "What the fuck!"

"Put the gag back on him!" Nero ordered.

"Ifeoma, why are you letting this man turn you against your family?" Afam fought as the men tried to hold him down to reapply the gag. "Who the hell does the modafucker think he is?"

"I am her husband!" Nero snapped.

"No, you're not. A fiancé is not a husband," her mother sneered.

"Yes, he's my husband. We got married on my birthday. Look, you can see our photos on the registry website." Ifeoma stepped forward, flashing her phone in their faces.

"Ewo!" her mother gasped, glancing at Afam. "Obu kwa eziokwu." *It is true.*

Afam's mouth was gagged so he couldn't speak. He just glared at Nero and his sister.

"I'm not even going to ask about your involvement with the Italians who came here to hurt me and my wife because Frank has already told us the details."

Afam made what sounded like a growl.

Nero ignored him and continued. "What I want to know, Mrs Nzekwe, is about your husband's involvement in my parents' death?"

"As if I'm going to tell you anything." She stuck her nose up in the air.

"Then you're going to watch your son lose his fingers. You can see Frank already lost one. Afam is next. I will take every finger from him until you tell me the truth. Boys, hold him down and bring the knife."

Afam fought as the men laid him flat on his chest. Two men knelt on his body while another cut off the rope binding his hands behind him. Then his fingers were splayed out on the concrete, ready for cutting.

"No, no, no," Mrs Nzekwe cried. "Please don't hurt my son."

"Then tell me what happened to my parents."

"Fine. I will talk." She hesitated. "Release Afam."

"Don't waste my time. I'm out of patience," he said in a harsh tone.

"Okay." She sagged. "As you know already, your father John Ezeilo and my husband, Victor Nzekwe, were friends who met at university. Your father studied Design Technology while my husband studied Production Engineering. So, it was no wonder they started up a business together when they returned to Nigeria. Things were going great, and the business was growing. At the time, one of the income streams was through the tannery and exportation of quality leather. Then suddenly John suggested that instead of exporting the rawhide to be finished in Italy and rebranded as Italian leather, they could finish it to a high level in Nigeria. He said he had an Italian fashion house who was ready to work with Zequer to manufacture the end product. That fashion house was owned by the Piedimonte family, and your mother was the creative designer. Victor wasn't happy about it. Neither was I. We saw it as John snatching more shares in the company through his wife. In the end, things got sour, and they fell out."

"Mother, don't tell me it's true. You actually had a hand in Nero's parents' death," Ifeoma accused.

Mrs Nzekwe shifted uncomfortably. "You have to understand we would have lost so much if it had ended up in court. Your father didn't have the ready cash to buy out his partner's shares. He hoped he could still convince him to stick with their original business model. He tried to renew the concession with the customer in Italy to continue supplying the raw hide. But John wouldn't budge. He said the Conti family were ripping us off."

"Wait a minute." Nero stiffened. "How did the Conti family get involved?"

"Mr Conti was the customer buying our raw hide material in Italy." Ifeoma's mother said.

"Do you remember his full name?"

"I never met him in person. But I saw the documents he signed. It was Tom-something. Like Thomas, but the Italian version."

"Tommaso?"

"Yes! Tommaso Conti. Do you know him?"

Nero's mind raced at a thousand miles an hour as some things clicked into place. He ignored her question. "Tell me how he was involved in my parents' death."

Mrs Nzekwe tugged the collar of her blouse. "Mr Conti wanted Victor to get rid of the John problem. He told Victor that if he got rid of the problem, he would renew the concession and Zequer could supply Conti with leather for the next ten years. We couldn't pass up the opportunity."

"So, you killed Nero's parents for wanting to add value to Zequer products. For wanting to turn it into a brand the people, the country, would be proud of. For promoting Nigerian leather, instead of buying it back as finished products under the guise of Italian leather. Way to go, Mother," Ifeoma spat in disgust.

"We were doing the best for our family and the company. The concession would have guaranteed jobs for at least ten years," her mother defended.

"Out of curiosity. Once my parents were out of the way, did Tommaso Conti honour the concession? Did you all make a lot of money?" Nero asked.

The woman lowered her head, not meeting anyone's gaze. "He renewed the concession, but he lowered the buying price. When Victor argued, Mr Conti told him he should sign the contract or face others finding out Victor had killed his business partner. Victor had to give into the blackmail and signed the contract. But Zequer started losing money from that point and hasn't really recovered. Victor had his first heart attack soon after that. Although he recovered, ten years to the date, he died from heart failure."

Nero should have cheered that the man got his comeuppance, but there was nothing to cheer. Still, he felt a little lighter because he'd discovered the answer he'd been seeking.

Ifeoma stepped up to her mother. "I knew you were not a good person. But I never thought you would stoop to killing someone who caused you no harm. Encouraging your son to hire assassins to kill Nero? Well, the two of you are going to join Dad soon. I hope you enjoyed your life because it's over."

Ifeoma swivelled and walked towards the door.

"Ifeoma, wait. I'm your mother. Your blood. Afam is your brother. Please don't do this."

Ifeoma didn't stop.

Nero followed her. He didn't need to stay to see what happened next. His wife needed him.

He caught up with her outside the vehicle and assisted her to climb into the car. They sat in the back, holding onto each other until Kane arrived and joined them.

"It's done," he said and started the car engine.

Nero nodded at him in the rearview mirror.

"What happens to their bodies?" Ifeoma asked.

"They will be returned to their house and arranged. He hung himself and she had heart failure."

"What about Afam's wife and the domestic staff?" Nero asked, concerned about the loose end.

"They were sedated when we took Mrs Nzekwe Snr and her son. By the time they wake up, the bodies will be back in situ."

"Thank you for everything you've done," Ifeoma said.

"Yes, thank you. You've gone above and beyond," Nero said. The man had thought about every scenario and built in a backup. Tonight would not have been a success without him.

"You're welcome," Kane said solemnly.

The rest of the drive was in relative silence. By the time they returned to the estate, grey tinged the far eastern horizon and dawn wasn't far off. Kane dropped them in the driveway before turning around and heading back out. He had to ensure everything else went according to plan.

Nero opened the front door and held it while she walked in and flicked the light switch. Orange glow filled the foyer as Max came into view from the corridor. Nero shut the door and locked it.

"Welcome," Max said.

"Thank you. How is Lucia?" Ifeoma asked.

"She's asleep. Florence stayed with her," he replied.

"Okay. We'll go up." Nero held Ifeoma's hand as they went upstairs.

They stopped outside Lucia's door and peeked in. Lucia was asleep on the bed, under the duvet, while Florence lay on the small sofa covered in blankets. They didn't stir, and neither Nero nor Ifeoma wanted to wake them.

Closing the door quietly, he tugged Ifeoma into their bedroom. A heavy sigh escaped her as they crossed the threshold, her fatigue evident. A sharp pain contracted his chest and his throat tightened, triggering his protectiveness.

Everyone saw the strong, capable woman. But this aspect of her, this openness, was solely for his eyes. And he would do everything to shield her from the world. Because it was his responsibility to comfort and heal her so that when she faced the world, they witnessed the fierce lioness.

Silently, he guided her into the bathroom. She stood almost passively as he helped her take her clothes off before doing the same with his. This was another proof of how close they'd grown to each other. How much she trusted him. She wasn't afraid to be vulnerable with him, to open every aspect of herself, just like he did with her.

Naked, he covered her hair with a shower cap. Then he helped her into the shower cubicle. Under the warm spray, he washed her body. After rinsing off, he grabbed towels and dried them both. Then he grabbed a negligee from the closet and tugged it over her head. He pulled on silk PJ bottoms.

Once dressed, she crawled into bed. He scooted up behind her, spooning her.

"Are you okay?" he asked, feeling the need to get her to talk.

"I'm drained," she said with a sigh.

"Same here. The past few weeks have been taxing."

He'd expected to feel relief after he exacted revenge for his parents' death. However, all he felt was an ache in his chest for his wife, who'd lost members of her family tonight. Good or bad, family was family. She was grieving.

She didn't reply immediately, and he just held her, happy to convey comfort and safety in his arms. She was his family now, along with Lucia. He would do anything for her.

"Do you think you will hate me with time?" she asked after a while.

"Hate you? Why?" His grip around her midriff tightened.

"Because my parents killed yours." Her voice sounded croaky.

"No, Ifem." He pressed his lips to her nape, tenderly. "I loved you years ago, before my parents died. Loved you when I finally met you in Rome. Why do you think I initiated the bonding ritual? I love you now that you've accepted me and my daughter into your heart. I will always love you."

She shifted, turning to him, and palmed his hairy chin, her eyes searching his. "You know we are bonded for life. There are no reversals, no divorce."

"Hurray to that. I'm not the one who runs away all the time," he teased, grinning.

"Hey, I only did that once," she laughed and his heart sang that she was in a lighter mood after the heavy night they had.

"And you broke my heart." His grin widened.

"Dim oma, I'm sorry. You healed my heart, freeing me to love again. So, I promise, I won't break your heart again and I will always love you." She leaned in and kissed him deeply.

He returned the kiss with love and passion. No matter what tomorrow brought, he'd found the heart and home he'd been searching for most of his life.

Thank you for reading Trophy Wife. If you enjoyed this book, please leave a review on the retailer website.

To find out when the epilogue is available and to read more about upcoming book releases and bonus content, sign up for my newsletter[1]

Lorenzo and Nkoli will be back in an upcoming novella. Kane has his own story coming soon, featuring Yadili old and new.

---

1. https://www.kirutaye.com/contact

YADILI SERIES

Prince of Hearts[1]
Killer of Kings[2]
Bad Santa[3]
Rough Diamond[4]
Tough Alliance[5]
Trophy Wife[6]

---

1. https://www.kirutaye.com/duke

2. https://www.kirutaye.com/xandra

3. https://www.kirutaye.com/bad-santa

4. https://www.kirutaye.com/rough-diamond

5. https://www.kirutaye.com/tough-alliance

6. https://www.kirutaye.com/trophy-wife

OTHER BOOKS BY KIRU TAYE

MEN OF VALOR SERIES:

His Treasure
His Strength
His Princess
Her Protector
Men of Valor box set (books 1 – 3)

The Essien Series:

Keeping Secrets
Making Scandal
Riding Rebel
Kola
A Very Essien Christmas
Freddie Entangled
Freddie Untangled

The Bound Series:

Bound to Fate
Bound to Ransom
Bound to Passion
Bound to Favor
Bound to Liberty

The Challenge Series:

Valentine
Engaged
Worthy

Captive
The Yadili Series:
Prince of Hearts
Killer of Kings
Bad Santa
Rough Diamond
Tough Alliance
Trophy Wife
Honour (featured in Love and The Lawless anthology)
PNR/Fantasy romance
Outcast
Sacrifice
Black Soul
Scar's Redemption
Haunted (featured in Enchanted: Volume Two anthology)
The Ben & Selina Trilogy
Scars,
Secrets
Scores
The Royal House of Saene Series:
His Captive Princess
Saving Her Guard
The Tainted Prince
The Future King
The Future Queen
Screwdriver
Viva City FC Series:
Tapping Up
Against the Run of Play